B.J. DANIELS

NEW YORK TIMES BESTSELLING AUTHOR

HEARTBREAKER

HQN

ISBN-13: 978-1-335-04519-5

Heartbreaker

Recycling programs for this product may not exist in your area.

This one is for Mariah Kowceun-Marino,
copresident of the Malta Hands All Around
Quilt Club, and one of the most talented women
I know. It is a joy to be copresident with you.
And an even bigger joy to watch
that creative mind of yours at work.

HEARTBREAKER

CHAPTER ONE

HER EYES FLEW OPEN, her fight-or-flight response already wide-awake. She jerked up in the bed, blinking wildly, terrified and yet unable to believe what she was seeing. Three hulking dark forms appeared out of the shadows of the huge master bedroom. One of the men tripped over her duffel bag on the floor where she'd dropped it. He swore as he kicked it out of the way.

She tried hopelessly to banish the men back into whatever nightmare they'd climbed out of, realizing the stumble must have been what had awakened her.

All she could think rationally was that this couldn't be happening, because these men being here tonight was so wrong.

But before she could open her mouth to speak—let alone scream—the largest of the three intruders reached her side of the king-size bed. Roughly he pushed her down and clamped a gloved hand over her mouth. *This was real.*

She finally screamed, but the gloved hand over her mouth muffled the sound. Not that it would have done any good if she had hollered to bloody hell. There was no one else in the house to come to her rescue—let alone anyone nearby. The house was high on the mountainside overlooking Flathead Lake, surrounded by acres of forest and as isolated as money could buy.

Frantically she shook her head as she met the man's

eyes, the only feature not hidden by his black ski mask, and tried to communicate with him that she wasn't the woman he wanted.

"Don't fight me," the man said in a hoarse whisper as he renewed his efforts to hold her down. "We don't want to hurt you."

But she did fight because they were making a terrible mistake and they didn't know it. That realization sent panic rocketing through her system. Her heart banged against her rib cage, her thundering pulse deafening in her ears. She fought to pull the clamp from her mouth.

If she could only explain the error they were making. Failing in her attempts to pull away his gloved hand, she struck out with her fists as her legs kicked wildly to free themselves from the covers. All she'd managed to do was make things worse. He leaned over her, pressing his body weight against her chest with his forearm, taking away her breath.

"Did you find it?" the man holding her down demanded of the other two. They had produced flashlights, she saw, and were now searching the room. She could hear one of them at the dressing table knocking over bottles of expensive perfume and rejuvenating skin creams.

Moments later, as she tried to breathe, she saw the smaller of the men motion to the larger man that he'd found something. "Got it." He pocketed what appeared to be a cell phone before the men turned to her.

Hope soared. They'd found whatever they'd come for. Now maybe they would leave the way they'd come in, like phantoms in the night. It wasn't as if she'd seen their faces.

Her slender thread of hope died as she heard the man holding her down say, "Help me with her." The words sent a fresh stab of alarm coursing through her. She fought even harder. Kicking free of the covers, she got a leg out and struck the smallest of the men in his masked face as he tried to grab her legs. She felt his nose give under her heel and make a loud pop. He let out a wounded cry as he backed off.

"Damn it," the first man said. "I need help here."

The other intruder, the one who'd been searching the room earlier, climbed on the bed, crawling across the king-size mattress toward her. She caught him in the jaw with her fist before he pinned her arms down as he climbed on top of her.

She struggled to breathe from the weight of him, gagging. What had he eaten tonight? Pizza with anchovies? She tried to turn her head away as she bucked in an attempt to throw him off her, but he was too heavy. All she could do was heave and squirm under him, horrified at what these men now planned to do with her. *To* her.

"Come here," ordered the man who still had her mouth covered. The one she'd kicked in the face approached, still holding one of his gloved hands over his bleeding nose. "Cover her mouth."

She caught the angry glint in the man's pale eyes before the men made the switch. She tried to tell them about the mistake they were making, but before she could get out more than a word and a breath, the broken-nose man covered her mouth roughly with his bloody glove. She gagged at the smell and feel of the warm, sticky liquid on her lips. But it was the look in his eyes that sent her heart rate off the charts.

He would kill her if he got the chance.

Panic had her inhaling sharply through her nose as she watched in growing terror as the first man pulled a syringe from his coat pocket. She fought with all the strength she had left in her. But even as she did, she knew it was useless. She stood no chance against three men. She felt him jab the needle into her neck as she continued to fight until her body went limp.

As she lay like a rag doll, helpless on the bed, she heard a sound that turned her blood to ice. Someone was tearing duct tape into strips.

CHAPTER TWO

FRANKLIN DAVENPORT HAD let the staff go for the night. He poured himself a drink even though he should have gone to bed hours ago. His estate on Whitefish Lake was blissfully quiet, just the way he liked it. Friends thought he had to be lonely after his wife's death all those years ago. But he'd had his granddaughter living with him until recently. He'd been sad to see Geneva go, but she'd wanted a house of her own.

For a while, she'd taken the drama with her. At sixty-five, he felt he deserved a quiet life after spending years accumulating his fortune. But with Geneva, there was always something. Recently it had been money. She wanted more. He wanted her to do something with her life. Anything.

He had cut her allowance and canceled her credit cards. You would think he'd beaten her, the way she went on about it.

Now the twenty-two-year-old wasn't speaking to him. It was a nice reprieve even though he knew it wouldn't last. He should feel guilty. Geneva was all the family he had. But with her, it was always something—just like it had been with her mother. The past few days he'd been enjoying the peace and quiet even though he knew it couldn't last.

His landline rang. He glanced at the time, wondering who would be calling him at this hour. His associates knew to call only during business hours. He let it ring, feeling only a little guilty. Geneva knew better than to call this late.

The landline quit ringing. He had a moment of silence before his cell phone started in.

With a silent curse, he put down his drink and pulled out his cell. Only a very few people had his cell phone number. His granddaughter was one of them.

He glanced at the screen. Geneva. He swore and let it ring yet again. What kind of trouble could she be in now? The last time she'd gotten arrested, she'd tried the landline first and then his cell.

But this time he suspected it would be another plea for money. She always made him feel guilty.

"It isn't like you can't afford it," she would say.

"Yes, I've worked hard my whole life for this money."

She would roll her eyes and say, "And you'll never be able to spend it all. I'm your only family. What is the point? Besides, one day I will have it all anyway."

"Unless I decide to leave it all to charity," he would threaten, and watch her pale in horror before he would give in and agree to buy her whatever it was she wanted.

He wasn't in the mood now for another tearful discussion about his decision to cut her allowance—especially at this time of the night. He should have done it the moment she dropped out of college. He should have done a lot of things differently when it came to her. He'd made mistakes with her mother, and now he felt as if history was repeating itself.

The phone quit ringing. He was ashamed of how glad he was that he hadn't taken the call. He hadn't talked to Geneva in almost a week. They hadn't just argued about money. His granddaughter had terrible taste in companions. He often thought she couldn't make a good decision if her life depended on it. But this latest boyfriend was the worst she'd brought home yet.

He started to raise his glass to his lips when his cell

phone began clamoring again, and he began to worry. Maybe something really was wrong. He would never forgive himself if she was in real trouble and he'd refused to answer the call.

Even before he touched the screen on his cell phone to accept the call, he knew this was going to ruin his evening.

"Franklin Davenport?"

The unearthly electronically altered voice made his pulse spike. He didn't remember saying yes, but he must have said something because the voice continued.

"We have your granddaughter. If you go to the authorities, we will kill her. Get ten million dollars together. We will contact you soon." The line went dead.

Over the pounding of his heart, Franklin Davenport listened to the silence on the other end of the line as the caller's words reverberated in his head. Picking up his drink, he downed it. For a moment, he thought about calling the cops since he hated being threatened. He had built a media empire by not being intimidated by anyone.

But while he might risk his own life, he couldn't risk Geneva's. No matter how much they disagreed, he loved his granddaughter. He tried her cell. It went straight to voice mail.

He stood for a moment before he placed a call to the one person he trusted with his life—and now Geneva's.

When Judge W. T. Landusky answered, he said, "Willie, it's Franklin. I'm so sorry to call you at this hour and wake you." His voice broke.

"You didn't wake me. I was reading. What's wrong, Franklin?"

He'd always known that if he were ever in trouble, Willie would be there for him. They shared a bond that he knew he could always depend on.

"I just got a call. My granddaughter's been kidnapped. The man who called said that they would kill her if I…" He couldn't go on for a moment. He cleared his throat and told his friend what he knew, answering the judge's questions. "Geneva…she's everything to me, Willie. I can't—" He couldn't finish.

Fortunately, he didn't have to. "If you hear from her, let me know. Otherwise, just sit tight and let me see what I can find out. I'm on my way."

"Willie," he said before the judge could hang up, "I have a tracking device on her phone. It's state of the art. I forgot all about it until this moment. Let me check it." He called it up on his phone, his fingers trembling, but his stomach no longer roiling as badly as earlier. Everything was going to be all right. He had to believe that.

The screen came up. "That's odd," he said, frowning. "It appears she's moving very fast, headed southeast."

SHE WOKE TO BUZZING. At first she thought it was only in her aching head. Her mouth felt dry as cotton. She licked her lips, remnants of memory teasing at her as she gagged at the taste. A terrified feeling settled in her stomach, making her afraid to come fully awake for fear it had all been real.

She slowly opened her eyes. Her heart dropped as she saw where she was—in the back seat of a small airplane. A bout of nausea hit her as the craft dipped and bobbed through the darkness.

Panic rushed at her, making her want to scream. She fought back the hysteria as her survival instincts kicked in. *Don't move. Let them think you're still knocked out from the drug. You don't want them to shoot you up again.*

Slowly, moving nothing but her eyes, she took in her situation. She was alive. She didn't think they had sexually assaulted her. Her hands were duct-taped in front of her at her wrists, but she could tell that her ankles were free. She was glad of that—not that she was going anywhere. At least not yet.

They'd dressed her in her jeans along with the T-shirt she'd been sleeping in and a sweater she'd never seen before. She could feel shoes on her feet. Wiggling her toes, she thought they were her sneakers. So where was her duffel bag? The men would have no reason to bring it along. It was probably back at the house. Her pulse spiked, but she quickly assured herself that her overnight bag wasn't the worst of her problems right now.

She dared a look to her left. The man with the broken nose was asleep, snoring loudly, in the accompanying seat. She glanced up front at the pilot in the seat diagonally from hers. She guessed that he was the largest of the men, the one who'd been giving the orders earlier in the bedroom.

From the smell of stale pizza, she surmised that the third man was in the seat in front of her. Outside the windshield, she could see nothing but darkness—at first. Then she saw what looked like a mountain coming up fast, and with a start realized how low the plane was flying. She could see the tops of pines not all that far below her window.

Where was he taking her that he was flying so low?

That frantic thought was quickly forgotten as she saw the pilot and the man in the front begin to talk animatedly, clearly trying to keep their voices down. She picked up only a few words over the loud buzzing of the plane's single prop engine, but she caught enough to terrify her.

Something was wrong. She heard the distress in the pilot's voice. *Lost.* They were lost? Her panic shot up along with her pulse. Could this get any worse?

As if sensing the sudden tension at the front of the plane,

the man next to her suddenly jerked awake. She quickly closed her eyes. Through her lashes, she watched him lean forward. "Shouldn't we be there by now?" he asked.

She noticed the handgrip of a gun sticking out of the man's jacket pocket as he unsnapped his seat belt to lean even farther into the cockpit to hear what the men were saying. Sensing that she might not get another chance, she took the calculated risk.

It had been years since she'd picked anyone's pocket, but apparently she hadn't lost her touch, she thought. She slipped the weapon out even with her two hands bound and tucked it down beside her, out of his range of sight. Letting out the breath she'd been holding, she assured herself that he was completely unaware that he'd lost it.

She leaned back, closed her eyes again and tried to stay calm. Having the gun made her feel more in control even though she knew it was a false security. There were still three of them. But when they landed, if the pilot could figure out where they were going, she would be ready. Maybe with the element of surprise, she could get herself out of this mess.

The three men were yelling now over the roar of the plane's engine. The pilot's exasperated voice: "Both of you just shut up."

Broken nose: "But shouldn't we have found the landing strip by now?"

Pizza man: "It has to be here, right? You said you knew where we were going."

Broken nose: "What? *We're lost?*"

The pilot: "Shut the hell up, Kyle. I don't need you getting on my case right now." He elbowed broken nose back into his seat. "I don't need to hear it from you either, Baker. Just look out your side of the plane and tell me if you see any lights."

Baker: "A landing strip in the mountains? You sure you got the coordinates right, Wes?"

Wes: "Obviously not. We're getting low on fuel, and it's so damned dark I can't see a thing. Baker, can you see anything off your side of the plane?"

Her euphoria at having a loaded weapon to defend herself deflated at their words. Lost and low on gas? A gun would do her no good unless they found the landing strip and even then, if it came to a wrestling match, Kyle would take the weapon from her probably before she could fire a shot.

The engine sputtered. She tensed and felt everyone else do the same. No one spoke. *This wasn't happening.* Heart in her throat, she heard the engine cut out, sputter and then fall silent as it quit altogether. She glanced outside but saw nothing but mountains and pine trees. No landing strip, no lights. The pilot was frantically trying to get the engine going again.

She felt the plane bob before it began to nose downward as the engine refused to start. The tops of the pine trees grew closer and closer. *The plane was going down.*

Tucking the gun under her, she felt foolish for what little hope the weapon had given her. What good was a weapon when she was about to die in a plane crash? She tightened her seat belt and heard Kyle frantically trying to put his back on. She leaned forward behind the front seat, preparing for the inevitable as she cursed her rotten luck. If she hadn't been in that house tonight, she wouldn't be about to die.

WHEN HIS CELL PHONE rang in the wee hours of the morning, Thorn Grayson knew it was the judge even before he answered it. It had been so long since he'd heard the old man's clipped, gravelly voice that he'd thought Judge W. T. Landusky had forgotten about him.

"To what do I owe this honor, Your Honor?" he said into

the phone, now fully awake. For years he'd been expecting this call. It wasn't as if he hadn't been warned that at any time he might be asked to do the man a favor.

The retired judge let out a growl. "This is not a social call."

"I didn't suspect it was, given the hour. What can I do for you, Judge?" Thorn had been one of WT's guinea pigs as part of a program the old man had funded himself to rehabilitate a handful of rebellious, troubled teens he believed would benefit from a second chance.

It had been a form of heavy-duty boot camp. If the judge was anything, he was tough. He'd held their feet to the fire, demanding they reach their potential through both education and training. As one of those Montana rebels who made it through the near impossible program, Thorn knew the man had saved him from a life of crime. He owed the now retired judge, and they both knew it. Landusky had saved his life and, although he would never admit it, he had a great affection for the cantankerous old man.

Now Thorn sat up, bracing himself. The one thing he was certain of was that the judge wouldn't be calling unless there was trouble. The kind that Thorn knew only too well.

"A single-engine plane went down in the mountains north of you about thirty minutes ago," the judge said. "I need you to find it."

He frowned. Just before the phone call had awakened him completely, he'd thought he'd heard a small plane flying low near his cabin, deep in the mountains north of Gardiner, Montana, and the north entrance to Yellowstone Park. He'd always been a light sleeper.

"Isn't the FAA all over it? Search and rescue? Local law enforcement?"

"No."

He cursed under his breath. So the plane had been flying under the radar and the pilot hadn't filed a flight plan. Someone hadn't wanted to be seen. "So why exactly *isn't* the FAA involved? Local law enforcement? Search and rescue? Legally, ethically and morally, isn't that proper procedure?"

"When did you become so damned law abiding?"

"When I met you, remember?"

Another growl and then, "This is a delicate situation. I wouldn't ask for your help if it wasn't."

"I understand. You have a downed plane and no one is looking for it."

"*You* are."

He chewed at his cheek for a moment. "Not even for you, Judge, until I get more information."

"You're as stubborn and difficult as always." The judge took a breath. "I received a call a few hours ago that a woman has been kidnapped. The kidnapper threatened to kill her if anyone notified the authorities."

"But if she is on a plane that crashed—"

"We need confirmation of that. We don't know for a fact that she's on it."

His mind was racing. "But you know where the plane crashed?" As the judge gave him the coordinates, Thorn quickly memorized them.

"The woman's cell phone has a tracking device on it. If she was on the plane, we need you to get her out as quickly and quietly as possible. If she is still alive."

"That's a lot of ifs. Who is the woman?" No way would the judge be involved in this unless the woman was some-one important.

The judge let out an impatient sigh. "Geneva Daven-port, the granddaughter of Franklin Davenport." *The media megamogul.* "She was abducted from her home outside of Big Fork earlier tonight."

Thorn swore. "This sounds like something you wouldn't normally touch with a ten-foot pole, so I'm guessing it's personal."

The judge's tone became even more clipped. "If you must know, Franklin and I served together in Nam. He saved my life. I owe him. It's a debt I take very seriously. I believe you can understand that."

He did. But he'd gotten out of this kind of work, and promised himself he was never going back. Even as he thought it, he knew, though, that he couldn't say no. Not to the judge. But he damn sure wanted to.

His mind was already working on the mission. It was time sensitive. He had to get to the plane, get to the woman, if she was still alive. At the same time, he knew someone would come looking for the plane and the woman. Someone besides him.

"What makes you think she's still alive?"

"Her cell phone. GPS indicated she is moving. Someone is still alive at the crash site. If it's not her, you'll have to deal with that."

"And after I find the plane and possibly this woman?"

"Don't call until you're back out and safe."

"You're that sure I'll be bringing her out?"

"I'm that sure you'll be coming out. Thorn, you know I wouldn't ask you to do anything you weren't trained to do. You *know* that country north of you. If anyone can find the plane quickly and get Geneva back to her family, it's you."

He felt a chill at even the thought of what he'd find back in those mountains. He'd promised himself he was done with twisted metal and death after what he'd seen in Iraq. But he'd also made a promise to Judge Landusky.

"I'll await your call." With that, the judge was gone.

JUDGE LANDUSKY STOOD for a moment, unable to shake the sudden doubt he felt. He told himself that he wasn't worried that Thorn could do this. The man had faced much worse than a few kidnappers and a spoiled, rich, young woman.

So what had him second-guessing himself? Maybe he was getting too old for this. That thought made him snort as he caught his reflection in his hall mirror. The man in the mirror had aged, no doubt about it. But he was still tall, broad-shouldered and in good shape. His hair had grayed, but he told himself it only made him look more distinguished. At sixty-five, he didn't feel a day over forty.

He might have retired as judge, but he wouldn't quit trying to make the world a better place until he was six feet under. He chastised himself for even thinking he wasn't up to whatever awaited him.

He wasn't worried about himself or Thorn, he realized as he picked up his suitcase and headed for the door. It was Geneva Davenport.

In his garage, he unlocked the door of his retirement present to himself—a low-slung midnight blue sports car. It had been the only impulse buy he'd ever made. Just seeing the car made him smile and at the same time shake his head. What had he been thinking?

As he started the powerful throaty engine, he turned his thoughts back to what Franklin had told him about his granddaughter and the trouble he'd had with her. Spoiled was putting it mildly. His friend had given her anything she wanted for years. He'd helped her get into numerous universities with healthy donations only to have her drop out of every one of them—or get thrown out.

When he'd asked for WT's advice recently while on the golf course in Florida, he'd given it freely. "You need to get tougher with her."

"Tough love?" Franklin had laughed at that. "I know you've turned a lot of kids around in your career, but Geneva doesn't need your boot camp. She's just sowing a few wild oats. She's a good girl. She'll snap out of it."

"She's no longer a girl, Franklin. She's twenty-two."

His friend had nodded, worry furrowing his brows. "I know you're right. It's just so hard. I want her to have everything she wants. I have all this money. What else am I going to do with it?"

"You're not doing her a favor," he'd told him.

Since both he and Franklin had now returned to Montana for the summer months, Franklin had told him that he'd threatened to cut off her allowance if she didn't straighten up and do something with her life. A self-made man, Franklin abhorred her attitude. Had Geneva been a male, Franklin would have taken this stand a long time ago.

He'd admitted that he'd made mistakes with her, and was trying to rectify them only to have her rebel even worse. The last straw had been the new boyfriend, Zac Judson. He'd canceled the credit cards he'd given her and reduced her allowance, insisting she get a job.

And now she'd been kidnapped? Coincidence? WT doubted it. He'd never met Geneva. He hadn't seen that much of Franklin except for a few golf games each year either in Florida or Montana. But he feared that whatever was going on, it had the potential to break his friend's heart.

He knew Franklin had to be as worried as he was that Geneva was behind this—and might have just gotten herself killed in a plane crash in the mountains.

CHAPTER THREE

SHE COULD STILL hear the terrifying shriek of metal being torn away as the plane hit the pines and began to come apart. First the wing on her side of the plane struck a tree and snapped off loudly. She'd felt cold air rush in, and had felt the plane plummeting through the darkness toward the ground as the other wing tore away. The fuselage kept moving, barreling downward through the tall pines, the metal shrieking as it careered into the trees before it finally came to a bone-shattering stop.

In the eerie silence that followed, she sat up and opened her eyes to the blackness outside. In the cockpit emergency lighting, she saw at once that the pilot was dead, crushed to death by the plane's engine practically sitting in his lap. For a moment, she thought everyone was dead but her.

Then the seat in front of her creaked as the man in it shifted. Baker, the pilot had called him. She held her breath, working her fingers under her thigh and around the grip of the weapon. She pulled it out very carefully, very quietly and rested it between her thighs, her finger on the trigger.

Baker shifted again, cursing under his breath. He glanced to his left, back at Kyle. From where he was seated, he couldn't see her without turning all the way around. She saw that the side of his face was bleeding. He picked a piece of broken glass from his cheek almost idly as he stared at the man in the seat next to her.

"Kyle?" Baker sighed when he got no response, and turned back, let out another curse as he tried to open his door. He had to put his shoulder into it several times before, with a rending squawk, it swung out. She felt the fuselage shift under her as Baker practically fell out. She realized that they were on the ground, the plane's wheels gone.

As he turned to look back, she closed her eyes and lay still, looking as dead as possible. She heard him let out a cry of pain followed by a curse as he moved away from the plane.

Opening her eyes, she saw him limping away from the plane and into the darkness. Where did he think he was going? He was obviously injured from the way he was limping and holding his left leg. She realized he might be back, which meant she had to move fast.

But before she could, next to her, Kyle stirred. To her horror, his gaze met hers. She saw the hate in it. She knew hate. She'd grown up in a place where hate and distrust were a way of life. His gaze hardened even before she pulled the gun she'd taken from his pocket earlier, but she didn't turn it on him. Once she did, she had to fire it or he would take it from her. She didn't want to kill anyone. So she waited for him to make the first move—and his last—if he did.

His hand went to his jacket pocket, his eyes widening with the realization that the weapon she held was his very own. "You bitch."

She could tell that he thought he could take the weapon away from her since her wrists were still bound with duct tape. He had no idea what she was capable of or what kind of experience she had with a gun. And right now she felt as if she was fighting for her life.

He let out a hoarse laugh and then froze as if in confusion. Blood ran from the corner of his mouth. As he wiped it across his lips with the back of his hand, he looked down at the blood. Then slowly, he opened one side of his jean jacket to peer down.

She gasped as she saw the tree limb sticking out of his stomach. He stared at it for a long moment before he tried to move in his seat and apparently couldn't, judging by the groan that erupted from him. She could see now where the limb had punctured the side of the plane, entering his body and pinning him to his seat.

Her stomach roiled, and she thought she was going to be sick.

His gaze came up to hers. He let out a sob, blood bubbling from his mouth. Then his eyes took on a vacant look before his head lolled forward. She waited, afraid that when she moved, he might grab for her. But he was gone, and suddenly she was desperate to get out of this plane, away from all of this death and gore.

Tucking the gun into her jeans waistband, she shoved the front passenger seat forward and crawled over it. As she dropped to the ground, she felt something tear at her leg. Pain seared through her, but she was so glad to be on solid ground she didn't even look to see how badly she might have been injured. She dropped to all fours, sucking in the fresh air as if drowning, and tried not to throw up.

It took a few moments to catch her breath and still the nausea roiling inside her. She was alive. But for how long? Baker could come back at any moment. She'd learned how to survive on her own at a young age. She called on that experience now as she tried to calm herself and consider what to do.

First things first, she had to free her wrists. While she could shoot the gun with her wrists bound, she'd have a much better chance of stopping Baker if her hands were free. Holding on to the side of the plane, she pulled herself up on still-wobbly legs.

The sky had lightened to the east, but the dark shadows of predawn still hunkered in the pines. Looking around, she didn't see or hear anyone. But she couldn't believe Baker would have gone far. Unless he'd panicked and was just trying to get away. Would he know how to get out of these mountains?

As she looked around her, all she could see were more pine trees and more mountains. She had no idea where she was or how she was going to find her way out. But she would survive. No matter what she had to do. It was how she'd lived a good portion of her life. She wasn't going to die on this mountainside.

In the glow of the emergency lights from the plane, she saw that she'd left the passenger-side door open. She could see a piece of jagged metal on the side of what was left of the plane. Limping over to it, she saw the blood smear on the metal and realized this was what had cut through her jeans—and her flesh—when she'd exited the plane. It was probably the same thing that Baker had gotten tangled up in, as well.

The sheet metal was jagged and sharp. She sawed at the tape, careful not to cut her wrists. This high in the mountains the June air was cold, but she knew that wasn't why she was trembling. As the tape gave way, she managed to rip it off using her teeth. As she did, she stared down at the sleeve of the sweater she was wearing. This definitely wasn't hers. Not green cashmere. She would have never bought something in this color even if she could have afforded cashmere.

Shaking her head at the path her mind had taken, she tried to concentrate on what to do next. If she hoped to stay alive, she would need warmer clothing because Montana mornings, especially in the mountains, were cold and she had no idea how long it would take her to get to civilization. And then what?

She couldn't think about that now. She glanced into the fuselage. All of the men had been wearing jackets when they'd abducted her from the bedroom. The thought of climbing back into the plane with two dead bodies turned her stomach. But it wouldn't be the first time she'd had to do something distasteful. She feared it wouldn't be the last.

This time as she climbed into the plane, she was careful to avoid the jagged edge of the metal that had cut her leg. The pilot had taken off his brown leather jacket, but it was behind him on the seat. She pushed against his shoulder, able to move him just enough that when she tugged hard, the jacket slipped free.

As it did, his wallet and cell phone fell out of a pocket along with a thick white envelope. She picked up all three items, pocketing the wallet and phone. The envelope felt heavy. Opening the flap, she saw a stack of hundred-dollar bills.

She realized that this was probably only a percentage of what he was getting paid for the job. Too bad the pilot hadn't found the landing strip where she assumed someone would have been waiting with the rest of his money. After all, when you kidnap Geneva Davenport, Franklin Davenport has the bucks to pay just about anything to get his granddaughter back.

Pocketing the envelope, she pulled the large leather jacket over the sweater and zipped it up. She glanced into the back of the plane at Kyle and felt her stomach turn again. Gingerly she reached in, turning her face away as she dug in the pockets of his jean jacket.

Like when she'd taken his gun, she felt safer by having his cell phone and wallet. Not that she had any idea what she planned to do with either because the last thing she could do was go to the police.

For a moment, she stopped to listen. She didn't hear Baker, but that didn't mean he hadn't returned and was now hiding in the pines waiting for a chance to jump her. Pulling the gun, she carefully climbed back out, avoiding the torn metal as she searched the shadowy pines for any movement.

The sky had lightened more. She saw no one, heard nothing but the steady thump of her heart in her chest. All her instincts told her that she had to get out of here before Baker came back. Or before someone came looking for the kidnappers and the plane…and her.

Abducted out of a sound sleep, then almost killed in a plane crash, her body was revved to the max. She felt as if she could wrestle a mountain lion. But first, she realized, she had to pee.

Even though there was no one in the plane who was going to see her, she stepped away into the far shelter of a stand of pines next to a rock cliff.

Dropping her jeans, she crouched. As she stared back at what little she could see of the fuselage, she heard a sound on the clear, morning air. A horse whinnied nearby, warning her that she was no longer alone.

DAYLIGHT FINGERED ITS way through the glistening boughs of the pines by the time Thorn caught a whiff of the fumes coming from the downed plane. He brought his horse up short in a stand of pines covering the side of the mountain. Dismounting, he tied up his horse, along with the extra saddled mare and his mule carrying supplies.

Since he had no idea what he would find, he'd tried to cover all the bases. For all he knew, the woman might be injured and unable to ride out of the mountains. On the mule was a collapsible cart that he used to drag dead game out of the mountains. He hoped it wouldn't come to that, but he felt ready for whatever he found up here.

Pulling his weapon, he crept to the top of the rise.

In the light of dawn, he could see one silver wing caught in the tops of the pines where it had come off on impact. A half dozen pines had been sheared off when the plane hit, leaving the debarked wood glowing in the new day. Past that he spotted the other wing gleaming among a pile of branches.

Cautiously, he made his way up the mountainside, following the wreckage of the plane. It hadn't taken him long to get to the crash site. If the woman was still alive, he knew he had to get to her as quickly as possible. But there was also a good chance that she wasn't the one with her phone. He had no idea how many kidnappers had been in the plane. Or how many of them were still alive and going to be a problem.

He hadn't gone far when he spotted the tail of the plane's fuselage sticking out from a stand of pines. He stopped for a moment to listen but heard nothing.

The judge believed someone had survived the crash because the tracking device had shown them moving around the area. Had that person tried to walk out of here already? He hoped not. He didn't feel like chasing anyone through these mountains. Only a fool would try to walk out unless the person knew exactly where he or she was. But if it was one of the kidnappers, he might be anxious to get away before someone came looking for the plane. Thorn knew the feeling. He wanted this over with as quickly as possible—and with the least amount of bloodshed.

He moved as silently as possible toward the downed fuselage. Even if someone had survived, the person might have since died of his or her injuries. Aware that the survivor could be one of the kidnappers, he stayed low, moving cautiously, his weapon in his hand loaded and ready to fire. It wasn't the first time he'd walked into a scene like this not knowing who or what he had to fear. But he had hoped never to have to do it again.

He felt the hair rise on the back of his neck as he saw that the passenger-side door of the plane was hanging open. Had someone exited just as the judge had said? Or had the door come open during impact? If someone had escaped, where were they now?

While this deep in the trees it was still dark, the sun had begun to scale the backside of the mountain. A squirrel chattered from a nearby tree. He heard his horse whinny and wondered if anyone else had heard it. His skin crawled with a feeling of déjà vu. He wasn't alone. He could feel it. Someone *was* alive, somewhere on this mountainside and possibly armed and dangerous.

In the next moment, the plane exploded in a deafening roar. Heat and debris drove him back as the fuselage became a ball of fire.

CHAPTER FOUR

THORN STOOD STARING at the fuselage, his heart in his throat. He was too late. If someone was still in the plane... Or had climbed back in for something...

Flames licked at the pines around the downed plane. Over the crackle and roar of the fire, he heard a branch snap off to his right—but not soon enough to react to the possible threat.

The woman came out of the trees, her eyes wide, but the gun in her hand steady as she pointed it at his chest and yelled, "Drop the gun and put your hands up!"

Caught off guard, he didn't respond at once. She fired a shot. Bark flew from the tree next to him as the bullet hit within inches of his head. Clearly, the woman knew her way around a weapon. He dropped his pistol and slowly raised his hands as he took in the woman staring him down.

"Geneva Davenport, I assume?"

She said nothing, narrowing her blue eyes at him. "Who are you?"

"Thorn. I'm here to rescue you."

She looked amused by that. Stray locks of her blond ponytail hung around a heart-shaped face smudged with soot. There was a small cut above her right eye, a very blue eye. She wore a too-large brown leather jacket that was obviously not hers, and sneakers without socks. There was blood on her left jeans pant leg.

What struck him was that she wasn't acting like he'd expected a megamogul's granddaughter to react. Hell, she wasn't acting like any woman who'd been kidnapped and almost killed in a plane crash would behave when faced with someone saying they'd come to rescue her.

Had he expected her to run into his arms crying? He'd at least expected to see relief on her face. The last thing he'd thought he would be doing right now was staring down the barrel of a gun.

"Geneva," he said, thinking she must be in shock. "It's all right. I've been sent by a friend of your grandfather's."

She eyed him suspiciously. "How did you get here so quickly?"

"I have a cabin not far from here. That's why I was sent. Your grandfather wants to make sure you're safe. I can get you out of these mountains to safety, and then you can call him."

"And why should I believe you?" She tilted her head toward the smoke rising from the charred fuselage. After the initial explosion, the fire had burned out quickly. He wondered if she might have a concussion. That could explain her behavior.

"I guess you'll just have to trust me. But we need to get out of here," he said, trying for patience. "That explosion won't go unnoticed." He knew she'd been through a lot, but the sooner they left, the better. "You need me."

She smiled at that. "So you say. But I wouldn't move if I were you. I've had a really rough night. I don't want to shoot you, but I will."

SHE CONSIDERED THE MAN. He looked nothing like the ones who'd abducted her. They had all looked like average Joes. Thorn, if that was his real name, looked like a mountain man, with his full dark beard and shaggy dark hair that curled out from under his weathered cowboy hat. Everything about him told her he was dangerous, maybe especially the look in his gray eyes.

He'd been sent here all right, she thought. That missing airstrip must be closer than the pilot had thought. Otherwise, how did this man find her so quickly?

Also she sensed that he didn't want to be here any more than she did. Kidnapping was nasty business. Maybe he didn't like being involved. So why was he? All she knew was that he *shouldn't* be here, and neither should she. How long would it take before everyone realized that?

"Geneva," he said in a calm, low, almost hypnotic voice as if talking to a child. "You need to trust me. I don't want any harm to come to you."

"That sounds like a threat."

He shook his head, clearly losing patience. "Look, Geneva—"

"Can you please stop calling me that?" she snapped, her head aching. She hadn't meant to say it out loud, but she still felt sick to her stomach from the drugs and woozy from hitting her head when the plane crashed.

"I'm sorry." He frowned, those gray eyes narrowing as he studied her. "What would you like me to call you?" Now he really was talking down to her as if she was a child.

She felt her finger on the trigger tighten. When was this nightmare ever going to end? *Yes, what would you like him to call you?* "How about JJ?"

"JJ?" His frown deepened, those eyes intent on her.

It was what her father had called her. Just the thought of him made her heart ache. If he could see her now. "I called myself JJ when I was little. It stuck." The best lies begin with a little truth, she'd learned.

"So not Geneva?"

She groaned inwardly. "My grandfather only uses the name Geneva when he's angry with me." That at least was true as well, kind of.

"Okay, JJ, now can we get out of here?"

He'd said she just needed to trust him. Trust didn't come easy to her even under the best of circumstances—and these were definitely not that.

She had a gun on him, one she hoped she wouldn't have to use, but it was definitely an option she was keeping open. She had no reason to trust this man and every reason not to.

"As I was saying, *JJ*, they will be looking for the plane. If they are nearby, they will have seen the flames. We have to go. *Now.*"

"How did you find me?" she asked, still not convinced that he wasn't in league with the kidnappers. How else had he known where to find the plane? He said he lived nearby. Near a landing strip where he'd been waiting for a small plane to arrive? He'd certainly found the plane quickly.

"There's a tracking device on your phone."

On *her* phone? She blinked in surprise, the gun wavering for just an instant as she realized that he meant on *Geneva's* phone.

It was apparently the opening he needed. She hadn't seen him move until he was on her. She got off another shot before he wrestled the weapon from her hands, but the bullet went wild. He threw her to the ground as if it was definitely not his first time overpowering someone.

Anger coursed through her and she fought him, not because she thought she could get free. She knew that like the others, he'd be too strong for her. She fought because she was mad and sick of the way she was being treated and furious at the injustice. This should not have been happening to her.

"Whoa," he said as he gathered her wrists in one large hand and pressed them above her head. His body held her to the ground no matter how hard she tried to throw him off. "I'm one of the good guys."

She looked into his gray eyes and scoffed. "Sure doesn't look like it from where I am."

"Sorry about having to get rough with you, but I don't take kindly to anyone holding a gun on me."

"Especially a woman?"

"Especially an *angry, scared* woman." His gray eyes softened, reminding her of the earlier dawn. She saw that there were tiny laugh wrinkles around those eyes. She guessed his age at thirtysomething—much like her own even though she still got carded in bars because she looked so young. Which was another reason the men who'd kidnapped her hadn't realized their mistake.

She stared at the man now, wondering what he would look like without the beard, and then wondering where that stray thought had come from.

As he started to search her with his free hand, she bucked and fought, but it did no good. He emptied the pockets of the pilot's leather jacket, first taking out the cell phones, then the wallets and finally the envelope stuffed with hundred-dollar bills.

His gaze fell on hers. "You took these off the men in the plane?" He made it sound almost as ghoulish as it had been.

"I wanted to know who abducted me," she snapped.

He seemed to consider that, studying her as if he wasn't so sure about her. If he only knew. Clearly, he'd expected her to be sitting on a tree stump crying and waiting to be rescued when he found her. He hadn't really thought she would run into his arms, had he? Maybe the real Geneva might have, she realized.

She felt a change in him. He was starting to question things. He was starting to have doubts. She wanted away from here as badly as he apparently had just moments before. She just wasn't sure she wanted him taking her anywhere. But the alternative might be him leaving her here as dead as Kyle and the pilot.

"There's something you should know," she said, shifting his suspicion away from her for a moment. "One of the men escaped the plane. I figure he hasn't gone far and that he will be coming back."

THAT STOPPED THORN COLD. He'd just assumed she was the only one who'd survived the crash. Then when the plane blew up... He froze on top of her and looked around, feeling the hair rise on the back of his neck again.

"You just decided to tell me that?" he snapped. "Is the man injured?"

"He was limping the last time I saw him."

"Which direction did he go?"

She gave him an impatient look. "Like I can tell you from down here."

Thorn considered the woman. She definitely wasn't what he'd been expecting. Still he'd assumed she would be glad that someone had come to rescue her.

Instead, she'd held a gun on him and was still fighting him. Hell, she'd actually fired two shots at him, one so close to his head that the bark from the tree next to him had pelted his face. Not to mention the fact that she'd been calm enough to go through two dead men's pockets and take their wallets, cell phones and an envelope full of cash. That didn't sound like a spoiled, rich, pampered young woman who'd been kidnapped in the middle of the night and barely survived a plane crash.

"I thought you said we had to get out of here," she said, glaring at him.

"*Now* you're ready to go?"

"I would like that just fine." She bucked under him and managed to get one hand free. Her fist struck him in the jaw.

He grabbed her wrist again. "Knock it off. You're going to hurt yourself." His words fell on deaf ears as she continued to fight him.

Instead, he dragged her up from the ground and over to a thick trunked pine tree, her swinging and kicking at him the whole time. She was a wild thing, full of spit and vinegar, as his grandmother used to say.

Pulling off his belt with one hand as he held her off with the other, he wrapped the belt around her waist and the tree. He tightened the belt until she could still breathe, but was no longer a danger to either of them for the moment.

"Nice right hook," he said, rubbing his jaw as he watched her try to free herself from the tree. "You are one stubborn woman, you know that?" He glanced around, listening, but didn't hear anyone approaching. Maybe the kidnapper was trying to walk out of the mountains. Or maybe not. It was bad enough having to fight this woman knowing there was someone even more dangerous out in the woods.

"The man who left the plane… Is he armed?"

She shrugged as she glared daggers at him and he considered what to do next. Fortunately, she'd taken the kidnappers' phones and wallets, so he had the IDs of the two before the plane blew up. But if there had been any evidence on board the plane, it was gone now. He couldn't help but wonder what had made the plane explode.

JJ WATCHED THE cowboy check the men's wallets and cell phones. Both phones were password protected, and there was no cell phone service up here on the mountain. She knew because she'd already tried when she was peeing in the woods. The men were Wesley "Wes" Brennan and Kyle Spencer, both of Kalispell, Montana. She'd never heard of either of them—not much of a surprise, all things considered.

Now as she watched the cowboy, she saw the way he studied the IDs in the wallets as if he hadn't known who the kidnappers were. Maybe he was telling the truth.

But then again, he could be working for the same person who'd hired the other men. That didn't mean he'd known their names. He'd said that a friend of her grandfather's had sent him. That was more believable than Franklin Davenport knowing a man like this one.

As she studied him, she tried to understand why this cowboy seemed more dangerous than the men who'd abducted her. Maybe because this one seemed to know exactly what he was doing, as if it wasn't the first time he'd taken a gun away from a woman or belted someone to a tree. There was also something about the way he moved, stealth-like. A panther on the prowl. No wasted movement. And those gray eyes. She felt a shiver. He looked at her with a calculating gaze that seemed to bore into her very soul.

She had no doubt there was a reason this man had been sent to find her. He wasn't like the others. He wouldn't have been piloting a plane low on gas and lost in the mountains. This man would have found the runway and collected the second half of his pay.

The thought jolted her. And now he was going to take her off this mountain—one way or another. She'd already felt how strong he was. She was at his mercy. She swallowed at the thought of how easily he could overcome her—or worse, kill her. But apparently whoever had sent him didn't want her dead. Didn't want Geneva Davenport dead, she corrected. At least that was her hope.

But no matter what this man said, he wasn't some innocent cowboy who just happened to live nearby. Not the way he'd handled her so far. The man had known exactly how to overpower her single-handedly, when it had taken three men and a drug to control her in the bedroom last night.

Her head throbbed, and she could feel the ache and burn of the cut on her leg. It had started to bleed again. She'd seen enough of the wound through the tear in her jeans to know it was a nasty cut that would require a tetanus shot. That was, if she ever got off this mountain alive.

She leaned against the tree and closed her eyes. She would not go down without a fight. But she had to wait for an opportunity to turn the tables on this cowboy. Meanwhile, she had little choice but to go along with him since she had no idea where she was or how to get out by herself.

The man was right about one thing. She needed him. Temporarily.

THORN STUDIED THE woman as he considered what he'd gotten involved in. Her big blue eyes were closed, her dark lashes lying against her pale skin. She had quit trying to escape. But that didn't fool him for a minute. The woman was a fighter. He'd have to watch her closely.

He tried to tell himself that she'd been through a lot tonight, just like she'd said. She was certainly feisty, and not bad to look at even after being kidnapped and nearly dying in a plane crash. But he was sure she knew that, and used it and her grandfather's position and wealth to her advantage. Still, maybe he needed to take a more gentle approach.

"You all right?" he asked, worried he'd gotten the belt too tight.

"My head hurts," she said without opening her eyes. "I hit it when the plane crashed."

"You don't have a concussion."

Those eyes, the color of a Montana summer sky, opened and shifted to him. "Thanks, Doc."

He sighed and reached for the cantina in his pack. "I thought you might like some water."

He held it to her lips, not sure she would drink, as stubborn as she was—and as suspicious. The water was cold, straight from the spring behind his cabin. To his surprise, she drank as if she'd been lost in the desert for weeks.

"Enough?"

She took a little more before she nodded. As he started to step away, he noticed that the cut on her leg was bleeding again.

"You're bleeding." She glared in answer. "I'm going to have a look at your leg. If you kick me, I will be forced to further restrain you."

"And you're one of the good guys?"

He crouched next to her and the tree. Pulling his knife from its scabbard, he carefully cut the jeans fabric open enough that he could see her injury better. The cut was jagged and fairly deep.

"You're not just some cowboy who lives nearby," she said, those blue eyes intent on him as he got to his feet. "So who are you?"

"Just a cowboy who lives nearby."

"Right," she said in disgust. "And you expect me to trust you?" she said under her breath, and she looked away from him.

He felt the two phones he'd taken from her weighing

down his jacket pocket. "By the way, which of these phones is yours?"

"Worried about the tracking device leading someone else to us? I've never seen either of those phones before."

"Where is your phone, then?" he asked.

She shrugged, making him suspect she was lying. "I assume the man who took off has the phone or it was destroyed when the plane blew up."

He studied her. She was lying about something. Her phone? Or something even more dangerous? "I'm going to have to go get my first aid kit."

"You aren't going to leave me like this," she cried, straining against the belt around her.

"My first aid kit is with my horse just over the rise. Stay here."

"Funny," she said as he walked away.

He hadn't heard his horse whinny, and now worried that the missing kidnapper might have found both horses and his mule. But as soon as he topped the rise, he saw with relief that all three were where he'd tied them. As he led the trio back to where he'd left the woman, the sun topped the trees, a golden orb against a cloudless summer day.

He couldn't help but wish he were down at his cabin right now instead of dealing with this…problem.

Back at the wreckage, he removed the first aid kit from his saddlebag. "This is going to hurt," he said as he opened the bottle of rubbing alcohol and met her blue eyes for a moment before she closed them tight again.

He poured the alcohol over her wound and saw her shudder. She bit down on her lower lip, but she made no sound. She was much tougher than he'd expected, he thought as he bandaged her leg. The cut was deep but shouldn't need stitches, so the bandage would do for now. They would have to change it often to keep it clean, but they had to get moving.

She was right about one thing. The kidnapper could come back. But it was more likely that it would be someone looking for the plane—and Geneva. Most planes had tracking devices on them. Since this one hadn't gotten wherever it was headed, there was definitely someone looking for it. Without Geneva, the kidnappers had no leverage, and he was betting that whoever was behind this hadn't been on the plane.

He rose to his feet and considered the charred remains of the fuselage for a moment. This was a simple kidnapping, right? He hated going into any situation without all the information available, but especially something this high up the ladder since Franklin Davenport was a powerful man. If it had been anyone but the judge who'd asked him to get involved…

He turned to the woman. "Have you ever ridden a horse?"

"It looks pretty simple. *You* can do it, right?"

He smiled at her sarcasm. "We need to get a few things straight before I let you loose. I didn't want to come back into these mountains after you. So I'm in no mood to put up with any more of you fighting me. I will get you out of here alive, and after that, you're your grandfather's problem."

She said nothing, her blue eyes hot as a welding torch flame.

JJ WATCHED HIM go to his saddlebags, her heart dropping as he pulled out a length of rope. "You are not going to tie me up."

He didn't bother to glance at her. "You've given me no choice."

Her pulse pounded in her ears. An even colder chill

tiptoed up her spine. "You didn't come to save me. You're making me your prisoner. You're one of them."

He didn't answer as he came toward her.

She pulled at the belt that had her bound to the tree, but the effort was wasted.

When he reached her, he grabbed her right hand before she could swing at him again, then he corralled her left. Holding her wrists in a viselike grip, he bound them together with the rope quickly and again, with obvious practice.

She was angry and scared, but she gave up fighting even though it was second nature to her. She had to be smart, save her energy, bide her time. She told herself that if he wanted her dead, she'd already be killed. That meant they would be riding out of here together. Why else would he have brought two horses and a mule?

Still, she didn't trust him. He'd known she'd survived the crash. He'd said Geneva's cell phone had a tracking device on it. Nothing like Find My Phone. It would have to be something more sophisticated. Which made her wonder who'd put the device on the phone. Geneva must have known her grandfather had been tracking her via her phone. Why else leave it in her bedroom, where the kidnappers had found it?

She assumed the men had kidnapped the woman they thought was the granddaughter of media mogul Franklin Davenport for money. That was the obvious motive. Unless there was more to it, she thought. Not that it mattered. She was neck-deep in this, and right now she didn't see any way out until she got free of this cowboy.

ALL THE FIGHT seemed to have gone out of her as Thorn finished securing her wrists. But he didn't trust it, fearing this tactic was more like the calm before a storm. He thought about the judge and his powerful friend. Neither was going to like the measures he'd had to take to subdue this woman.

"I'm going to remove the belt, but if you give me any trouble, I will hog-tie you and throw you over the mule I brought. Your choice—ride out in the saddle or tied to a mule like a sack of potatoes. I'm good either way."

"You skipped charm school, right?"

He smiled. "In my business, it's not a requirement."

"And what business is that?" she asked.

He shook his head as he pulled the belt free, expecting her to run or attack. To his surprise, she did neither as he helped her over to her horse. He figured she'd try to take off the moment she settled in the saddle, so he had a good hold on her reins.

He hoisted her up. True to form, the instant her perfectly rounded bottom touched the saddle, she gave the horse a good kick, making the mare jump forward. Still holding the reins with one hand, he jerked her off the horse with the other, and then picked her up off her feet by the front of the leather jacket she was wearing.

"You do that to my horse again and—"

"You're choking me."

"Nothing compared to what I'd like to do to you." He held her in the air for a few moments longer, before he set her on the ground and gave her a shake. "If it was up to me…"

"Yes, we know what you would do if it was up to you. So do it," she said defiantly.

He snorted. "You seem capable enough to get out of these mountains by yourself," he said, considering her. She looked in good shape, and she definitely had the spirit and determination. "Somehow, I don't think it would be the first time you've had to rescue yourself." That alone surprised him. Then again, everything about this woman surprised him from the moment he first saw her holding a gun on him.

"There's one problem I don't think you've considered," he said patiently. "The kidnappers. They need you. Which means they're looking for you to make sure you don't surface before they get their money." He saw her eyes widen. "I thought you might have missed that part." He looked into all that tempting blue, trying to gauge just how much more trouble she was going to be. More than he needed, that was for sure. "I will do my best to keep you safe until you are returned to your grandfather. Still want to take your chances alone with the kidnappers?"

"Why should I believe anything that comes out of your mouth?" she said, her voice breaking. "You could be taking me straight to them." It was the first time he'd seen a crack in her kick-butt veneer. Under all the attitude, he now saw that she was exhausted and possibly more frightened than even she wanted to admit.

He took off his Stetson and raked his hand through his hair, never taking his eyes from her or letting go of her. "I swear, you're more obstinate than me, and that is saying a lot." He cursed. "Look, you don't have to trust me."

"Don't worry, I won't."

He sighed. "So are you going out of here on a horse or on a mule?"

She looked away for a moment. He saw the stubborn set of her jaw. The damn woman would rather stay here alone than let him help her?

He waited her out, though he'd long ago lost patience with her. Whoever was behind this would be looking for the plane. He had to assume that they knew where it had gone down and would be coming soon. He could feel the clock ticking while she made up her mind.

When he was about ready to hog-tie her to the mule, she finally spoke. "You're taking me to your cabin first?"

"To my cabin to pick up my truck, and then I'll take you to your grandfather. You can call him from the cabin. There will be cell phone service. Ready?"

She nodded, and he helped her up on the horse. Taking the reins, he walked to his own. Swinging up in the saddle, he pulled her horse up next to his, the mule on a tether behind him.

They rode out the same way he'd come in. A thunderstorm was supposed to blow in later today. It would make tracking them harder, but not impossible.

It could lead whoever found the plane—or the missing kidnapper—right to his cabin.

CHAPTER FIVE

THE SUMMER DAY rose golden. Sunlight shimmered in the boughs of the pines, sending up the rich scent into the morning air as they rode down out of the mountains. Thorn watched the woman tip her face up to the sun and close her eyes. She looked good considering everything she'd been through. He'd seen the injection mark on her neck and assumed that's how the men had gotten her from her house to the plane. He would have loved to hear her side of the story, but was determined to do only what was asked of him and wash his hands of her as quickly as possible before getting back to his simple, quiet life.

She was clearly trying to relax in the saddle and hide the fact that riding the horse terrified her. He could tell that she'd never ridden before. Every time the horse shuddered or stumbled, she jolted, hanging on to the saddle horn for dear life.

Thorn hid his smile, amused that he'd discovered the one thing the woman might truly be afraid of—a horse— after living through a much more harrowing experience.

The plane had gone down on the other side of the mountain from his cabin. The ride out, once they got past the rim of the cliffs at the high ridge, would be easy—if no one tried to stop them. He kept a lookout for the other kidnapper, though he doubted the man had come this way. There were no fresh boot tracks on the trail.

Thorn also figured they would have seen him by now if the man had circled back. They'd lost valuable time back at the crash site arguing. He'd wanted to ring the woman's pretty slim neck. He told himself that of course she would be suspicious after everything that had happened to her.

But something kept nagging at him. He'd never heard of Geneva Davenport before today. She'd defied his expectations of the woman he thought he'd gone into the mountains to rescue. But what did he know of rich, pampered granddaughters of superwealthy men? Maybe they grew up to be exactly like this one. It wasn't like he'd had much contact with the outside world the past few years.

He couldn't even imagine growing up with too much money. He'd been the stereotypical kid who grew up with parents who drank, fought and moved from job to job, state to state, a lot. He could have turned into a serial killer—he had the same family background as a lot of them, according to the judge.

Instead, he'd merely started acting out by drinking, lying and stealing cars.

He figured if he hadn't gotten caught and ended up before Judge Landusky, he would be in prison right now.

He glanced over at JJ. What would she know about a life like that? Nothing.

By the time they reached the rock rim along the top of the mountain and rode under it, he was pretty sure they weren't going to run into the missing kidnapper.

He reined in. From here they could see mountains for miles. No one would guess that there was a town right below them or a river that ran through the middle of it. He pulled out his cantina, took a drink and held it out to her.

She held up her tied wrists. "Can't you—"

"No."

She glared at him. "I have to go the bathroom."

"Then I hope you aren't modest because I'll be tagging along with you."

"I'll hold it."

"Your choice." He put the cantina away and took some jerky from of his pack. He'd made it himself from this year's elk. He offered her a piece, and to his surprise she accepted. They ate in companionable silence for a moment. He knew he shouldn't, but still he had to ask. "Where were you when you were kidnapped?"

"In bed."

"At your house?"

"Alone," she said, and took a bite of the dried meat.

"There were three of them?"

She looked over at him as if she could tell he wanted to hear the details. He thought she would deny him that and was surprised when she didn't. "I was sound asleep. Something woke me. I saw three masked men. The one I now know was Wesley Brennan covered my mouth with his gloved hand and held me down while the other two, Kyle Spencer and the man he called Baker, searched the room."

He frowned. If this was a simple kidnapping… "What were they looking for?"

She shook her head. "They found her phone."

"*Her* phone?"

"My phone. I told you my head hurts. Anyway, Baker pocketed it, and then the two came over to the bed to help hold me down so Wesley could inject me with some kind of drug."

Thorn could imagine the fight she'd put up. He was well aware of how she acted when cornered.

"Were you conscious before the plane crashed?"

She nodded. "Kyle was asleep in the back with me, but

he woke up to lean forward to see what was going on. The pilot said he was lost and the plane's fuel was running low. I saw Kyle's gun sticking out of his jacket pocket. My wrists were bound together with duct tape, but I managed to take it without him being the wiser. I hid it from his view, planning to use it when we landed."

He couldn't help but raise a brow. "You were going to shoot them?"

"Only if they forced me to."

This young woman was no shrinking violet. Far from it. "That was clever of you. When did you realize the plane was going to crash?"

"I overheard the pilot talking even though I pretended to still be knocked out. Then I braced for the crash." She took another bite of the jerky.

"When did the one kidnapper bail?"

"Baker? I thought everyone was dead, but then I felt him move in the seat in front of me. He said Kyle's name, then, thinking everyone was dead, he opened the door and jumped out before taking off through the trees. He seemed…scared."

Thorn would imagine so. He had to know that the plane would be found. He glanced over at her. "You must have been scared too."

She either didn't hear him or ignored that as she continued, as if lost in her story. "I was about to get out of the plane as well when Kyle came to. I thought I was going to have to shoot him, but a tree limb had punctured the side of the fuselage and pinned him to his seat." She hesitated a moment, then looked away, adding, "He died, I got out and not long after that, there you were."

She'd left out only one thing. "I thought I heard something right before the plane exploded." She said nothing.

"Odd, if the plane was running low on fuel that it would explode—not on impact, but later."

"You think someone purposely blew it up?" Her voice wavered as if realization of how close she'd come to dying was finally starting to sink in.

"Why would anyone want to blow up the plane knowing you were inside?" he asked more to himself than to her. Wouldn't the kidnappers need her for the exchange? Why kill her and the men who'd abducted her?

Her eyes widened as if she was wondering the same thing. He looked into all that blue, feeling as if he were on a slippery slope above a tropical bottomless pool. She looked even more wary. "I thought we were in a hurry to get out of these mountains?"

He put the rest of the jerky away. "Look, I didn't come all the way back into these mountains to harm you. If that were true, I would have broken your neck and left you beside the plane and no one would have been the wiser."

JJ HID HER real shudder with an exaggerated pretend one. "And you keep trying to convince me that you're one of the good guys." She shook her head. "You've killed people before." When he didn't respond, she continued. "If any of this were legit, there would be cops, Feds and FAA crawling all over this mountain. Not some—" she waved her jerky in his direction as if not sure what to call him "—*cowboy* coming for me with two horses and a mule."

"Easy, you don't want to hurt Gertrude's feelings. You could still end up on that mule." He spurred his horse, pulling hers and the mule along with him, as he started down through the pines.

He'd asked her a lot of questions. She thought she deserved some answers, as well. Rehashing what had happened to her had felt like she was talking about someone else being kidnapped. The irony of that wasn't wasted on her. If she hadn't been in that bed last night... While all of this had a surreal feel to it, she worried it was going to get painfully real before it was over.

"So who are you?" she asked as her horse trotted alongside his.

"I told you. My name's Thorn."

"No last name?"

"None that you need."

"What do you do?"

"Do?"

"For a living?"

"I'm retired."

She shot him a look. "*Retired?* How old are you? Forty?"

He smiled. "Not quite."

"Are you married?"

JJ didn't miss the way the muscle in his jaw bunched. He looked away. "Not anymore. If you still have to go to the bathroom—"

"I'm fine. Divorced?"

"Widowed." He spurred his horse so hers dropped back. Clearly, he didn't want to talk about it. She was surprised she'd gotten as much information out of him as she had. She thought she had a lot to hide, but apparently she wasn't the only one.

They continued down through the pines, back into the cool shadows and then out again. Ahead she could see the roof of a cabin.

He slowed their horses. She watched him looking around warily. Did he think Baker might be here waiting for them? To what? Ambush them?

Everything must have looked just as he'd left it because

he spurred his horse and led hers and Gertrude the mule toward the cabin.

He'd said he hadn't wanted to come up into the mountains after her. She wondered what he'd been offered. Obviously, something he couldn't refuse. She could tell that he was anxious to turn her over to Franklin Davenport. *And get back to what?* she wondered as she looked around.

But she had to admit, she felt relieved. The man had told the truth about the cabin at least, she thought as he led her toward the barn. The newer log cabin was small, the barn and outbuildings old. She saw an ancient pickup parked off to one side. She didn't see another vehicle.

It made her wonder what he did here. Surely he didn't live here year-round. But if not, what did he do the rest of the time?

She glanced at the road out of his mountain retreat. The land fell away toward the river far below. She saw a familiar arch in the distance, and suddenly she knew where she was. The Roosevelt Arch was located at Yellowstone Park's north entrance. That meant that the small town of Gardiner wasn't far away.

So the kidnappers had flown her from Big Fork all the way here before the plane had gone down. There was probably a landing strip somewhere near Gardiner. Was that where the pilot had been headed and had just gotten turned around?

She thought about what he'd said about someone blowing up the plane. Had there been explosives on board the whole time? But why would someone want to kill Geneva Davenport?

When she looked in Thorn's direction, she realized that he'd been studying her again. She was sure her relieved expression had shown on her face. She'd been afraid that his cabin would be miles from civilization. Now that she knew it wasn't, she was relieved.

He dismounted and started to help her down from her horse. His gaze met hers. "I'd like to untie you."

"Please do."

"I could ask you to behave."

She smiled. "But what would be the point, right?"

With a laugh, he grabbed her waist in his two large hands and lifted her, slowly lowering her to the ground. She held out her wrists for him to untie the rope.

For a moment, he merely studied her. The man wasn't stupid.

"I'm through fighting you, okay? I just want to go... home." The word stuck in her throat. She hadn't had a home in so long, let alone anyone to go home to, that it wasn't a word she used. Her stomach growled at even the thought of a well-stocked refrigerator and a stove to cook on.

He must have heard the anguish in her voice as well as the rumble of her stomach because his expression softened. "You must be hungry."

"I'm starved," she said honestly. All the piece of jerky had done was whet her appetite. "I didn't have much to eat yesterday."

"Let me put the stock away and if there's time, I'll make you something to eat."

"If there is time before what?" she asked, suspicion tingeing her tone.

He sighed. "Before I take you to your grandfather."

She stood at the entrance of the barn and watched him put the animals away. Even if she'd had the energy to run, she couldn't. She needed food. She also needed his trust— and his pickup. It was her only chance. She had to escape before he turned her over to Franklin Davenport and the authorities. Once they realized she wasn't Geneva Davenport, that she hadn't had permission to be sleeping in the woman's house last night and that she had a criminal record…

Exhaustion threatened. She leaned against the doorway to the barn, surprised by Thorn's gentleness with the animals. She lowered herself onto a bale of hay by the open door.

She liked watching his big, sun-browned hands. They were the hands of a man who worked outside, who knew hard manual labor. They stirred something in her she hadn't felt in a very long time.

A shaft of summer sun cut through a hole in the roof. He stepped into it, the light accentuating the angles of his face. He was strikingly attractive even with the full beard, she thought with a jolt. She saw now why he was so strong. He'd taken off his jacket and wore only a T-shirt. His muscled arms bunched as he lifted off the saddles and packs. His T-shirt rode up as he hung up the tack, exposing his washboard abs, his skin a warm tanned brown even though it was early summer. She looked away, the heat of the sun, the rich smell of hay, the man making all of this feel too intimate.

She must have dozed off, coming awake with a start when she felt someone touch her arm. Her eyes flew open. Off balance, she shot to her feet, confused as to where she was for the moment. He grabbed her arm to steady her.

"It's okay," he said softly. "You're okay."

She didn't feel okay. She could feel the clock ticking. How long did she have before he turned her over to Franklin Davenport and the questions began?

As they walked down to the cabin, she wiped a hand across her face. It came away blackened, no doubt from the explosion earlier. "Is there any chance I could get cleaned up before we leave?" She did need to wash, but she also wanted to put off the inevitable as long as she could.

"I need to make a phone call first," he said, making her heart drop.

Once he talked to whoever had sent him to find her, he'd know the truth because by now someone would have found her duffel bag on the floor of Geneva's bedroom with her purse and phone inside—not to mention her car was parked in Geneva's three-car garage on the lower floor of the house. Or the real Geneva Davenport could have surfaced by now.

Either way, she was screwed.

CHAPTER SIX

THORN PUSHED OPEN the door to his home, took a quick glance inside to make sure it was empty and motioned JJ in. He watched her expression as she looked around the small cabin, taking in the fireplace, chair and bookshelf that made up his living room. She glanced at the bed and the chest of drawers next to it before peeking around the low partition into the kitchen, which was similarly simple: sink, stove, just enough butcher-block counter to cut meat, refrigerator and freezer.

He figured she'd grown up in boundless space and luxury. He hated to think what she thought of his cabin since everything was basically all in one room.

It had served his purposes just fine, but now he was seeing it through her eyes. He'd bet her bedroom was larger than his entire cabin.

"Tell me about her."

"I beg your pardon?" he asked behind her.

"The woman who broke your heart so bad you swore never to love again and moved here." She made a sweep of her arm, taking in the interior of his cabin in a way that made it clear what she thought of it.

He clamped his jaw shut, feeling his teeth grind. "She was my wife. She was killed. It was my fault."

JJ turned to face him, shock and sympathy in her expression. "I'm sorry."

"Right. You think you have me all figured out. You don't."

She nodded, but she'd seen right through him—right to the heart of it even without any details. This was why he kept the world at arm's length.

"How long were you married?"

He stared at her. She wasn't going to give up? "Really, you want all the gory details?"

Hands on her hips, she sighed. "Maybe I just want to know more about the man who...*rescued* me. After all, you're supposed to be the only thing standing between me and the people who want me dead. So yes, I'd like to know who I'm dealing with. I want to know about the woman you've never been able to get over."

He groaned inwardly. "Doesn't it worry you that I just told you I got her killed?"

She looked at him, waiting, as if they were talking about the weather instead of the biggest heartbreak of his life. "What was her name?"

"Bethany." His throat threatened to close. It had been so long since he'd spoken her name out loud.

JJ nodded and looked toward the kitchen. "You said you might have something to eat here?"

The sudden change of topic threw him for a moment. "I have elk steaks and frozen vegetables from last summer's garden."

"Pretty self-sufficient, huh?"

"I try to be. Aren't you going to ask me how I got her killed?"

She shook her head. "You'll tell me when you're ready. That's if I'm still around." With that she limped into his tiny kitchen.

"You know how to cook?" he said after her.

She laughed. It seemed to fill the cabin with sunshine.

He shook his head as he followed her.

"The bathroom is *outside*?" JJ asked as she squinted out the back-door window. He had stepped to the sink to fill kettles with water and get them on the stove to heat.

"I'll take you." He finished what he was doing.

"Seriously?" She shot him a disbelieving look. "I can see the outhouse from here. I think I can find my way there."

"It's finding your way back that worries me," he said as he stepped past her to open the back door. She sighed, clearly aggravated with him. Too bad. She'd given him no reason to trust her even as far as he could throw her.

She stepped out, and he let her lead the way through the sunshine toward the outhouse, looking around as he went. Unlike her, apparently, he hadn't forgotten about the missing kidnapper. She didn't seem as concerned, which caused him even more worry. Everything about her attitude seemed...off. She wasn't acting like a woman who'd been kidnapped and was anxious to go home. She hadn't even mentioned calling her grandfather.

He scanned the mountainside. The view was so familiar; he knew every tree, every rock, every bush. He saw nothing unfamiliar. No movement.

She scoffed at his concern for her safety. As she reached the outhouse, she stopped. Wind lifted the strands of blond hair that had escaped her ponytail. "Tell me you aren't going inside with me."

Thorn opened the door, his pistol still strapped at his side. The small building was empty. Had he really thought the kidnapper might have been hiding there? JJ gave him an amused look as if to say he was being ridiculous. Probably. Which made him want her out of his care as soon as possible.

"What did you think was in there? Baker, the missing kidnapper?"

Without answering, he held the door open for her and

she stepped inside, grabbed the door out of his hand and slammed it. There wasn't a lock. He heard her let out an exasperated sound from inside and smiled as he stepped around to the side. He was glad to exasperate her a little since she certainly had him.

He saw that dark clouds had gathered off to the west. The thunderstorm the forecasters had predicted looked as if it was on its way. Right now, though, there wasn't a cloud above him, but he could feel the breeze freshening as the day wore on.

Stepping just far enough away from the outhouse as to give her some privacy and himself some, as well, he pulled out his cell phone and made the call, keeping his voice down.

"I found the plane," he said into the phone when the judge answered.

"Is she…?"

"I have her." He quickly filled him in on what she'd told him about the kidnapping and plane crash.

He heard the relief in the old judge's voice. "Any problems?"

"Nothing I couldn't handle."

"In that case, I guess I'd better ask what kind of shape she's in."

"She cut her leg but it should heal okay. Has a bump on her head. I had to tie her up to keep her from killing me, but other than that…"

"Really?" Landusky sounded as surprised as Thorn had been.

He thought of the woman in his outhouse. "She's…something else."

"I have no idea what that means. But as long as she is alive and safe, that's all I need to know for now. I'll notify Franklin and get back to you."

"Make it quick," he said into the phone, but the judge had already disconnected.

He heard the outhouse door start to creak open and was beside JJ in a few long strides.

"Aren't you being a little overly protective?" she asked as he walked her back to the cabin.

He didn't bother to answer. Maybe she felt safe here, but he knew better. Until her kidnappers were caught, she was in danger. He reminded himself none of that would be his problem soon. All he had to do was deliver her. After that, the judge and her grandfather could decide what to do next.

"I made a call," he said once they were inside the cabin. "Your grandfather is being notified that I found you and that you're safe. Once my contact calls back, I'll take you to him."

"Great."

Except she didn't sound like it was truly great. "If you'd like to call him, you can while I make us something to eat."

"I'd like to clean up first."

"I thought that might be the case." He went to the stove to check the three large kettles of water heating. Her grandfather was waiting for her call and she didn't want to call him? Maybe that wasn't strange. Maybe they weren't close. Or maybe there was friction between them. JJ wasn't a child. Maybe she resented the fact that because of her rich grandfather she'd been kidnapped.

It seemed strange, though. Wouldn't she want to relieve his mind herself that she was all right? It made him suspicious. Surely she wasn't involved in her own kidnapping. Although it wouldn't be the first time, especially involving the granddaughter of a very wealthy man.

He studied her out of the corner of his eye. She looked to be in her midtwenties. That was an age where grandpa might have decided it was time she made something of her life and quit living off his money. Which in turn could have led to the kidnapping and ransom demand to get back at him.

Reining in his thoughts, he reminded himself that she'd almost died. Also, there was the needle mark on her neck. Maybe once she got cleaned up and ate something, she'd want to call him.

"I thought you might like a quick bath while I cook us something to eat." He saw her surprised expression as well as a yearning desire flash in her eyes before she realized what bathing in his cabin would require.

JJ LOOKED AROUND in confusion. "And where exactly would I take this *bath*? Maybe it's just me, but I don't see a bathtub."

He stepped to the back door and returned with a large galvanized tub, which he set in front of the fireplace.

"You can't be serious."

He didn't answer as he set to work. Within moments he had a warm blaze going in the fireplace. "I've got water heating on the woodstove. Sorry, no bubble bath, but I do have bath gel. I'm not completely uncivilized."

She had to admit, it was more than a little tempting. She wanted to wash the smell of her ordeal from her skin. Also, she was in no hurry to leave here and go to her…grandfather's. One look at her and Franklin Davenport would blow a cork. Before he had her arrested. She would love to put that off as long as possible.

But at the same time, taking a bath in the middle of this cabin with this man…

"I promise you will enjoy the bath," he said as he brought out the first kettle of hot water. He added bath gel, the scent rising on the steam into the air in the small cabin. "But only if you're not overly modest. Up to you," he said as he took the empty kettle back to the kitchen. "I guess it depends on how badly you want the bath."

JJ heard the challenge. She looked longingly at the tub in front of the fire as he continued to add water. She could feel the grime on her, not to mention the dried blood, hers and possibly others. She watched him finish filling the tub, almost salivating to climb in until finally she met his gaze. "Do you have a shirt I could borrow?"

He stepped to the bureau against the wall beside the bed and pulled out a flannel shirt. "You can undress over there," he said, pointing toward the bed. "While I cook." He stepped behind the short wall that separated the kitchen from the living room and bedroom. He stood a good three feet taller than the wall, but he turned away and she heard the rattle of pots and pans.

JJ had never been overly modest, and given what she'd been through, stripping off her clothes in this man's cabin seemed like no big deal. Still, she hurriedly discarded her dirty clothing and peeled off her bandage, anxious to climb into that tub of hot, wonderfully smelling water. She could hear him in the kitchen chopping something, his back to her.

Naked, she pulled on his flannel shirt. It was huge on her, falling down past her knees. She rolled up the sleeves and padded barefoot toward the tub. He was still chopping in the kitchen and apparently paying no attention to her.

She saw that he'd thought of everything. On the hearth next to the tub, he'd laid out two towels, and a bottle each of shampoo and the bath gel along with a washrag. She tested the water with her fingers before she shrugged off his shirt and stepped into the tub.

It wasn't very deep, but deep enough that she could slide down and get water up to her neck. Taking the bath gel, she began to wash her body, lathering the outdoors-smelling gel on her skin, the firelight playing off her wet limbs. She couldn't remember ever enjoying a bath this much.

She rinsed off and was considering how to wash her hair when she heard him behind her.

"I can help with your hair," he said. She started to say that she could handle it, when he pulled the tie releasing her ponytail and then ordered her to "Lean forward."

She did as he poured warm water from a kettle over her head. She was blindly reaching for the shampoo on the hearth when she felt his hand already holding the bottle. A moment later, he began to work the shampoo into her thick long hair.

It felt luxurious. She realized that she'd been holding her breath. Now she let it out as he massaged the shampoo in, using those big hands and strong fingers to massage her scalp. Eyes closed, she couldn't help herself. She relaxed into it, hypnotized. No man had ever washed her hair. While titillating, it was comforting.

But it seemed so out of character for this man. How could he be so cold and calculating, even violent, and yet so gentle? She remembered how he'd been with his animals.

She leaned into his hands. A pleased moan escaped her lips, followed by a chuckle from him. Her eyes flew open. *Had he washed his wife's hair like this?* Careful, she warned herself. One act of kindness and she was putty in his hands? Not if she was smart. Hadn't he said he got his wife killed?

WT COULDN'T HELP being anxious. He'd gotten Thorn into this. Worse, he was circumventing the law to help his friend Franklin. He told himself that once Geneva was safe, he would insist the authorities be called.

Thorn had the woman, so why couldn't he relax? Because from what little the man had said, Geneva had been a problem. He winced as he remembered Thorn saying that he'd had to tie her up. Franklin would just love that. But he hoped his friend would be so thankful to have his granddaughter back that he wouldn't be worried about possible rope burns.

That Geneva was a spoiled prima donna didn't surprise him. Franklin had told him stories about his granddaughter's bad behavior. He imagined how Thorn would have reacted to her, and found himself smiling. Geneva Davenport would have been shocked by Thorn, as well. Talk about an immovable object. Of course he wouldn't put up with her giving him any trouble. He had a job to do, and knowing Thorn, he would have just done it—despite the woman.

Sighing, he was just thankful that Geneva had survived the plane crash with what sounded like minor injuries. Did she realize how lucky she was—especially since the plane had blown up after she'd gotten out?

Of course, this didn't mean that it was over. If she set this all up... WT knew Franklin would want to deny the obvious. Unless the young woman really was innocent. He reminded himself that he'd been a judge a large portion of his adult life, and still believed in innocent until proven guilty.

But he also wasn't one to ignore the evidence. Well, he told himself as he neared Whitefish Lake, where Franklin had an estate by the same name, deciding what to do with Geneva from here on out would be up to his friend. He knew Thorn would be glad to be rid of the woman.

Once Thorn brought her to Franklin's home, he could go back to his solitary life in the mountains even though WT hated to see the man hiding out from the world. But there was nothing he could do about that. He'd tried to warn Thorn about his wife, but he'd been too in love to listen. It was something neither of them had ever mentioned after the tragedy. WT knew it would always be there between them like a wedge.

Because of that, he was half surprised that Thorn had

taken the assignment. Then again, Thorn Grayson was a
man of honor. He would consider the request payment of a
debt. Paid in full, WT thought, once Thorn delivered Geneva to her grandfather.

THORN HAD THOUGHT food might tame some of the wild
out of this woman. Turned out, a bath and shampoo had
done the trick. He'd felt her relax for the first time since
he'd laid eyes on her as he'd washed her hair. He knew it
wouldn't last, and it didn't. She'd let her guard down for a
few minutes, but he could now feel the tension and wari-
ness back in her.

Washing her hair had been an impulse, one he now regretted as he recalled how much his wife had liked him
washing her hair. It wasn't a memory he needed right now.
"Ready to rinse?"

She nodded and leaned forward, the spell broken. He
poured the warm water over her hair to wash out the suds.
The soapy liquid ran over her shoulders and down her back.
He tried not to notice her pale bare skin, the tiny freckles
along her shoulders or the slim back that disappeared into
the soap bubbles. He added the conditioner to her hair,
worked it in and rinsed her hair again. When he stopped
pouring, she lifted her head, wrung out her hair and waited
for him to leave the room.

"It's often slippery getting out," he warned as he touched
her arm and felt her start. "Let me help you. Promise not to
look." He couldn't help being amused. She really didn't believe he was one of the good guys. Not that he could blame
her. He wasn't so sure of that himself.

As she rose, his arm keeping her steady, she reached for
one of the towels. He took the second one and wrapped it
around her from the back, this time looking away as he
realized how long it had been since a woman had stirred

anything in him. As he reminded himself who she was, he didn't need her being the one to remind him of his lost love.

She stepped out of the tub onto the rug next to it, and he quickly returned to the kitchen with the empty kettle. "I'll rebandage your leg before we leave."

He'd felt her gaze on him as he'd left the room. He hoped she was feeling guilty for suspecting he might have had other intentions when he'd suggested the bath in front of the fire—let alone the shampoo. And yet, if he was honest with himself, he shouldn't have suggested either.

This was a job. Not even one he'd wanted. Once he turned her over to her rich, powerful grandfather, he'd be done.

And yet he couldn't forget the feel of her thick hair in his fingers or the glow of her skin fresh from the bath. He was still a man, although it had been a very long time since he'd felt any longing for what he'd denied himself.

"I hope you like elk," he said from the other side of the partition, surprised at the tightness in his chest, in his voice. Out of the corner of his eye, he saw that she was wearing his flannel shirt.

"I do."

He thought she might have eaten anything at this point. He heard her stomach rumble as she stepped around the wall and into the kitchen, coming up beside him in the tight space. Her hair was wrapped in a towel. There were droplets of water still clinging to her lashes. She looked… sexy as hell, her cheeks flushed from the heat of the bath. He glanced away as he felt an ache in his chest he hadn't felt in a very long time.

"Oh, that smells good," she said with such enthusiasm that he had to look at her again just to see if she was joking. He doubted this woman had ever had to live on elk meat. Hell, he doubted she'd even tasted it before.

FRANKLIN DAVENPORT PACED the floor in front of the marble fireplace in his large living room on Whitefish Lake, hoping he'd done the right thing.

He'd heard nothing from the kidnappers. Nothing from Geneva. Nothing more from the judge after the last call that informed him that his granddaughter had been found alive. He'd been so relieved that he'd had to sit down.

"Then I don't have to worry about raising the ransom money," he'd said into the phone.

"I would go ahead and make preparations, just in case," the judge had said.

"Just in case what?"

"I like covering all my bases," his old friend said. "Go ahead and make the arrangements. I will be there soon."

Except WT hadn't arrived yet. He'd said Geneva would be calling him as soon as she had cell service. Except she hadn't called. He desperately needed to hear her voice, to know that she really was all right. He thought of how stubborn she could be. Was that why he hadn't heard from her yet? Or was there a problem? Was she injured and couldn't call?

The judge had told him not to talk to anyone. But in order to raise the ten million, he'd had to call his lawyer and his chief financial officer. They were also on their way.

At the sound of the doorbell, he rushed to it and threw the door open. "Willie," he said, relieved, but not as relieved as he would have been to see Geneva standing there.

The judge looked the same from when he'd seen him on the golf course in Florida this winter. Neither of them were the broad-shouldered, tall and strong young men they'd been when they'd met in the military. But they'd both taken care of themselves and were still solidly built for their years. They both had full heads of hair, though both were gray. It made them look distinguished, he liked to say.

Willie spent hours fishing the Gulf of Mexico from his Florida retirement home in the winter months, while Franklin played golf near one of his numerous homes in the south. Both also had homes in Montana where they spent the summer months. So they were both tanned with what he liked to think of as character lines. Their faces, though, were now etched with worry.

Franklin shook the man's hand, not surprised by his strong grip. On impulse, he pulled him into a quick awkward hug. He'd never been so glad to see anyone. He'd learned while building his fortune that there were only a few people you could trust with your life, let alone your granddaughter's. The judge was one of them.

"I can't tell you how much I appreciate—" Willie waved the rest of his words away. "I'm so glad you're here. I've been going out of my mind."

"You haven't heard from the kidnappers again?"

He shook his head. "Do you think they know that we have Geneva?"

"When the plane didn't make it to its destination, they would know something had gone wrong," the judge said. "Let's sit down, and I'll tell you everything I know."

"But Geneva is safe?"

"She's with someone I trust."

Franklin let out a long breath and felt his eyes burn. He turned away to lead his friend into the living room. "Can I get you something to drink?" Willie shook his head and took a chair. As he did, Franklin saw him check his cell phone.

He felt a sliver of worry work its way under his skin as he started to make himself another drink, but instead poured sparkling water into a tall glass with ice and a slice of lemon before he went to sit across from the judge. "I had hoped she would call. I need to hear her voice."

"She will soon be on her way here," Willie said.

He tried to relax, but every time he saw his old friend check his cell phone, he felt his anxiety growing.

"Here's what I know given the information you gave me for the tracking device on her phone," the judge said. "Your granddaughter was abducted from her home, taken to a nearby private airfield where she was flown southeast toward Gardiner in a small four-passenger plane. The plane crashed in the mountains north of town. The pilot and another man were killed in the crash. Geneva was uninjured except for a cut on her leg, which my contact bandaged when he found her. Unfortunately, the plane was destroyed, but your granddaughter apparently took both men's wallets and cell phones before that, so we know their identities. It shouldn't take much to find the person behind the attempted kidnapping."

Franklin put his face in his hands for a moment. He couldn't even imagine what his granddaughter had gone through. Let alone that she would have the sense to take the men's wallets. But if Willie said she was all right... He lifted his head. "Thank you."

"I wanted to speak to you first. Under the circumstances, I think the best way to get your granddaughter home safely would be with my contact. If you disagree, he can put her on a plane in Bozeman and you can pick her up at the Kalispell airport. He's standing by, awaiting your decision. Let's not forget that she will be in danger until the kidnappers are found. My advice is to have my contact bring her to you. That way, we'll know she's safe."

"I'll go along with whatever you think is best," Franklin said even though he felt impatient to see for himself that Geneva was all right. "I trust you, Willie. If your...contact will get her here safely, then by all means."

"It will take a while to drive from where she was found."

"I'm just glad she's okay."

WT nodded. "Then I think what we need to do is talk about how to proceed from here."

"I've had to call my chief financial officer and my attorney. They are both on their way."

His friend frowned. "Did you tell them—"

"Nothing yet. I was waiting for you, but I need their help to put together such a large sum of cash. I don't have ten million lying around. But we aren't going to give the money to the kidnappers now anyway, right?"

"The kidnapping has failed, but, Franklin, that doesn't mean the person won't try again. Once Geneva is here safe, then we need to call the FBI and let them handle it from here on out."

"I thought you said the kidnappers were dead?"

"One of the men in the plane got away, but my impression was that the three men were working for someone else. The pilot had an envelope on him with a large amount of cash, so it appears he was paid, at least partially, for the job."

"You think the person behind the kidnapping will try again?"

"It was a brazen move to demand ten million dollars. I would think the person would be even more desperate to get his hands on the money now. Two of his accomplices are dead, but there is one out there who might be able to identify him. That's if the person behind the kidnapping knows that things have gone south."

Franklin stared at him. "You mean he might not know that the plane crashed?"

"Possibly. Or he might think that *you* don't know, in which case, you should be getting a call to tell you where to deliver the ransom demand fairly soon."

"I did as you said and got together what I could in such

short notice." He motioned to a briefcase by the door. "There's just under four million in there, all unmarked bills."

"Good. I doubt even the Feds will be able to find the kidnapper quickly. Which means your granddaughter will have to stay close to home until it is safe."

Franklin swore. "And given what I've told you about my granddaughter..." He sighed. "She's so damned head-strong—just like her mother. And right now she's furious with me. We've been arguing over her latest boyfriend, money, everything."

He finished his sparkling water and rose to get a real drink. As he did, his doorbell rang. He hurried to the door, opening it to find his chief financial officer. Behind him, coming up the walk, was his lawyer. "Your timing couldn't be better," he said, and led the two of them into the living room.

"Judge W. T. Landusky, this is my chief financial officer, Curtis Hunt, and my personal lawyer, Helen Mars."

Willie had gotten to his feet, shaken Curtis's hand and was turning toward the woman when Franklin saw all the color drain from his friend's face.

"Helen?" Willie said as he was about to shake her hand, and stopped dead.

"You two know each other?" he asked, looking back and forth between the two of them.

"Hello, William. I'm surprised to see you." But Franklin noticed that she didn't seem surprised at all.

CHAPTER SEVEN

HER STOMACH RUMBLED AGAIN. JJ had always had a good appetite. But it appeared that her ordeal had left her famished. Also, this could be her last meal for a while, she thought. Maybe her last meal ever if this man was working with the kidnappers. They'd drugged her, almost killed her in a plane crash... She had to believe that getting out of this alive was questionable. Especially if this cowboy had anything to do with it.

She watched him dish up two plates of what appeared to be elk hash. She could see carrots, potatoes and onions chopped up with the meat, all of it in a rich dark gravy. He handed her a plate and a fork.

"Let's eat in front of the fire."

She took hers in and sat on the edge of the hearth, leaving the only chair for him.

"Take the chair," he said, being the perfect gentleman.

She shook her head as she pulled off the towel to free her hair. It fell around her shoulders. "I'm fine here by the fire. My hair is still wet. The heat feels good." With obvious reluctance, he took the chair, looking somewhat chagrined. "You don't get a lot of company, I'm guessing," she said, stating the obvious.

"My choice," he said, keeping his gaze on his plate as he ate.

JJ dug in, as well. "This is delicious," she managed to say between bites. "You're a good cook."

"Self-defense. It's cook or starve."

She suspected he enjoyed cooking more than he was willing to admit. Most men, at least the few she'd come across, would have slapped down an elk steak in the pan and called it good.

They ate in a companionable silence. For a while, she'd let herself forget about the call Thorn was waiting on— or what the person on the other end of the line would tell him. By now, Geneva might have turned up. Everyone was going to want to know whom Thorn had rescued from the kidnappers' plane and what the woman might have to do with this whole mess.

She had just taken her last bite when his cell phone rang. Thorn rose and took both of their plates into the kitchen. She sat on the hearth, afraid to breathe. Maybe she should make a run for it now. Once everyone realized the mistake that had been made, there would be questions. Questions whose answers could land her in jail—if not worse.

But she knew she wouldn't get far on foot, and she darn sure wasn't stupid enough to try to ride a horse bareback out of these mountains.

"Yes." She heard Thorn as he answered.

She waited for him to say something else, her heart in her throat. He seemed to be listening. She could only imagine what the person on the other end of the line was telling him.

"No, she's all right. I just fed her." He made it sound as if she was a stray dog he'd picked up and was now caring for until he could take her to the shelter.

More silence, then finally, "All right. I'll do that."

She heard him disconnect, pocket the phone and step around the edge of the partition. Her body tensed as she raised her gaze to his, not sure what she was going to see there. But his expression gave nothing away. Nor did his words.

"It's time to go. I'm driving you home."

JJ nodded, afraid to speak for fear that her voice would betray her. Their gazes held for a moment. She felt a quiver of electricity move through her as she recalled his fingers in her hair. A tingle worked its way up her spine, the warmth that had spread through her now gone.

Just because he'd been kind to her… She reminded herself that she still didn't know who had hired him to come after her or where he was really taking her. He'd offered to let her call her grandfather, but he hadn't mentioned it again since she'd had her bath and something to eat. Had he been relieved when she'd declined to make the call earlier?

What if she had wanted to call Franklin Davenport? Would he have let the call go through or made an excuse? As far as she knew, no one had called the authorities. Two of the kidnappers were dead. Didn't someone need to contact the sheriff? All Thorn seemed interested in was turning her over to whoever had sent him into the mountains after her.

She couldn't help the fear and distrust. It was ingrained in her from early childhood, and something not easily overcome. What a mess. She'd stumbled into all of this by accident. And right now she didn't see any way out.

Rising on trembling legs, she said, "I should get dressed."

"Wait."

She felt her heart drop.

"I need to rebandage your leg."

She let out the breath she'd been holding and sat back down as he went to get his first aid kit.

He was fast and efficient, his fingers nimble, as if he'd also bandaged his share of body parts in his life.

After he finished, he rose and said, "I'm going out to start the truck. It hasn't been run for a while." He was watching her closely again. No doubt afraid to leave her alone while he got the vehicle.

"What?" she said, hoping her voice sounded light instead of terrified. "We don't have to ride out on horses?"

"Sorry to disappoint you." He still hadn't moved. She realized he didn't want to leave her because he was afraid she'd take off out the back door. It had crossed her mind, but she wouldn't get far on foot—especially with him hot on her tail, so to speak.

"Thank you for the bath. I'll get dressed and we'll go. I feel so much better now. But if you don't trust me, you could bolt the back door." She glanced in that direction before turning back to him. "You could tie me up again, but it would make it hard for me to dress, now, wouldn't it?"

He shook his head, clearly not amused, before he opened the door and looked out. Apparently not seeing any problems, he said, "Stay here until I come back for you."

"Right, I know the drill. Otherwise, you'll take me out of here on Gertrude."

He turned those gray eyes on her. "Wear anything of mine you can find that fits you." With that he disappeared out the door.

She hurriedly wiped her fork off as well as her plate, telling herself she was being foolish. Leaving her fingerprints was the least of her problems. Then she went through what little clothing she could find of his and dressed in too-large sweats she had to roll up and tie tight around her waist. She covered them with a T-shirt, and pulled on a large hooded sweatshirt over the top.

JJ rolled up her dirty clothing and put it into the only thing she could find—a large paper sack. She set it by the door. She had no intention of leaving any evidence behind, but even as she thought it, JJ knew it wouldn't matter. Once someone found her duffel bag with her purse and phone in Geneva Davenport's bedroom—let alone her car in the garage—it would be all over for her.

From outside came the roar of a truck engine. Time had run out. She knew enough about the man to know that nothing would keep him from turning her over to whoever had hired him. Maybe he was a good guy, which meant she'd soon be coming face-to-face with one of the richest, most powerful men in Montana, Franklin Davenport. Or maybe Thorn wasn't a good guy, which meant she'd soon be in the hands of the kidnappers again.

At the sound of him returning, she finished dressing and turned as he came through the door. She could hear the pickup running just outside. Apparently, he seldom drove it and he'd wanted it to run for a while to charge the battery.

She saw him stop just inside the door to look around the cabin. He had an odd expression on his face, as if wondering if he would ever see it again. He seemed to shake off whatever he'd been thinking as he stepped to the fireplace to extinguish the last of the flames and scatter the logs.

JJ hadn't moved, her heart thudding in her chest. As he went into the kitchen, his cell phone rang, and she heard him take the call with his usual, "Yes?"

She hesitated for an instant, torn between her fears. Thorn had been kind to her, but that didn't mean he wasn't working with the kidnappers. Even if he wasn't, she couldn't let him take her to Franklin Davenport.

Seeing her chance, she took it.

CHAPTER EIGHT

WITH HER PAPER bag of dirty clothes in hand, JJ threw open the cabin door, raced to the pickup and jumped in, locking the doors. She shifted the pickup into gear and tromped on the gas. As she did, she said a silent thanks to her eighth grade boyfriend, the car thief who'd taught her how to drive a stick.

Out of the corner of her eye, she saw Thorn come charging out of the cabin. He grabbed for the pickup's door handle, so close his fingertips grazed the side of the door. But not finding purchase, he stumbled back as the truck's tires spit dirt and rocks.

She roared off the mountain without a clue where she was going or what she was going to do. But the one place she wasn't going was to Franklin Davenport, where the mistake would be immediately disclosed with one look at her. She and Geneva were both blonde and had a passing resemblance, but that was all.

Glancing back in the rearview mirror, she saw him standing in the yard, staring after her. She told herself he was lucky to be shed of her, whether he believed that right now or not.

He'd come to her rescue, fed her and even helped bathe her. But that didn't mean he hadn't also been hired to make sure she didn't get away. If he worked for whoever was behind the kidnapping, then he was probably in trouble for losing her. But she had no doubt he could take care of himself.

If he worked for a friend of Franklin Davenport's…well, she suspected losing her would be more of a hit to his pride and his reputation. Either way, he would be angry and set on finding her.

Fortunately, there was little he could do about that. Since he lived so simply, he apparently had only one form of transportation, this truck—other than his horses and a mule.

She felt only a little guilty. That phone call he'd gotten right before she'd made her break? She suspected it had been the person who'd sent him into the mountains for her, letting him know that he hadn't rescued Geneva Davenport.

That the woman he had was an impostor.

If he didn't know, he would soon enough. It was only a matter of time before the mistake was realized. Geneva would return from her secret liaison with the man her grandfather had forbidden her to date, and the truth would come out.

There would be some confusion since not even Geneva would know who'd been sleeping in her house. Franklin would be so happy to have his granddaughter back that…

Her happy ending burst like a soap bubble as she recalled Thorn's words. The kidnapper would still be out there. A man like Franklin would do everything in his power to find out who'd been behind the attempted kidnapping.

And he had the perfect place to start—the woman who'd been sleeping in his granddaughter's bed. Once they found her duffel bag with her cell phone inside it and her car snug in Geneva's three-car garage, they would know exactly who she was. Geneva would recognize her name. And once they called the cops…

She groaned, wondering if she should just turn herself

in. The thought made her ill. She'd promised her father on his deathbed that she would never go back to the life she'd lived before he'd found her.

Just the thought of her father brought tears to her eyes. She was trying to make him proud, really she was. None of this was her fault. All right, she had to admit, some of it was her fault.

She thought of the real Geneva Davenport and assured herself that the young woman was safe, since no one but JJ apparently knew where she was. The kidnappers had thought they had the granddaughter of wealthy Franklin Davenport, so they wouldn't be looking for Geneva.

Instead, they would be looking for her, she thought as she came over a rise in the road and she saw the small town of Gardiner, the north entrance to Yellowstone Park. The Yellowstone River cut through the middle of the town. The highway either went into the park or north to Livingston. Where was she going? What was she going to do?

It was Saturday so she didn't have to worry about work until Monday, but eventually she would have to call in and say what? That she was sick, and hope this would all blow over? Or maybe she should just quit before she got fired.

First she would need a phone. Hers was back at Geneva's house in her purse in her duffel bag on the bedroom floor.

She groaned as another disturbing thought struck her. Were the kidnappers already looking for her? Baker could have reached a phone by now. He would have his own cell phone as well as Geneva's. He could have reached an area where he'd gotten cell reception. Would he tell them that she was dead? They still thought she was Geneva Davenport. That should buy her some time, right?

But only until Geneva surfaced. Or until they realized their mistake. Or until they got the ransom money for her kidnapping. Either way, once they found out that she was alive, they might see her as a loose end, one that needed tying up and quickly.

As the road descended toward the river and the town, she saw a ball cap, faded and dusty, lying on the truck seat next to her. Picking it up, she put it on along with the sunglasses from the dash. When she glanced in the rearview mirror, she didn't even recognize herself.

She turned north to follow the river toward Livingston, her mind racing. She figured she had one of three options. Turn herself in, return to Geneva's house overlooking Flathead Lake near Big Fork and retrieve her purse, her duffel bag and her car if they were still there and the authorities weren't, or run.

Once she had her belongings and car, she wouldn't have to run or turn herself in, she realized.

Her heart ached as she thought again of her promise to her father. *At least try to save yourself.* Once she had the duffel bag and car, no one would know she was ever in that house. No one would know who she was. She'd been careful not to leave any prints at Thorn's cabin or outhouse. It wouldn't take her long to make sure she hadn't left anything at Geneva's house and hopefully, she wouldn't leave any evidence in this truck. Why, though, had she told Thorn to call her JJ? Because she couldn't stand to hear him call her Geneva another time.

Groaning, she told herself that her only hope was getting her duffel bag and car from the woman's house. If the cops were there, then she would turn herself in.

Did she really dare return to the scene of the crime? Right now, it seemed her best option. Wouldn't the authorities be crawling all over Geneva's house, though? Unless... Unless they hadn't been called—just as they hadn't been called when the plane went down.

THORN WATCHED HIS truck disappear around a curve in the narrow road. He still had his phone in his hand. He could hear the judge asking what was going on. He disconnected, not having time to explain.

Taking off at a dead run toward the barn, he cursed himself for trusting the woman. He couldn't understand her behavior, and hadn't from the start. He'd been about to take her home. Why would she run now?

His instincts told him that something was desperately wrong with all of this, and had been from the start. He couldn't help but wonder how deep the woman was in it. He'd been taking her to her grandfather. Or was that the problem?

Or was it Thorn himself? Did she still not trust him, still think he was in league with the kidnappers? Not that it mattered. He was involved whether he liked it or not. He swore again as he rushed into the barn.

Hadn't he had a bad feeling about this from the get-go? He wouldn't have touched it if it hadn't been the judge. He knew he should call WT and tell him what was going on. But he wasn't ready to admit that he'd let the woman get the best of him. Once he found her, once he knew what her story was, then he would call. Until then…

He went straight to the tarp-draped hulk in the corner. Jerking the cover off his motorcycle, he swung a leg over it, cranked up the engine and took off.

He had no idea what the woman's problem was. But he was about to find out.

FRANKLIN'S CELL PHONE RANG, stopping him from saying anything further. He quickly glanced at the number and didn't recognize it. He said as much to the judge as his phone rang again.

"Answer it," Willie said, and cleared his throat. "If it's the kidnapper, tell him you need more time to get the rest of the money. Let's see how desperate they are to finish this quickly. It will give us some idea as to whether or not they know what we do."

As he took the call, Franklin couldn't help noticing that his friend hadn't taken his eyes off Helen. What the...?

It was the same mechanically altered voice as the one that had called Franklin to tell him Geneva had been kidnapped.

"Do you have the money ready?" the voice asked.

He looked at Willie, who had risen from his chair and come over to listen. The judge nodded and whispered, "Tell him how much you have."

"There's someone with you. I told you not to call the cops or what would happen." The voice sounded angry.

"It's not the cops," Franklin said quickly. "It's a friend who's helping me get the money together. You can't possibly think that I have ten million dollars lying around."

"How much do you have?"

"About four."

"Four?" A curse, then, "It's not enough."

"It's all I've been able to raise with such short notice. I need more time." For a moment, he feared that the kidnapper had hung up. Willie held up his phone. He saw what Willie had written on it. "Before we go any further, I want to speak to Geneva." More silence. He looked to the judge, afraid they'd pushed the kidnapper too far already. Was it wise to make demands?

"I need to speak to Geneva," he repeated, his voice breaking. Calling the kidnapper's bluff felt as if he was playing Russian roulette with his granddaughter's life. She was his princess. She meant everything to him. There was no amount of money he wouldn't pay for her safety. But he had to trust that the judge knew what he was doing.

"She can't come to the phone for such a small amount of money. If you want to see her again, then you'll come up with the rest and quickly. I'll call tomorrow about where to take it. You'd better have it by tomorrow night if you ever want to see your granddaughter alive again. If you involve the authorities, I will kill Geneva. Is that understood?"

This time there was no doubt. The line had gone dead. He disconnected and, shaking with fear, looked to Willie.

"They don't know that we have Geneva," the judge said. "Or that we know about the plane crash, but they're worried that we're going to find out. They want the ten million bad, so they're willing to take the gamble and it's bought us some time."

He nodded, hoping Willie was right. He knew he couldn't have picked a better man than this one when it came to trouble. His friend's color had returned to his face from earlier, but Franklin would have been blind not to sense something between him and Helen. "The two of you…" He made a motion through the air.

"We're old friends," Helen said quickly, and changed the subject. "Did I hear you correctly? The kidnappers don't have Geneva? And what's this about a plane crash?"

WT ONLY HALF LISTENED while Franklin filled Helen in on what had happened. He was still in shock, and it took a lot to rattle him. When Helen had walked in the door earlier, he couldn't believe his eyes. He'd never thought he'd see her again. He could have been knocked over by a feather.

It had been years, and yet she looked so much the same. She'd aged, just as he had, but if anything, the passing of time had made her more beautiful.

He felt like a teenager again at just the sight of her, and wanted to kick himself. At sixty-five, a lot of water had flowed under the bridge. But it sure didn't feel like that right now looking at her.

Franklin had conferred with Helen and Curtis for several hours before ordering in food for all them. WT had realized that he wasn't going to get a chance to talk to Helen alone. He'd been busy trying to reach Thorn, and was growing more worried by the moment.

Earlier on the phone, he'd heard Thorn swear, followed by a slamming door and then a disconnect. Since then, all the judge's calls to him had gone to voice mail.

The only explanation WT could come up with was that Geneva had either been taken by someone—or she'd gotten away somehow. He couldn't imagine Thorn letting that happen, unless he'd lowered his guard. If Geneva had taken off, then that made her look even more guilty of this crime.

But WT had to believe that Thorn would find her. The man was a bloodhound. He'd get on her scent and track her down, or die trying. That's also what worried him.

He realized Helen had asked him a question. He looked up from his phone.

She smiled at him. "We were just about to have a drink," she said. "Join us?"

He shook his head, feeling off-kilter. The last thing he needed was alcohol. Seeing Helen again had definitely added to the feeling. But he was also worried. From what Thorn hadn't said, he knew Geneva had been giving him a hard time. Not that Thorn couldn't handle just about anything thrown at him.

Making him more anxious was the fact that Franklin had called in Helen and Curtis. Curtis had been on his laptop since he walked in. He didn't seem interested at all in the kidnapping. But Helen had hung on Franklin's every word.

Was she flirting with his friend? The thought made his chest tighten with jealousy even though it had been years, and he and Helen definitely hadn't ended on the best of terms. Wouldn't she enjoy knowing how many times over the years he'd thought about her? How many times he'd questioned breaking up with her.

To see her again, here…

His cell phone rang, startling him. He'd been lost in thought. He checked the screen. As he excused himself to take the call, both Helen and Franklin were watching him with interest. He had the strangest feeling that she'd been purposely trying to make him jealous.

The moment he closed the den door behind him, he took the call. "Thorn, is everything all right?"

"I'm afraid not."

THE SUN HAD gone down by the time JJ reached the turnoff to Geneva's house. Dusk was setting into the pines as she started up the narrow steep dirt road after hours of driving. The small upscale development had been built high in the Mission Mountain Range. Each house sat on a roomy twenty acres in the secluded woods for privacy.

The gate partway up the mountain was locked during off-season, but left open during the summer to make it easy for residents. Geneva wintered with friends either down south or in Europe. Only in the past eighteen months had she hired a contractor to build her a house to her exact specifications.

At the top of a rise, JJ turned left and followed a narrow paved road back into the huge home Geneva had built. She didn't see another soul anywhere as she drove up to the house. It faced the lake, with huge glass windows across the front and a three-car garage. A few lights shone behind the tinted windows, coming on automatically as programmed.

JJ saw no sign of police. No sign of crime scene tape.

She pulled into the drive. Nothing moved. She left the truck running and got out to open the garage. If they were waiting for her...

As she keyed in the passcode, the main garage door rose smoothly. She held her breath. As the truck lights illuminated a bumper she felt her pulse jump, but it was only her car that she'd left here. It seemed like it had been in another life. Next to it was Geneva's SUV. The third space was where Geneva parked her convertible sports car; it was still empty.

Even as she pulled the truck into the garage and closed the door, JJ told herself that she could be walking into a trap. The FBI could be inside.

But only if Geneva's grandfather had called them, which seemed unlikely given that he'd sent a cowboy to rescue her instead of the authorities.

That didn't mean that someone else wasn't waiting inside, though. By now the kidnappers could have realized that they'd grabbed the wrong woman. It was the not knowing that was keeping her on edge as she opened the mudroom door.

She let out the breath she'd been holding when no one arrested her the moment her shoes hit the marble floor. Or grabbed her and injected her with more drugs.

Hurriedly she punched in the security code before the alarm sounded. She froze, listening, afraid the house code might have been changed.

Apparently it hadn't, she realized with a sigh of relief.

Her first instinct was to run upstairs as quickly as possible, since the sooner she got her duffel bag… If it was still here.

But she hesitated, giving it a moment before she moved. As she stood listening to the dead quiet in the house, she had a stray thought.

How had the kidnappers gotten in to kidnap her in the first place? She'd just assumed they'd broken in, but then the alarm would have gone off and awakened her. The front door required a security code to open—just like the garage, and even the entrance in from the garage.

She considered how many people Geneva could have given the code to. Look how easily she had given it to a woman she'd never met in person. A few months ago Geneva had given JJ the passcode for her house. While in-flight to the French Riviera, the woman had called the travel agency and asked for Jenny Foster, like she always did when she wanted someone to handle all of the arrangements.

When JJ had come on the line, Geneva had told her that she'd forgotten one of her travel bags and needed it over-nighted to her. She'd already been in the air when she'd remembered.

"I know it's an imposition, but would you mind going to my house, retrieving it and sending it to me? I would be forever grateful." The woman had given her the pass-code immediately when JJ said she would be happy to do that for her.

She'd assumed that all of the woman's close friends must have been on the same flight from the noise in the back-ground. When she'd gotten to the house, she couldn't be-lieve what she'd found. The place was a mess, as if Geneva had thrown a party and left without picking up.

JJ hadn't been in the house long before a cleaning ser-vice arrived, making her wonder at the time why Geneva hadn't simply called the service instead of sending her all the way out to the house.

But then again, she did a lot for the woman. She had been Geneva's travel adviser and planner for over two years and had handled all of her travel arrangements including reservations and VIP accomodations. JJ had become her go-to girl for anything the woman might need.

Often while on the phone, she could hear Geneva talking to friends in the background. JJ had learned more than she'd wanted to about the young woman's rich, privileged life.

The realization that the kidnappers must have had the security code for the front door meant that at least one of the kidnappers must be someone close to Geneva. A scary thought, but JJ figured the cops would figure it out. Once they were called. In the meantime Geneva was safe. JJ had made her reservations for a two-week rendezvous with her latest boyfriend, Zac Judson. He was the older man that Geneva's grandfather couldn't stand. Zac was one of the reasons Franklin Davenport had cut up the credit cards he'd given her and cut her allowance to the bare minimum.

JJ knew all of this from being on the phone with the talkative Geneva every time she called, which was often. It was why JJ wasn't worried about the woman. She knew exactly where she was staying since she'd made the reservations for her at a posh resort in Palm Springs, California.

She listened for a few more moments before she headed for the stairs to the third floor master suite. She wasn't about to take the elevator. She hated closed-in spaces, especially right now.

A sense of urgency filled her as she climbed. *Just get the duffel bag and get out.* Even as she thought it, though, she worried that she might have left one stray blond hair in the bed that could be used to get her DNA and her identity found through her criminal record. She couldn't take the time to wash the sheets, dry and remake the bed like she usually did.

She had bigger worries, she told herself. As she climbed, she had flashbacks of being carried from the house. Maybe she hadn't been as out of it as she'd thought she had.

Out of the blue, she thought of Thorn back at his cabin. He must be furious. By now he would have called the cops. There was probably a BOLO out on her and his truck. Well, eventually it would be found in Geneva's garage. Let him deal with it when it happened. By then, she would be long gone.

For just a moment, she felt guilty. Especially if he was telling the truth and he really was one of the good guys. He hadn't wanted to be involved in this any more than she had. She wondered what he'd think when he found out who she was and why she'd ended up in the middle of a kidnapping.

Seriously? That's what you're thinking about at a time like this? What some cowboy hermit thinks about you? She shook her head as she reached the top floor. With each step, she held out even more hope that she was going to get out of this unscathed. Maybe no one had been here. Maybe her duffel bag was still in Geneva's bedroom, right where she'd left it. Once she had it and her car in the garage, no one would know she'd been here.

There would be some confusion about who was kidnapped, but all Franklin Davenport would care about was that his granddaughter was safe. The kidnappers who were still alive would cut their losses and go back to their normal lives. They weren't stupid enough to try to grab Geneva again, right?

She reached the landing, her heart a wild frightened bird's wings beating in her chest at the thought that she really might be home free. At the closed door to the master suite, she stopped to listen. The house felt so eerily quiet. Had it felt like that last night and she just hadn't noticed it?

A chill washed over her. She shivered. Just a few more steps and this could be all over, she thought as she pushed open the door, remembering the incredible view of the lake from the bedroom. The view had been why she'd chosen to sleep in the master bedroom instead of taking one of the guest rooms—a near fatal mistake in retrospect.

JJ pushed the door open and gasped.

CHAPTER NINE

JJ TOOK A step back as she tried to hide her shock. Thorn sat on the end of the king-size bed in the middle of the master suite, his gaze on her, her open duffel bag beside him. He looked relaxed, but she knew better. She'd seen how quickly he could move.

"JJ," he said, and nodded as if now everything made perfect sense. "Or should I call you Jenny Jo Foster?"

"I can explain."

He laughed. "Why should I believe anything that comes out of your mouth?"

She flinched at her own words thrown back at her. She considered running, but there was no place to go. He had her duffel with her purse inside it. He knew who she was, and he had proof that she'd been in this room last night when the kidnappers had abducted the wrong woman.

"How did you—"

"Motorcycle parked in my barn. I used to race them, and I still love to go fast and push myself, when challenged. Also, I didn't have to stop for gas as many times as you did in my old truck. I'm assuming you used the credit card you found in the glove box."

She nodded, acknowledging that he'd outsmarted her. He'd been waiting for her. She wondered how he'd found the place, how he'd gotten in, how he'd known this was where she'd been headed. Apparently, he'd been one step ahead of her since he had someone feeding him information, she reminded herself.

She shifted on her feet. "May I have my duffel bag?"

"No."

"I'd like to change my clothes. Yours are a bit…baggy." She pulled the extra sweatpants fabric out a good eight inches. He placed his hand over the duffel bag protectively. "What are you going to do with my things?" she asked him.

"What do you think? I'm going to give the bag and its contents to the authorities."

She'd been listening for the sound of sirens, but heard nothing but the pounding of her heart as he rose slowly from the end of the bed. "If you were going to call the authorities, you already would have." She saw that she'd hit on the truth. "So let me change."

Stepping forward, she took the duffel from him and headed for the bathroom, knowing he would be right behind her. As she started to close the door, he stopped her, putting his flat palm against it to keep it from shutting.

"Don't do anything stupid like try to climb out the window, okay?" he said.

JJ glanced at the window, which was three stories above the ground. "That *would* be stupid," she agreed. "Do you mind? I'd like to change without you standing there watching me."

He removed his hand. "I'll be right here."

"I wouldn't have it any other way," she said, and pulled the door shut, locking it. Not that locking it did any good if he decided to come in.

She quickly changed into jeans, T-shirt and a hooded sweatshirt that actually fit. From her purse she took out what cash she had, her only credit card and her phone. She stuffed them into the pockets of her hoodie. Then she brushed her hair and tossed the brush back into the duffel, ready, she told herself, to face whatever was coming.

"JJ?"

Opening the door, she smiled. "Worried I was going to tie the towels together and give that bathroom window a shot? Sorry, I never got my knot-tying badge in Girl Scouts. All thumbs, unlike you. So what now?"

"Now you're going to tell me the truth." He motioned to one of two chairs in a sitting area by the wall of glass. The view really was amazing, even in the evening like now.

But her gaze was on the cowboy in front of her. She was caught. At least for the moment. All her instincts told her that they needed to get out of here. It didn't feel safe.

"I'm at a disadvantage," she said. "You know who I am, but I don't even know your last name. I'd like to know the name of the man who chased me clear across the state."

"Grayson. Thorn Grayson." He grabbed the other chair, swung it around and placed it directly in front of her— blocking her escape. "Now where is Geneva Davenport and what the hell were you doing in her bed last night?"

"You make it sound so sordid. I was alone."

"Sit down and start talking."

"Fine." She sat, trapped. One thing was clear at this point. Whoever this man was, he would keep chasing her. He was relentless. Now he'd caught her. He knew who she was. There was no getting out of this. Unless she could convince this cowboy to help her. But that would mean telling him everything. "It's a long story."

He leaned back, crossing his arms as if he had all night.

She frowned at him, realizing that was the case. "I know nothing about you."

He smiled at that. "You don't need to know anything about me."

She raised a brow. "But I'm supposed to bare my soul to you?" She thought of earlier in his galvanized tub in the front of the fire. She'd bared a lot more than her soul already.

"If you have nothing to hide…"

She scoffed at that. "Who has lived to this age and has nothing to hide?" Her eyes narrowed at him. "Including you? Why don't you tell me about your wife."

He seemed to grit his teeth, and shifted in his chair as if to rise. "If you'd rather tell your story to the cops…"

She thought he was bluffing. Wouldn't he have already called them if he were going to? "One question first."

He looked at her with obvious impatience as he settled back into the chair.

"Why?"

"Why what?"

"Why haven't you turned me over to the cops already? Why did you go to all the trouble of even tracking me down? All you would have had to do was give the cops a description of your pickup and let them find me. You could have just gone back to your…life."

She saw that hit a sore spot.

"Clearly, you don't get my life. But then you are in no position to judge, are you?" He had her there. "Once it became abundantly clear that things weren't as they seemed, I wanted answers. I want them directly from you. Also, you took my truck. Gertrude and I have a history."

"Gertrude? Isn't that also the name of your mule?"

"I named the mule after my truck. Now would you please quit stalling?" He leaned back. "So why are you so afraid of the law?"

"I have a record."

"And you think they might suspect that you were involved in the kidnapping?"

"I can't imagine how," she said even though she could. At the very least, she'd trespassed. That could get her fired if not worse. Geneva or her grandfather could press charges, and she had enough financial problems as it was.

"Tell me how it was that you were kidnapped from Geneva Davenport's bed," he said.

"I was house-sitting. Kinda." She glanced away for a moment, his gray gaze too intense.

"*Kinda?* How did you get into the house?"

"I know the security code. Geneva gave it to me. I'm her travel adviser and planner. I arrange luxury accommodations for her and make sure she has everything she needs when she arrives."

"There's such a job?"

JJ sighed. "It's what I do. Look, I don't think we should stay here. Maybe there is somewhere else we could go to talk about this. I just have a bad feeling."

"A bad feeling?" He seemed to consider that. "Or you're stalling."

She rolled her eyes. "Have you always been so suspicious?"

Before he could answer, his cell phone rang. He checked the screen and then rose to take the call. "Yes?"

Her heart dropped. She'd just about bared her soul to him, and she had no idea who he was talking to on the other end of the line. She hadn't been lying about that bad feeling. It felt even stronger now. She glanced toward the open doorway as he turned his back to talk to whoever was on the other end of the call.

Her mind whirled. Was he talking to his associates in crime? He'd known the passcode to get into the house—just like the kidnappers. If he had broken in, the alarm would have gone off. The cops would have been all over this place when she arrived. Unless he'd gotten the passcode from Franklin Davenport, but knowing Geneva, JJ doubted the young woman would have given it to her grandfather. Not that he probably couldn't get it.

She picked up the chair she'd been sitting on and swung it, catching Thorn in the back. Grabbing her duffel bag as he went down, she sprinted toward the door without looking back. She flew down the stairs. Her heart was pounding so hard she couldn't hear if he was behind her or not. She doubted being hit by even an expensive well-made bedroom chair could keep the cowboy down.

She was almost to the lower level when the front door burst open. As she tried to skid to a stop, two men she'd never seen before rushed her. She swung the duffel bag, but her target only jerked it out of her hand and threw it aside. She kicked the other one in the groin and started to turn to run back the way she'd come, when he grabbed her and punched her in the face. Stars danced before her eyes an instant before everything went black.

THORN STRUGGLED TO his feet at the sound of an engine revving up outside. Had he really turned his back on the woman again? Rushing out of the bedroom, he caught sight of a man dumping JJ into the back of a large SUV, then climbing in. The driver hit the gas even before the door closed, and the vehicle left in a haze of smoke boiling up from the tires on the pavement.

He knew he'd never be able to get to her before they took off. But he headed down the stairs at a run anyway. He'd risked his neck for nothing because before he reached the main floor, the SUV turned the corner and disappeared in the pines on the road down to the main highway.

Swearing, he turned back into the house. Spotting her duffel bag lying on the floor, he picked it up and headed to the back of the house where he'd left his motorcycle. The only thing he could do at this point was to go after her, cussing her the whole way. What had she been thinking, hitting him with that chair and running?

He raced out the back of the house and leaped onto his bike. Flathead Lake's slick surface had turned to silver in the moonlight.

His back hurt from where the chair had knocked the wind out of him and sent him sprawling to the floor. He should have known not to turn his back on her.

What about what she'd told him? She was Geneva's travel agent? If she was telling the truth, Geneva Davenport had given her the passcode to her house.

Unless all that had been nothing but a fairy tale she'd spun for him. Damn the woman. He was trying to help her. But even as he thought it, he reminded himself that it wasn't the job the judge had asked him to do. He was no closer to finding Geneva. If JJ had been telling the truth, then she knew where the woman was because she might have made the arrangements for Geneva to travel somewhere, which would explain why JJ was supposedly house-sitting—*kinda*.

He heard his cell phone ring and knew it was the judge again. He'd cut him off in midsentence to chase after JJ. When he'd called later, he'd had to tell WT that he didn't have Geneva. That there'd been a mix-up.

Now he had to fix this. As far as he knew, Geneva Davenport was still in trouble. But so was JJ, he told himself as he went after her. And JJ might be the only person who could help him find Geneva and finish this.

He roared down the road in time to see the dark SUV turn onto the main highway and head south. He slowed, letting a car or two go by before he also turned onto the highway. He had no idea where JJ was being taken or by whom. He assumed the kidnappers must still believe that they had Geneva, which meant she was safe for the moment.

But why wouldn't they believe that she perished when the plane crashed and later exploded?

Because the missing kidnapper from the plane, Baker, must have seen JJ alive and by the plane before it blew up. Or seen Thorn and JJ at some point as they were leaving the site. Either way, the kidnappers now thought they had Geneva *again*.

He hated to think what they would do to her when they realized they had the wrong woman—and had from the beginning.

"FRANKLIN, MAY I speak to you in private?" WT said as he returned to the dining room. He could see that his friend was about to protest, about to assure him that anything he had to say could be said in front of his attorney and chief financial officer.

But he must have seen the judge's expression because he stopped himself and rose. "If you'll excuse us. Please help yourself to dessert."

Franklin led him into his den. "Is it Geneva?" he asked, sounding terrified.

"The woman on the plane wasn't Geneva."

His friend blinked. *"What? Are you telling me she wasn't kidnapped?"*

"It's a little complicated. A woman who was staying at your granddaughter's house *was* kidnapped. We believe the kidnappers thought they had Geneva. At this point, I don't think they know any different."

Franklin lowered himself into a chair and rubbed his forehead. "I don't understand."

"I don't have the whole story yet, and neither does my... contact. But we should soon. We have to assume that Geneva is still in trouble. I think you should continue to raise the money for the ransom demand."

His friend nodded slowly. "So we have no idea where she is."

WT shook his head. "I'm sorry. And I think we should keep this to ourselves."

Franklin rose to his feet wearily and faced him. "I noticed something between you and Helen."

"It's a long story." And definitely not one he wanted to get into.

"You don't trust her? Or is it Curtis? He's young but—"

"I don't trust anyone right now, and won't until Geneva is back here and we know exactly what's going on. You shouldn't either."

JJ WOKE UP slowly to rocking. It took her a moment in her foggy condition to realize she was on a bumpy gravel road. She had no idea how long she'd been out or where they were taking her. She didn't have long to think about it.

"I hope to hell you didn't kill her," she heard one of the men say from the front of the vehicle.

"I checked. She's still breathing."

"The boss said to bring her to him when we found her, but he definitely needs her alive."

As the vehicle came to a stop, she groaned inwardly. Her jaw felt as if it was broken. She opened her mouth, closed it and opened it again. It hurt but it seemed to still work. To her surprise, only her wrists were bound with tape—just like they'd been on the plane, only this time behind her.

She appeared to be in the cargo area of a large SUV. When it stopped, she tried to sit up, but a hand pushed her back.

"Stay down!" a man ordered. "Or I'll hit you again."

"The boss won't be happy about you hitting her," the driver said, and the other man told him what he could do with his comment.

She heard what sounded like the driver waiting for a line of traffic to pass. A moment later, they were moving again.

Was there only the two men that she'd seen when she'd come racing down the stairs? "Where are you taking me?" No surprise that no one answered her. She thought she caught the scent of water. Did that mean she was still around Flathead Lake?

The driver braked to a stop, killed the engine and got out. She could see the tops of dense pine trees out the window and realized she could be anywhere.

The back of the SUV opened.

The man who'd been holding her down slid out, grabbing her ankles and pulling her toward him. As he did, he drew a pocket knife and flopped her over on her stomach. Grabbing her bound wrists, he began sawing through the tape. "Not so uppity now, huh."

As her wrists were freed, he jerked her out of the SUV by one leg. Still dizzy from the blow to her head, she stumbled and would have fallen if he hadn't caught her. With one hand holding her upper arm tightly, he buried his fingers in her hair until he had a handful. "You know what happens if you fight me again."

She could only assume, but all the fight had gone out of her. The second man appeared and grabbed her other arm.

They half dragged her toward what appeared to be a small old cabin in the woods. Through the pines, she could see the lake and what appeared to be a huge new home being built on the lakeshore.

JJ realized that she could no longer hear the traffic on the highway, and realized just how alone she was here with these two men. If they'd brought her to this isolated area to kill her, they'd picked the perfect place.

The driver pushed open the door into the cabin. She blinked as musty cold air rushed out of the dim darkness. Looking around, she felt as if she'd been transported back to another time. The cabin appeared unchanged from maybe the 1940s, with its knotty pine walls, old bar signs and fishing photos. It smelled like an antique photo album, she thought as the two men hauled her into the living room area.

At first she thought there wasn't anyone else in the room. Until she saw a figure move from the shadows and into the light of the front window.

THORN FOLLOWED ON his motorcycle, making sure he kept a car or two between him and the dark colored SUV. They'd headed south along the lake, passing cherry orchards and U-Pick signs, before he saw the SUV's blinker come on as the driver waited in the traffic before it pulled up and turned off the highway.

Thorn wasn't worried about the men spotting the tail. He didn't think they had seen his motorcycle behind Geneva's house. They'd come right to the front door as if they knew exactly not only what they wanted, but also how to get in.

Had they come to the house looking for JJ? Or Geneva? Or did they know the difference yet? Because of that, he didn't have any idea who they were or what they were planning to do with JJ.

All he knew for sure was that they had her and he was getting her back. Ahead, he saw the SUV turn off and disappear into the pines. He drove past with the rest of the traffic, but turned back the first opportunity he had.

By then there was no sign of the SUV as he followed the narrow dirt road it had taken into the pines. He hadn't gone far when he caught the glint of the SUV's bumper partway down the hillside. On this side of the lake, the land dropped away steeply to the water.

Thorn slowed and pulled over. Cutting his engine, he hid the bike in the undergrowth and then headed through the trees toward the SUV. As he approached, he spotted the cabin just off the road. Farther down the hill, he saw the shine of bare new wood, and realized a huge house was being built right on the water far below the cabin.

He wondered how the men who'd taken JJ had access to this place. Whoever had hired them could own the land, but why bring her here in that case? It crossed his mind that the men might be part of the construction crew. They would know about the cabin, and since it didn't appear anyone else was around over the weekend, knew they could use it. But use it for what purposes? He had his handgun in its holster under his jacket, but picked up a chunk of firewood as he neared the cabin. He preferred not to kill anyone if he could prevent it.

Hearing nothing, he worked his way cautiously toward the door. He told himself that they hadn't brought JJ here to hurt her, but he couldn't be sure of that. The hillside felt unearthly quiet, as if anything could happen here without the rest of the world knowing.

JJ STARED AS the figure materialized from the shadows. For a horrible moment, she thought that she was about to meet Franklin Davenport. All she knew about the man was what she'd overheard Geneva telling her friends when she'd called to make travel arrangements at the agency. And that was plenty.

Geneva had made him sound like a tyrant who used his power to get anything he wanted. The kind of man who could crush someone like JJ without giving her a second thought.

But as the man stepped forward, she realized he wasn't the distinguished older man she'd seen in the newspaper articles. He looked to be no more than fifty, with pale eyes and a head of dark wavy hair. He looked as if he'd been spending the weekend on the lake, dressed in shorts, polo shirt and boat shoes. He was handsome in a dark, intense kind of way. She had no idea who he was or why she'd been brought here. He definitely wasn't Zac Judson, the man Geneva had been dating. She'd seen a photo of the two of them at the house.

The man sighed as he moved toward JJ. "You've done a great job of avoiding me. Until now. I don't think you realize who you're dealing with, although you should. No one rips me off. Especially you." His eyes seemed to narrow, brows furrowing with each step, until he was only a few feet from her in the dimly lit cabin.

When he finally spoke, his voice was low. "Who the hell is this, Ryan?" He looked at the man on her right, the one who'd been driving.

"Boss?" Ryan said, sounding confused.

Then the boss shifted his gaze to the one on her left. "Bobby?"

The men flanking her glanced from their boss to her and back in even more confusion. "It's Geneva Davenport," Bobby said, sounding nervous. Not as nervous as JJ.

The boss let out a laugh that held no humor. "How did you come up with that?"

"We took her out of her house. The lights were on. She came hauling down the stairs…" Ryan said, no longer sounding sure of anything. He looked over at JJ and frowned as if she'd somehow tricked him.

The boss shook his head. "This isn't the woman I asked you to bring to me."

"What?" She felt Bobby squeeze her arm tighter as if he somehow blamed her for this.

The boss raised his voice, sending some of the dust molecules in the cabin airborne. *"You got the wrong woman!* That is not Geneva Davenport."

Ryan looked over at her again. "I don't understand."

"Clearly," the man said, and made a small motion with his hand.

"Find Geneva and don't bother me again until you have the right woman," the boss said, and headed for the door that opened onto a small porch on the lakeside of the cabin.

Ryan released his grip on JJ's arm as he looked at her. "Wait, what do you want us to do with her?"

The boss stopped at the door and turned back. He seemed to study her for a moment. "You say you found her in Geneva's house?" He nodded toward JJ. "Maybe you can explain how it is that they could make such a mistake?" he asked her, as if truly hoping for the answer.

She swallowed the lump in her throat. "I was at the wrong place at the wrong time?" Her mind was whirling. What did this man want with Geneva? If he was the head of the kidnapping operation, then wouldn't he know about the plane crash? Her head ached from lack of sleep, from one terror after another and from this latest blow to her skull. She felt as if her brain was no longer tracking.

Not just that. These men looked like construction workers, with their canvas pants and work boots. She thought
about the house being built on the lake below the cabin.
Were they somehow connected to that?

"Do you even know Geneva Davenport?"

"Not really."

"But you were in her house."

"I was...house-sitting for her."

He let out a laugh. "Well, that explains that. You do look
a little like her. Did she tell you where she was going when
she asked you to house-sit?"

One lie just followed another. "No," JJ said, wide-eyed.

He seemed to think about that for a moment before he
motioned to Ryan, the man who'd been driving the SUV.
"Well, if she asked you to house-sit, she knows you, which
means we might have to trade you." He looked at the men.
"Let's hang on to her for a while until we get this all figured out."

She started to tell the truth, that Geneva hadn't asked
her to house-sit, that she had no reason to make any kind
of trade, but he didn't give her a chance.

"There's a root cellar under the floor over there. That
should keep her until you find the real Geneva Davenport.
Make sure when you do find her, that she has her check-
book with her. Put her down there and drag something
heavy onto the trapdoor."

JJ knew her face must have shown her horror. Her pulse
was already pounding in her head, and her jaw hurt from
where she'd been hit. "Don't worry, I promise you won't
be there long." He turned to his men again. "Then get out
of here," he ordered. "I don't want to see either of you until
you have the right woman in tow."

She thought about fighting the two men still holding

her, but she was running on fumes. Even if she could get away from the men, she knew she couldn't get far before they caught up with her.

But the thought of being in the root cellar terrified her. She had this thing about spiders, let alone dark, airless spaces. She still couldn't believe this was happening. Her day had started before sunrise with a plane crash in the mountains.

She could feel dusk descending over the cabin as Ryan held her arm tightly and Bobby knelt to open the trapdoor.

The moment he opened it, an awful smell rose from the damp earth below the cabin. JJ thought she would heave, but Ryan didn't give her a chance. He pushed her forward. She pushed back with all her strength, which wasn't enough. Her body stopped just inches from the hole in the ground.

Bobby grabbed her by the hair and dragged her forward over the gaping blackness. She screamed as she lost her balance, but her throat closed so no sound came out. Ryan grabbed her to keep her from falling headfirst into the root cellar.

"Don't kill her," he said to his partner, who clearly wasn't listening. As Bobby let go of her hair, she windmilled her arms as she fought to regain her balance. If Ryan hadn't grabbed one of her arms, she would never have found the ladder at the edge.

He forced her down the ladder into the cramped dark space and then closed the trapdoor over her, forcing her to duck.

She heard him drag something over the top of the door as she clung to the ladder, hunched over and trying to breathe through her mouth. She blinked but saw nothing. The blackness sent a whole new level of fear rocketing through her.

JJ knew she couldn't stay like this, bent over, clinging

to the ladder, yet she was afraid to step down the last rung for fear of what might be down there. She had to move, though, and as she did, her bare arm brushed a cobweb.

Frantically, she tried to get it off her skin only to have what felt like a spider run down her arm. This time she didn't have any trouble screaming. But it made a hollow sound, one that she figured never got past the trapdoor above her head.

Fighting her growing panic, she tried to calm down, to think. There had to be a way out of this. The thought made her laugh, almost hysterically. She'd thought the same thing in the airplane when she'd taken Kyle's gun, and look how that had turned out.

She didn't know how much time had passed. She'd thought she'd heard the SUV drive away. Her head had filled with static as she tried to hold it together.

Then she heard a sound overhead. Footfalls. She took a step back. Something scurried away behind her, sending a chill up her back. She looked up and saw a tiny thread of light coming through a crack in the trapdoor. Another footfall, and then someone stepped on the crack, blotting out the light.

WHEN THORN HEARD someone exit the cabin from the front, he quickly moved out of sight around the side of the building. He could hear voices inside the cabin. The two men who'd taken JJ?

He debated rushing in, gun drawn, but knew that was too risky. He had no way of knowing if there were others in the cabin besides the two who had abducted her. All he could do was try to see inside.

Moving around the side of the building, he found a window, wiped at the glass and was able to see into an antiquated living room. As he started to scan the rest of the interior, he heard a boat start up on the lake below the cabin. He caught only a glimpse of the craft as it sped away, a dark-haired man at the helm.

His peripheral vision registered movement as two men hurried from the cabin and headed to the SUV. They didn't have JJ with them. His heart pounded. What had they done with her? Had he hesitated too long?

The SUV's engine started. He listened as the driver backed out the vehicle and roared up the road through the pines. He moved swiftly, terrified his hesitation had cost JJ her life. Rushing into the cabin, he stopped dead.

From where he stood, he could see the entire cabin. It was empty.

Where was JJ?

CHAPTER TEN

JJ HELD HER BREATH. Had the boss come back? Had he changed his mind about leaving her here? Or had he decided to get rid of her?

She tried to move away from the crack in the floor, as if there was anywhere to run, and collided with more cobwebs. Frantically she brushed at them, a cry escaping her lips. Above her, she heard a sound.

"JJ?"

She couldn't believe it. *"Thorn?"* She fought not to cry, her relief so quick and overwhelming, followed by a stray thought. *Better the devil you know than the devil you don't.* It was something her mother used to say.

"Thorn!" she cried at the top of her lungs, then she climbed up the ladder to beat on the bottom of the trapdoor with her fist. Dirt and other things she didn't want to think about fell over her. She cringed but heard him moving whatever had been slid over the trapdoor. And then he was opening it, letting in the light and the air and taking away the darkness.

He reached for her, grabbing her hand as she scrambled on shaking legs out of the root cellar and into his arms. He held her tight. "It's all right. I've got you. It's all right."

They stood like that for a long time, him holding her, her trying to catch her breath and not cry. After a moment, she finally felt better and stepped from his arms, feeling guilty.

This was the man she'd hit with a chair, she reminded herself and he'd just rescued her. Again.

On the heels of that thought came another. *He needs you to help him find Geneva. You still have no idea who this man really is. Or what he really wants with Geneva. Or with you.*

That thought was like a blast of icy water.

THORN FELT THE change in her, but he hadn't wanted to let her go even as she stepped from his arms. Those men had put her in a hole. He wanted to chase them down and put them into the same hole and leave them there.

He'd heard the terror in her voice coming from under the floor, saw it etched on her face and felt it in her body as he'd pulled her out and into his arms. She'd looked so small, so vulnerable, as he'd held her. He'd wanted to sweep her up and carry her far away from all of this.

But he couldn't. As he'd brushed cobwebs from her hair, he reminded himself that he didn't know who this woman really was and how she'd gotten involved in all this.

"Let's get out of here," he said as he saw that her strength and determination had returned, along with her suspicion of him.

She looked up at him for a moment before shifting her gaze away. "Thank you for getting me out of there."

He nodded. As he led her out of the cabin and up the road, he listened to make sure that the men weren't coming back. He felt the steady still-angry beat of his pulse and heard only the breeze in the tops of the pines.

As they moved through the growing darkness, all around them the pines were black in the growing darkness. Through the trees he caught glimpses of the mountains, now purple against Montana's midnight blue big sky.

They were almost back to the spot where he'd hidden his motorcycle, when JJ let go of his hand and stopped walking. "I need to know why you came after me."

He turned to stare at her. "Seriously? You need to ask?"

"I guess I do."

He shook his head. "How many times do I need to tell you that I'm one of the good guys?" he asked, not knowing what else he could say, let alone how he could convince her.

Then in frustration, he grabbed her and pulled her into him. His mouth dropped to hers and the next thing he knew, he was kissing her with a passion he'd forgotten he'd ever possessed.

THE KISS HAD taken her by surprise. That and her reaction to it. She'd parted her lips to say something as his mouth had dropped to hers. But any words were lost as he pulled her tighter into his arms and deepened the kiss, stealing her breath and her senses.

At the sound of an approaching vehicle, he let go of her abruptly. Off balance, it took her a moment before she could get her feet moving again. He grabbed her hand to steady her and led her through the pines to his motorcycle. Were the men coming back?

"Get on," he said, his voice sounding hoarse as he climbed on the bike and motioned for her to join him.

Since her options were limited, she swung a leg over the bike behind him. Her arms wrapped around his waist as he started the motor and kicked it into gear. The bike jumped forward, forcing her to hang on tight as he gunned it.

Thorn took a curve fast on the narrow dirt road as he raced up the hill toward the highway as if he was still angry. Angry with her? Or angry with himself for kissing her?

She felt numb, as if she'd been in shock since three men had abducted her from her sleep last night.

They reached the highway. Thorn had to stop to wait a moment for traffic.

"I'm sorry. I really appreciate you rescuing me back there," she said.

He grunted in answer before hitting the throttle, and they were off, roaring down the highway through the growing darkness.

She felt her hair blow back, a golden wave behind her. She tightened her arms around Thorn's waist and leaned her cheek against his back, reveling in the feel of speed and wind as the warm summer night rushed past. Touching the tip of her tongue to her lower lip, she thought of the confusing kiss. Confusing because it had been so unexpected. And because she had no idea what it meant.

Even more confusing had been her reaction to it. For a while, she'd lost herself in the kiss, in this cowboy's arms.

Thorn whipped in and out of the traffic on the narrow winding road, headed north. She caught glimpses of Flathead Lake through the pines, the surface a silver gray in the darkness.

JJ knew she should be terrified at how dangerous this was. But with Thorn driving, she felt surprisingly safe. She leaned against his warm strong back and tightened her hold on him as the bike sped down the highway, the two of them feeling like one on the motorcycle.

She tried not to think about what had happened and what would happen now. Or about the men after her. Or about the cowboy who'd just kissed her. She had no idea what had possessed him. He'd made it clear he wanted to be rid of her when he'd thought she was Geneva Davenport.

So had anything really changed now that he knew at

least some of the truth about her? She couldn't let her guard down again until she knew what was in it for this cowboy. Clearly, he was doing everything he could to keep her alive. Because he needed her if he hoped to find Geneva. But then what?

She thought again of the kiss and hated that it had awakened something inside her. Something she didn't want awakened at this time of her life any more than she wanted this cowboy to do the awakening. He'd kissed her because he wanted her to trust him. That's all it had been.

But at this point, she didn't trust anyone, maybe especially this cowboy who kept rescuing her—for what end? Did it even matter? She was in so much trouble, she'd never be able to dig herself out.

Closing her eyes, she let herself enjoy this moment of freedom. There was nothing she could do but be swept along through the growing night. She breathed in the summer evening, rich with the smell of water and pine trees and campfires on the beach, and realized that she felt young and alive for the first time in years.

It was as if she'd been untethered, freed from more than a dark, damp root cellar. She'd been abducted from her regimented, goal-oriented life and lost all control. She couldn't see the future any more than she could see farther than what the motorcycle's headlight illuminated ahead. Why not throw caution to the wind? Or maybe she no longer felt terrified because she'd used up all her terror sometime during the last almost twenty-four hours.

She closed her eyes and let the summer night blow past, knowing this might be as good as it got, especially if Thorn was taking her to the cops. Or worse, Franklin Davenport. Who would ever believe she wasn't involved in all this?

Geneva Davenport, she thought. Once she contacted Geneva at the resort where JJ had booked her a suite for two weeks, this would be all cleared up.

Even as she thought it, she knew it wouldn't be that easy. But it would definitely be a place to start since she was apparently the only one who knew where Geneva was.

Right now the woman was probably sitting by a pool in Palm Springs, sipping a drink adorned with an umbrella without a care in the world. Geneva didn't even know she was in trouble and that a lot of dangerous men were looking for her.

Not yet anyway.

CHAPTER ELEVEN

THORN SLOWED THE motorcycle to turn into the out-of-the-way bar and grill somewhere near Columbia Falls. A neon beer sign blinked through the pines. Only a few pickups were parked out front. He pulled around back, out of sight of the highway, and cut the motor. In the quiet that followed, he could hear cars on the highway. But none of them braked and turned in as he felt JJ lift her cheek from his back and take her arms from around him.

He turned to watch her climb off the bike, her gaze on the weather-beaten siding on the run-down bar.

"A friend of mine just bought this place. Him and the bank," Thorn said. "He hasn't started fixing it up yet." He glanced toward the short row of cabins even farther back in the pines. "Come on," he said as he dismounted and started for the cabin that had the number three on it, only the three was hanging upside down by one nail. "It's not as fancy as you're used to," he said as he pushed open the door.

She smiled at the inside joke. A closed-up scent wafted out as he reached in to snap on the light. It wasn't as bad as he'd expected. Then again, he figured his friend had cleaned it up for him. The bed was made, and the cabin looked as if it had been recently scrubbed down.

He shoved her duffel bag at her. "Here, you left this behind at the house." If he wanted to make her feel guilty, he had.

She looked like she might cry as she took it. "Thank you.

And thank you for getting me out of there." She shuddered and bit down on her lower lip.

He nodded, unable to imagine how scared she would have been down in that hole. As they stood there, he wondered if he should say something about the kiss. Maybe apologize, although he wasn't sorry. "Toss your duffel on the bed and let's go over to the bar. I don't know about you, but I could use something to eat. It's been a long day."

JJ nodded, stepped in to drop her bag on the bed. He watched her dig out a brush. "Mind if I jump in the shower real quick?"

Why hadn't he thought of that? "Sure. Sorry."

"I'll make it fast." She headed for the bathroom. When she came back out only minutes later, he could see that she'd corralled her thick blond hair into a ponytail. She looked young, her cheeks flushed from the wild ride and the wind, her blue eyes bright as the summer sun. He felt an ache in his belly, wondering if he'd ever been that young even though he wasn't that much older than her.

"I could use a beer," he said, and stepped back to let her lead the way. They walked through the darkness toward the rear of the bar, following the sound of country music. Once through a screened door, they passed along a hallway with restrooms and storage areas before they reached the dark bar with its knotty-pine walls and scarred wood floors.

A half dozen men and women were seated at the bar with another half dozen at the tables on the far wall. His friend spotted him and motioned to a room off the side. Thorn and JJ stepped into it and his friend joined them, closing the door behind them.

IT HAD TAKEN a while for JJ to get her land legs back under her after that wild motorcycle ride, but the shower had helped. She had gotten the feel of the root cellar off her skin, if not off her mind.

As she stepped into the small room with Thorn, she took it in. There was a table and four chairs and nothing else in the room. She suspected there had been poker games in here in the past. She still felt off balance from everything that had happened. Being here with Thorn, in this bar from another century or two, wasn't helping shake how surreal all of this felt.

She watched Thorn's friend slap him on the back, pulling him into a hug before the man turned to her.

"This is my friend Miguel."

The stocky dark-haired man grinned. "You must be JJ."

She couldn't help her surprise. Thorn hadn't had a chance to make a call since rescuing her. *So he'd been that sure he'd find me and bring me here at some point?* Well, the man had never lacked confidence, that was for sure. She smiled and shook Miguel's hand. "Great place you have here."

Miguel laughed. "It will be once I get it fixed up."

"No, I like it the way it is. It's perfect," she said.

"Well, I can promise you that the food is good," the proud owner said. "How about I get you something to drink. Two beers?" He looked to JJ. She nodded. Miguel grabbed Thorn's hand again, pulling it close to his heart. "It's been too long, old buddy." With that he was gone.

JJ couldn't help being touched by Miguel's obvious affection for Thorn. It made her change her perception of him. The man had at least one good friend. She suspected there were more. So why did he live high in the mountains like some kind of hermit? Even as she questioned it, she knew it had to do with his deceased wife. He'd said he'd gotten her killed. She wondered if she would ever hear the whole story, or if they would part ways long before that happened.

Thorn took a chair at the table. Miguel had closed the door behind him, cutting off the loud jukebox music enough that they would have no trouble hearing each other once they started talking.

That was what this was about, right? It took her a moment before she dragged out a chair and sat down, dreading what was coming. She'd pulled off this life of hers for several years now without a hitch. Just her luck that some fools decided to kidnap Geneva Davenport.

Miguel brought in two beers, a bowl of fried hot corn tortillas and a tub of salsa. The smell was enough to make her stomach rumble. The last meal she'd had was elk hash earlier at his cabin. That seemed like days ago.

Thorn took a sip of his beer, watching her over the rim of his glass before he reached for one of the chips.

JJ helped herself to a couple of chips, heavy on the salsa, and washed them down with a gulp of the beer. How many people were looking for them? Her gaze settled on Thorn. She couldn't even be sure which side of the law he was on. He said he was one of the good guys, and so far it definitely seemed that way. But still, it appeared that no law enforcement had been called in, and there were at least two men dead and a plane crashed in the mountains.

"So," Thorn said as if feeling her questioning gaze on him. "Let's hear it. You were about to tell me the story of how you ended up in Geneva Davenport's house last night."

She took a sip of her beer. "There are several ways to look at this. In a way I saved Geneva. If she'd been here instead of me…"

He chuckled. "That's how you're going to try to sell it? Good luck with that."

"Fine." She leaned back in the chair, cornered. One thing was clear at this point. Thorn had saved her again. Or had he caught her again? Either way, he had her. He knew who she was. There was no getting out of this. Unless she could convince this cowboy to help her. But that would mean telling him everything, including the truth.

"Where do you want me to start?" she asked, still stalling. She didn't tell anyone about her life. She certainly didn't want to open those old wounds to this man.

"How about the beginning? Tell me again how it was that you were kidnapped from Geneva Davenport's bed."

"As I said, I was house-sitting. Kinda." She glanced away for a moment, his gray gaze too intense. She could feel it boring into her soul.

"Right. You said Geneva gave you her security code. So you're friends along with being her travel agent?"

JJ sighed. "Not exactly. We've never met in person. She asked me to come by and pick up something she forgot and overnight it to her once. A while back. That's how I knew her passcode to get into the house. She's one of my clients at the agency where I work. I got to know her because she travels a lot. I take care of everything from having a luxury SUV waiting when she lands to booking a hotel, making restaurant reservations, buying her a new swimsuit from a shop she likes and having it delivered so she can step into it the moment she arrives at the hotel."

He raised a brow. "You do everything for her but apply sunscreen. I got that. Still it doesn't explain why you were sleeping in her bed. Or did she ask you to keep her bed warm?"

She mugged a face at him and leaned back in her chair again. It was late, and it had been a very long day. "I had booked her a resort, and I knew she wouldn't be home for two weeks."

"So you decided to curl up in her bed and stay for a while? This is starting to sound like a fairy tale."

"I guess you could say that it is. I'm homeless."

He blinked. "But you just said you have a job, a job where at least one of your high-end clients trusts you."

She had to look away out of shame. "I can't afford a place to live." He raised his brow in disbelief. Was she going to have to tell her entire life history to this man? It appeared so, since he was waiting for a rational explanation and she only had one, the truth.

Fortunately, Miguel came in with two steaming plates of food. He put them down and quickly left, no doubt sensing the tension in the room.

Thorn motioned to her plate. "I'm sure you can eat and talk."

She picked up her fork. The meal smelled so good, she took a quick bite. It was delicious. She took another bite and saw that he was still waiting. He wasn't going to let her get away without telling her whole story. She realized it was like ripping off a bandage. Just get it out and be done with it.

"I was raised by my mother until I was fourteen. She was a meth addict. We lived in Billings." She took another bite, chewed and swallowed. She noticed that he hadn't touched his yet. "I never knew where my next meal was coming from. I won't bore you with how I survived, but I ended up getting a juvie record because of it. Then one day I came home from school, and there was this man there I'd never seen before. Turns out that he was my father."

She raised her gaze and looked into his face, waiting for his reaction. To her surprise, he merely nodded as if he'd heard the story before. There was no surprise, no judgment.

If anything, Thorn's expression had softened, his gray gaze not so fierce. She felt herself relax a little.

"I'd always wondered about my father, but my mother had never told me anything about him," she continued. "Turns out, he hadn't known that I existed, but one look at me and he knew I was his. He saw my living conditions, and he paid my mother to let him take me. From then on, he raised me, paid for my college, gave me a...life." Tears filled her eyes at the memory of how her father had sacrificed to make sure she was taken care of. She made a swipe at them, turning away.

When Thorn spoke, it was barely above a whisper. "I'm guessing something happened."

She nodded and made another swipe at her tears. "My father got sick. Cancer."

"I'm sorry."

"I was a junior in college when I found out. I quit college even though he fought me on it, and I took care of him just as he had taken care of me."

Thorn picked up his fork. "He didn't have medical insurance?"

"Not enough. I found out after he'd passed that he had mortgaged everything he had to put me through college. I got a job at the travel agency, but I couldn't save the house. I looked around for a place I could afford to live and still pay off the medical bills. I found an affordable studio and got my car broken into the first night. Then at my job, I was asked to house-sit. I realized I could couch surf and not pay rent. It would help me pay off the medical bills faster. I keep a suitcase in the back of my car and a duffel bag with just what I needed."

She knew it was trespassing. She knew she shouldn't use

her position at the travel agency to even get house-sitting jobs. Worse to sleep over when she wasn't invited.

But she used every dime she made to pay down the medical debt. As it was, it would take her years. She'd lived hand-to-mouth with her mother long enough that she'd learned to survive on little. Her father wouldn't have approved, and that bothered her more than the fact that she could get caught and arrested.

She'd never dreamed she would get kidnapped while doing her version of house-sitting.

He shook his head as he began to eat his meal. "This explains a lot." He glanced down and then back up at her. "But why didn't the kidnappers realize they had the wrong woman?"

She shrugged. "Geneva and I are both blonde and have similar features I guess, and since they found me in her bed..." She felt raw and exposed. She'd always been strong. But she'd never let anyone close enough after her father's death, to know the truth about her life. She couldn't help feeling ashamed. She should have known what her father had gone through to give her the life he did. What he'd sacrificed. She'd just been so happy living with him that she'd never questioned it. That was one reason she was determined to pay off every cent of his medical bills. She owed him that much and more.

They both fell into a long silence as they finished their meals. As Thorn pushed away his empty plate, she asked, "The person who asked you to find me..."

"He's the judge I went before when I was young. I wasn't hired. This debt you feel you owe your father, it's more like that. The man who asked me to find you saved me from prison. Like your father, he saw that I got an education. I owe him."

She nodded in surprise. "I have a record from when I lived with my mother. Car theft."

He laughed. "Seems we have more in common than either of us thought."

"Does this judge know that the kidnappers took the wrong woman?"

"I called him after I found your ID in your duffel bag and told him there had been a mix-up, but that's all he knows. But since you made the arrangements for Geneva Davenport's trip, you know where she is, right?"

JJ nodded as Thorn's cell phone rang. He glanced at it and said, "I have to take this." But as he rose to leave the room, she touched his arm. He must have seen the fear in her gaze. "It's going to be all right." He left the room, closing the door behind him.

FRANKLIN LOOKED UP as his friend came back into the living room after he'd stepped out to make a call.

"Could we speak in private?" Willie asked.

He merely nodded and followed his friend into the den. "Well?" He couldn't help feeling impatient as Willie closed the door. He would soon have the money. Ten million dollars. The price for his granddaughter's life. He would have paid twice that much to make sure she was safe.

"You might want to sit down," the judge said solemnly. "I just got off the phone with my contact."

Franklin dropped into a chair, his heart lodged in his throat. "Geneva?" He listened as the judge gave him an update.

"Your granddaughter had given the woman staying at her house the passcode. Geneva wasn't home, but I suspect she knew the woman resembled her. Geneva also must have known about the tracking device on her phone, because she left it in her bedroom. The kidnappers searched for it and took it before they left in the plane that crashed."

"What are you insinuating? That Geneva set this woman up?" He wanted to leap to his feet, to argue that his grand-daughter would never do something like that, yet he couldn't find the strength to do either.

"I'm not sure what to think at this point," Willie said. "But I'm not ruling out that there's a chance Geneva's involved in the kidnapping. Or her boyfriend is. Either way, she's in danger."

He shook his head, not wanting to believe the evidence against his granddaughter. "We haven't been close for some time now. She keeps secrets from me. If she's involved in this, then that boyfriend of hers is to blame." His friend said nothing. "Zac Judson."

Willie pulled out his phone. "What do you know about him?"

"Just what little Geneva shared with me. They met after she got sailing lessons for her birthday. Zac was one of the instructors. He grew up in the Houston area. His father is a boatbuilder." He saw that the judge was waiting for his take on the man. "He's close to forty, too old for Geneva, and too…experienced." He waved a hand through the air. "She led me to believe that he came from money."

"You don't think he does?"

Franklin shook his head. "The one time I met him, I saw him looking around the estate. There was a hungry look in his eyes. It was one of the reasons I took Geneva's passport from her purse. I also cut her allowance to just necessities, which in her case is more than most people make in a year. But the boyfriend? He looks like a gold digger to me."

The judge was searching his phone. "I've found a Zach-ariah Judson in Houston, but he's in his sixties."

"The man's father." He watched Willie keep searching.

"Okay, here's a Zac Judson." The judge looked up from his phone and turned the screen toward him. "Is that Geneva's boyfriend?"

"That's him."

Willie tapped the keys on his phone. "He's had his share of run-ins with the law. Assault and the sale of illegal drugs at the top of the list."

Franklin swore and pushed himself to his feet. "I need a drink."

"I'd take one of those now too," WT said.

JJ WISHED SHE could believe that everything was going to be all right. That once she contacted Geneva, all of this would somehow get sorted out.

She could hear Thorn just outside the door talking to his friend Miguel after taking the call. She'd finished her meal, too nervous to sit still. She kept thinking about Geneva and how to go about telling her what had happened. The only way was to admit she'd been staying in the master bedroom at the woman's house. Geneva needed to know what was going on. What if she changed her plans and came home early? The woman needed to know that there were some desperate men looking for her.

Deciding to get it over with, she pulled out her cell phone and hurriedly called the hotel where she'd made reservations for her client. The line rang four times before the front desk finally answered.

"Geneva Davenport, please." She had to at least warn the woman.

"Just a moment."

She glanced at the door and silently pleaded with the desk clerk on the other end of the line to hurry. She was beginning to trust Thorn, wasn't she? He'd saved her twice today. But she didn't kid herself. He also wasn't letting her out of his sight until this was over. And that's what made her afraid to trust him entirely. He could throw her to the wolves, once he paid his debt to the judge by finding Geneva.

The hotel clerk came back on the line. "I'm sorry, but we don't have anyone by that name registered."

That wasn't possible. "I made the arrangements myself for her. Davenport. Please, can you check again?"

"I'm sorry, it appears someone with that last name *did* have a reservation, but the person never arrived and we were unable to reach the party, so it was canceled."

JJ disconnected as Thorn came back into the room. He glanced at the phone in her hand and then at her face. "Geneva," she said, and swallowed the lump in her throat. She'd been so sure the woman was safe as long as the kidnappers thought *she* was Geneva—and the real Davenport heiress was beside the pool in Palm Springs.

"Geneva never made it to the hotel I booked for her."

CHAPTER TWELVE

THORN STARED AT HER. All the color had drained from her face. He could see that she hadn't been worried about the real Geneva Davenport because she'd thought she knew where the woman was—and that Geneva was safe.

"She wasn't expected back for two weeks," JJ said, sounding scared. "She couldn't be reached because she left her phone behind in her bedroom. I assumed that she left it behind because she knew about the tracking device her grandfather put on it. She didn't want anyone to know where she was going."

"Except her travel agent?" he asked skeptically. "But her kidnappers were looking for something in the bedroom, right? Isn't that what you told me?" He saw her shiver. "Did they find anything else besides her phone?" She shook her head. "Then apparently, other than you, all they wanted was her phone. So they'd known it would be there. My question is, how had the kidnappers known her phone would be in her room?"

"I don't know. Because they thought I was Geneva and when they found the phone, they assumed it was mine, I mean hers." He could see that her suspicions had taken her to the same result his had, but she was having trouble accepting it.

"What can you tell me about Geneva?" He listened as she told him that over the past two years, she'd come to know the woman's business by overhearing her conversations when she called to make travel reservations.

According to JJ, the headstrong, clearly spoiled twenty-two-year-old was often at odds with her grandfather when she called JJ to book a trip. Her grandfather hadn't liked anyone she'd dated, Geneva had related to her friends in the background. He also tried to control her by threatening to do away with most of her apparently rather large allowance.

But recently Geneva had hooked up with someone who'd been the last straw with her grandfather. A man named Zac Judson, whose father owned Judson Boats.

A few days ago, Geneva had called to make reservations. JJ had asked where she would like to fly. Palm Springs, California.

JJ repeated the conversation and what she'd heard.

"Someone in the background said, 'But I thought you were going to the French Riviera?'

"'I wish. My grandfather took my passport. Can you believe that? It wasn't enough to cut off my money, but he made it so I can't even leave the country. Jenny, would you make the reservations for two weeks? I really need a break.'"

Thorn considered everything she'd just told him. "Is it possible she knew you would stay at her house the night she left?" He could tell that she'd been expecting the question because it was one that she'd been asking herself.

"You think she set me up."

"Don't you?"

JJ shook her head. "I know she's rich and spoiled and self-centered."

"And angry at her grandfather over…money," he said. "So she comes up with this scheme to get ten million dollars out of him and free herself from his control. She left her phone behind that she knew had a tracking device on it and told the kidnappers to be sure and retrieve it when they grabbed you. JJ, she set you up. She knew you were sleeping at her house. Probably from hidden surveillance cameras in the house."

"But how could she know I would go there last night?"

"Because you'd done it before."

"One other time. Maybe a couple of times."

He couldn't help giving her a sympathetic look. "You played right into her kidnapping plot."

"I KNOW IT looks that way," JJ had to admit. She saw his expression. "I can tell that you think I'm naive. But it just doesn't feel right."

"I guess I'm surprised you're that…trusting of a woman you've never met and only taken orders from over the phone. *I'm* trying to save your life, and you still don't trust me."

She knew he had a point. He'd come to her rescue again, hadn't he? True, he'd thought he needed her to find Geneva, but he'd risked his life for her. "Maybe I'm starting to trust you." She thought of the kiss. He hadn't planned on that. "Keep working at it. Seriously, I think you're making progress."

He shook his head at her. "I know you don't want to believe it. But Geneva calls you to book a trip for her, letting you know that she'll be gone for two weeks. *You have a place to stay for two weeks.* I'm surprised she didn't ask you to house-sit, but then you might have told someone— or even invited another person to stay even if she told you not to. By now she realizes you don't really follow rules."

"Sounds like you have *me* all worked out anyway." She knew he made a good argument, but it wasn't one she wanted to hear. She'd been so sure that Geneva hadn't known that she stayed in her house when she was gone. The cleaning service always came on Saturday morning to put clean sheets on the bed and clean the entire house. JJ was always gone by then, knowing that any trace of her was scrubbed and vacuumed and dusted away. There wasn't any way Geneva could have known, unless Thorn was right and there were hidden cameras in the house.

"She wanted you to know that she would be gone," Thorn continued. "Then she probably notified the kidnappers when you were asleep in her bed."

"If you're right, then why wouldn't they take my duffel bag and get rid of my car? Had anyone checked her house, they would have found both. So much for Geneva's clean getaway."

"Why would she worry about your car and duffel bag? She would have ten million dollars and be gone. Or maybe they planned to take care of those details later—before things didn't work out the way they had it planned. If anything, the police would think you were involved in the kidnapping, because eventually they would ID your body in the wrecked plane and know you weren't Geneva. At that point, they would assume she was dead since I'm betting she planned to disappear."

"You can't think the plane crash was part of the plan."

He gave her another patient look.

"You think I was supposed to die in the plane crash."

"Or the explosion."

What if Thorn was right? She felt her skin crawl.

That would mean that the pilot had been given the wrong information. Maybe the engine had been tampered with? Or the fuel supply? Or there was an explosive device on board? "That is so cold-blooded. Why would—"

"For ten million in ransom money."

She frowned. "Then the men who abducted me didn't know I wasn't Geneva."

"Probably not. But at least one of them has to know by now that he was set up," Thorn said.

"Baker. I wonder if he got out of the mountains, and if he did…" She stopped to look at the cowboy. "He's looking for the people who hired him and his buddies."

Thorn nodded. "If Geneva was behind it, he'll be looking for her next."

JJ felt sick, and yet when she thought of the woman she'd listened to talk about her problems while on the phone with her… "Maybe what I can't see is her putting something like this together. Also, those men who took me to the cabin? They thought I was Geneva. They're still looking for her. But I don't think they were involved in the original kidnapping. I think she owes their boss money. Apparently he's been trying to collect for some time and his patience had run out."

Thorn seemed to consider that. "Which could also explain why she cooked up this plan to get the money. Now that things have gone south, she's probably bailed," Thorn said. "If she left the area at all."

Geneva was young and impulsive. If she was involved, then JJ wondered if she had any idea how much trouble she was in. How much danger she was in. JJ could see her bailing and leaving her hired kidnappers high and dry. Not to mention the man and his crew who were also looking for her. JJ could attest to how angry and anxious the man was to find her.

Thorn sighed. "And now neither group has her—or the money—and if either of you shows up before they get it…"

"A week ago, Geneva asked me what it took to become a luxury travel adviser," JJ said. "She was interested in learning more about the job. Does that sound like someone who was planning her own kidnapping?"

"JJ," Thorn said, "she was befriending you. She wanted to make sure you would be sleeping in her bed last night."

She knew she was clutching at straws. Thorn had made a good argument that definitely made Geneva look guilty. But even if she was, JJ didn't believe that she was working alone. "I guess I could believe it if her boyfriend, Zac Judson, was behind it."

"You don't trust him? What do you know about him?"

"Just what I've heard over the phone. Her grandfather doesn't like him at all, which could say something about him. If she really went away with him like she had planned when she made the reservations for Palm Springs, he has to be in on it, right?"

Thorn pushed to his feet. "Even if she can trust her boyfriend, Geneva is in trouble. If we could find Baker, he might just lead us to who hired him—and probably tried to kill him." He pulled out the two phones that JJ had taken from the men in the plane before it blew up. "Let's start with these guys, but not tonight. I don't know about you, but I've had enough for one day." As he rose, he flinched as if his back still hurt, reminding her of earlier.

"I'm sorry I hit you with the chair. In retrospect, it was a mistake."

"It's all right. You've been through a lot. Seriously, we're no good to Geneva like this. In the morning, we'll find her, and we'll get this all sorted out."

Miguel came into the room to see if they needed anything else. Music from the bar flowed in with him.

"The food was delicious," JJ said. "Your recipes?"

He smiled. "My grandmother's. She was quite the cook.

I used to watch her make tortillas." He patted his hands together. "I make my own now just like she did."

"Thank you for everything," Thorn said, and looked at her. "If you don't mind, I think we'll stay the night in your cabin." That was news to her. The cabin was small, and there was only the one double bed. "We both could use some rest."

"Let me know if there is anything else you need," Miguel said. "Stay as long as you like."

As they walked over to the cabin, JJ admitted that she was exhausted after the long day she'd had. Apparently, she'd proved earlier that she could sleep anywhere—except in a small bed with the cowboy.

"If you're worried about where we're going to sleep, don't be," he said, as if reading her mind. She saw his amused grin. "I'll sleep on the floor." He glanced over at her. "You'll be perfectly safe, I promise." He made an X over his heart as if that would reassure her. He looked like he wanted to say something about that kiss earlier, but she cut him off before he could.

"What are you going to do with me when, as you say, we get this all sorted out?" she asked.

They'd stopped at the door to the cabin. A small dim bare bulb hung over the door. It was enough to see that he was frowning down at her. "*Do* with you?"

"I'm just wondering at what point you plan to turn me over to the authorities."

"I'm not."

"Not *yet*. Not until you find Geneva."

"What is it you want me to say? I thought we agreed that you were going to help me find Geneva because you seem to know more about her than even her grandfather does. Also, until we do, your life is in danger too. If I'm right, you were supposed to have died in the plane crash. You didn't. That makes you a loose end someone is going to want to tie up." He pushed open the cabin door, but she didn't move. "Look, you're safer with me than you would be on your own. Haven't you realized that by now?"

Was she? She thought of the kiss and her reaction to it. That certainly hadn't felt safe. "I'm not your problem."

He scoffed at that. "You became my problem when the judge asked me to find you. Well, find Geneva. Instead, I found you." His gray gaze locked with hers. "The only way to clear your name and not end up dead or in jail is to stick with me."

"You're that good at whatever it is you do?"

"Yeah, I am." He looked away. "I was trained in the military. Is that what you need to hear? JJ, what do I have to do to make you trust me?" He shook his head in obvious exasperation.

"How do I know that when we find her, you won't kill us both, take the ten million and disappear?"

He swore. "The way your mind works scares me."

"Me too," she admitted. "But I like to cover all the bases."

"I know the feeling," he said. "That's why I think Geneva is up to her ears in this." Thorn seemed to study her for a long moment. "You have to be the most fascinating woman I think I've ever met. And the most stubborn, impossible and frustrating. You've made it difficult, but whether you like it or not I'm going to keep you alive. We're going to find Geneva, and then we can part ways. Is that what you need to hear? You can go back to your job at the travel agency and—"

"You can go back to your mountain hermit retreat?"

He sighed and looked away. She was too tired to be having this discussion. True, she wanted to find Geneva. But maybe she just wanted this cowboy to know that she had options other than turning her life over to him, which felt dangerous to her. Especially after that kiss earlier.

Or maybe she just didn't trust not being on her own like she had been since her father's death—just like she'd been as a girl. That was something she knew and trusted. Depending on this cowboy was taking a risk, and that scared her. "What if I decide to go to the cops with all of it and let *them* find her?"

His smile transformed his face in the overhead light. She was struck again how handsome he could be when he wasn't trying to intimidate her. "Jenny Jo? If you were going to the cops, you would have already done it. Involving the authorities could get Geneva killed and you locked up."

"I thought you were so sure that she was behind her own kidnapping."

"Right now, I'm not sure of anything except that we both need rest. So stop arguing with me. *Please.*" He motioned for her to enter the cabin.

She hesitated only a moment, because he was right. She was exhausted and probably not thinking straight. She'd already made mistakes. Could she really afford to make another one that might have disastrous consequences?

But she didn't kid herself that getting too close to this man wasn't dangerous, even without having kidnappers on her trail. His kiss was imprinted on her lips—not to mention what it had stirred up inside her. But more dangerous was leaning on someone else. Especially this cowboy with his own painful past.

CHAPTER THIRTEEN

"WHAT DID YOU tell this judge of yours about me?" JJ asked as she stopped in the middle of the room, avoiding the only bed and the thought of their sleeping arrangements. She felt anxious. Tomorrow they would try to find Geneva. He was so sure she knew how to do that. It was what happened after they did that worried her. She felt as if she was getting in deeper into something even more dangerous.

"I told him that the woman in the plane wasn't Geneva. That there was a mix-up. That you're not involved in the kidnapping."

That surprised her. "You told him that you had me."

He chuckled at that. "Until you get it in your head to take off again."

She met his gaze and held it. "What are you risking here?"

"No more than you're risking."

"Your judge doesn't want to see me? Question me? Franklin Davenport doesn't?"

He sighed. "I'm not turning you over to anyone."

"Not even your judge?" That surprised her.

"No, not even to him. Now could we please get some rest, and tomorrow I plan to find Geneva and turn her over to her grandfather, guilty or not. Are you going to help me?"

She thought about the young woman who always asked for her at the travel agency. "I definitely want to find her before anyone else does."

"That reminds me. I need to look at the cut on your leg."

"It's fine." She started to step past him, but he grabbed her arm.

His gaze held her in a viselike grip much like his fingers, though he was barely touching her. "Let me look at your leg."

She sighed and sat down on the foot of the bed. He knelt before her and pushed her jeans pant leg up for him to see the cut.

"You should see a doctor to make sure it doesn't get infected."

"It doesn't look that bad. Can't you tape it up?"

"You'll have a scar."

She smiled at that. "It won't be my first or probably my last."

He looked up at her, a smile playing at his lips. "You live that dangerously?"

"Seems that way." She met his eyes. They appeared silvery in the cabin's light. Her chest tightened. It had been ages. She'd kept her head down for so long, working and paying bills, that she'd forgotten what it was like to have a man look at her that way.

Thorn cleared his throat and rose. "I'm going to take a shower." She thought about his fingers in her hair, the scent of shampoo filling the air. How long had it been for him, she wondered. Was his wife the woman he'd helped shampoo her hair in front of that fire? Or was the cabin and that life after whatever had happened to the woman?

He started to turn toward the bathroom, but then glanced back toward the cabin door.

She saw at once what he was thinking. "Going to lock me in?"

He gave her a tired smile. "It crossed my mind, probably the same way leaving crossed yours."

JJ let out a sigh and rose from the bed. "I know you think I'm difficult. But I've been on my own for a good part of my life. I'm okay with that. It's trusting my life to others that I have trouble with."

"Has there never been a man in your life, other than your father?"

She felt heat rush to her cheeks. "It isn't like I haven't dated." There'd been some boyfriends in high school and college, but after her father died she'd been too busy to even date.

"You've never been in love."

She started to argue that maybe she'd come close a couple of times, but he didn't give her a chance.

"I'm sorry, that's none of my business," he said. "And I understand about going it alone. It's easier than taking a chance on someone who can rip out your heart and stomp on it." He met her gaze. "Sorry."

"Do you want to talk about her?"

"No." He gave her a sad smile. "Don't try to go it alone this time, okay?"

"I'm too tired tonight. But if you don't trust me, please, nail the door shut. Or I suppose you could tie me to the bed."

A smile curled his lips. "Hmm. You tied to the bed. If I wasn't so tired…" He shook his head and sighed. "Just holler if you need me."

She dropped onto the foot of the bed, realizing it was true. She was too tired to run, and what would be the point anyway? He knew who she was. The only way forward at this point was with his help. They would find Geneva. They would find out what was going on. They would put an end to it, and if she was lucky, she'd get out of this free and clear.

The thought seemed impossible at this moment. She would need to call the travel agency and get a few days off. As if that's all it would take to find Geneva. She had no idea where the woman had gone.

Worse, it wasn't just JJ and Thorn looking for her. And because of that, none of this made any sense. How could one twenty-two-year-old be in so much trouble?

She could hear the shower running in the adjacent room. She tried not to imagine Thorn naked, soapy and all those muscles rippling under the spray. To her surprise that image wasn't what sent an ache to her center. It was his smile and the way his gray eyes lit for just a moment sometimes, hiding the pain inside. And the guilt he felt over the death of his wife. Or was there more to it?

JJ looked toward the bathroom door, wondering about her. With a start, she realized she hadn't seen a photo of his wife in the cabin. That seemed strange now that she thought about it.

But Thorn was right about one thing. She'd never been in love. She'd never met a man who made her heart beat fast and hard. Until now, and under the circumstances, that made her want to put distance between them.

Only a fool couldn't see that the last thing on this wounded cowboy's mind was another woman. He was doing this because the judge had asked him to. Because he was the kind of man who finished what he started. And he needed her to help him find Geneva Davenport. That was his only motivation, finishing the job he'd started. Then he would head back to the mountains and his…life.

And JJ would go back to work, back to her…life.

Feeling as if she didn't even have the energy to change into something to sleep in, she forced herself to reach for her duffel bag. She withdrew a large T-shirt and, quickly stripping down, pulled it on before climbing between the sheets.

The minute her head hit the pillow she fell into a dark, deep, dreamless sleep.

WHEN THORN CAME out of the bathroom, he half expected JJ to be gone. He hadn't been looking forward to chasing her down again, but he'd known he would. To his relief, there she was, curled up in the bed sleeping soundly.

He stepped closer. Sleep had smoothed out the worry lines in her forehead. It had softened everything about her. Without her usual intensity, she looked…peaceful—and damned beautiful. He stood over her, watching her sleep, jealous that she could just drift off so quickly. His sleep had been haunted for so long… This was what the sleep of the innocent was like, he thought. The sleep of a person with a clear conscience. Or at least fairly clear.

Shaking his head, he yearned for that kind of rest, but knew he wouldn't get it—especially on the cabin floor. He looked longingly at the side of the bed that lay empty, with her curled against the far side. Did he dare? It would be like crawling into bed with a sleeping mama lion and just hoping she didn't wake up and claw his eyes out.

Still… He stepped around to the side of the bed and carefully pulled down the covers, watching for any change in JJ as he did. The bed groaned under his weight until he settled in, keeping what space he could between them in the double bed. Thankfully she had not awakened.

She'd brought his wife out of the shadows, and now Bethany's ghost seemed to move restlessly through his thoughts. He'd banished her, exorcising her from his life, just so he could have a day without thinking of her. Now JJ had called her up from the grave. He realized he would have to deal with her. Maybe it was time that he buried her for good.

He must have fallen asleep, which surprised him, because when he woke he no longer felt the pull of exhaustion. He blinked and looked down to see that as wonderful as a good night's sleep had been, he had a problem.

JJ was asleep on his bare shoulder. If he moved even a fraction of an inch... If he even breathed...

JJ SIGHED, A long sigh of pleasure, and then stretched. She was still caught up in the amazing dream she'd been having. It wasn't until she lifted her head from the warm, smooth-skinned shoulder that she screamed.

The man leaped from the bed, holding up his hands. He was bare from the waist up, but wore jeans below that. "Nothing happened. I swear."

She blinked, the scream slowly dying in her throat as she recognized him. "Thorn?" He'd shaved off his beard and cut his hair. She couldn't have been more shocked by the transformation—or the fact that she'd awakened lying on his bare shoulder.

"I was so tired and you looked so comfortable in the bed," he said, still holding up his hands. "I'd apologize for climbing into bed with you, but that's the best night's sleep I've had in years." He stopped talking for a moment and frowned. "You're staring."

"It's just that you look so...so different." She shook her head. "You're...gorgeous."

He let out a nervous laugh. "Thanks, I think. I'm glad you didn't add what you thought of me before."

"What were you doing hiding behind all that hair?" She saw that she'd struck a nerve, and wished sometimes that she didn't often say what she thought.

"We should get going," he said as he started to turn away.

She wanted to curl back up on his shoulder and escape in sleep. Mostly she wanted to pick up that dream where she'd left off. She had just been getting to the good part.

But the moment was lost. She looked down to see that she still had her T-shirt on, and her panties. Nothing had happened, just as he'd said. But the remnants of her dream seemed to hover around her, a faceless lover's tender touch still making her skin tingle.

"I'm going to take a shower."

"I left you two clean towels," he said, his voice a little too low and seductive for this early in the morning. Especially with him looking so damned good.

"You really are one of the good guys," she joked as she felt his gaze on her.

"That's what I keep telling you."

JJ climbed out of bed, grabbed her duffel and headed for the bathroom. After a quick shower, she dressed in the spare pair of jeans and T-shirt she had in the bag, along with clean socks and her sneakers. She'd washed her long, thick hair, dried it with the towel the best she could, and now pulled it up in a ponytail. As she did, she couldn't help but think about Thorn's hands tangled in her hair, his fingers gently massaging her scalp.

She shook off the memory of waking on his warm, strong shoulder as she pushed out of the bathroom to find him standing in the open doorway, his back to her. He looked so different that it still startled her. He was dressed in jeans that hugged his slim hips and firm behind, and a Western shirt that spanned the expanse of his broad shoulders. She saw that he had a jean jacket slung over one shoulder.

"I didn't realize that you had time to pack clean clothes," she said.

"Miguel lent me a few things," he said, turning to look back at her.

When he shifted in the doorway, she saw his high cheekbones and strong jaw in the morning sunlight. For a moment, it took her breath away because she knew that this man was her faceless lover from her dream.

His gaze settled on her, and he seemed to do a double take. "Wow," he said, and started to say something more. But whatever it was going to be, it was cut off as his cell phone rang. He quickly turned away to take the call.

WT HAD SPENT the night in Franklin's guest room, but he hadn't slept well—and not just because of the news. Geneva Davenport was in the wind. And now both women were in danger.

"I'm sorry I got you into this," he said when Thorn answered his call now. "I had my reservations about the kidnapping. I should have listened to my instincts. I think it's time to call the authorities and let them handle it."

"No. JJ doesn't believe Geneva is behind this."

"JJ?" He heard something in the younger man's tone. A tenderness that surprised him. It had been heartbreak that had sent Thorn into the mountains to live in a cabin in the woods, to never love a woman again. WT could understand the sentiment only too well. Had something changed?

"I have to finish this. I'm going to. If you call in the authorities now—"

"It is much more dangerous than when I asked you to go into the mountains to look for the plane," WT said. "I can't ask you to continue."

"You're not. I'm doing this, but I'll need your help. I

need to know if Geneva got on any other flights on Friday or if she and her boyfriend, Zac Judson, are still in the area. Also, there's some property on the lake. I need to know who owns it. And who is doing the construction on the property." He gave him what information he had on the place where JJ had been taken.

"And you aren't going to tell me what this is about?"

"JJ was abducted a second time from Geneva's house. She doesn't believe it was the kidnappers. Instead, it appears that Geneva owes someone a lot of money and hasn't paid. The people involved want Geneva and are still looking for her. Apparently, they intended to trade JJ for her. So right now, there are people looking for both of them."

The judge swore silently. It was much worse than he'd thought. He'd questioned his judgment involving Thorn in this. The man had been so broken for so long after his wife's death. What if this was more than he could handle? "I thought I was only involving you in a simple rescue mission." It had sounded so straightforward, and Thorn had been so close by. He'd known the man could find the downed plane and get the woman out if she was alive. He'd just never expected that the woman wasn't Geneva Davenport. Or that things would get even more complicated, drawing Thorn in even deeper.

Thorn continued as if WT hadn't spoken. "Also, I need the addresses and anything you have on the two dead kidnappers." He'd given him the names Wes Brennan and Kyle Spencer. "I need to find the one that got away. Baker is all I know. It would help if I could get into their phones, but they are both password protected."

"Thorn—"

"You asked me to find Geneva. That's what I'm doing. Has there been any word on the plane?"

WT sighed. He knew this man, knew how tenacious he was. Wasn't that why he'd called him? He wanted the best person he could think of to find his friend's granddaughter. Sighing, he said, "It's been found. I would imagine the FAA is investigating since the plane was reported stolen from an airfield near Kalispell Friday night."

"Who owned the plane?"

"A corporation that owned a corporation and so on. I'm trying to sort it out and so is the news media. When I have some names, I'll let you know. In the meantime—"

"Just don't do anything stupid," Thorn said. "Like going to the authorities." The line went dead.

Thorn wasn't going to turn back. He wouldn't stop now even if ordered to. WT knew all he could do was help Thorn any way he could. He'd make a few calls. He'd get the information Thorn needed and hope it would be enough to keep him and the woman he called JJ safe.

But now he was worried about what Franklin would want to do. He might change his mind and insist on going to the authorities. Or he might refuse to go through with the ransom drop when the kidnappers called back. But until they knew for certain that the kidnappers didn't have the real Geneva...

And if Geneva was behind this, from what he'd learned about her? WT sighed, not sure who they could trust. He thought about the man's chief financial officer. He'd hardly noticed the man. Since Helen had walked in, he'd only had eyes for her.

But this morning with only Franklin and Curtis in the dining room, he considered the man. The CFO was much younger than WT would have thought, midforties at most. Blond, blue-eyed and attractive, he wore an expensive tailor-made suit, and chunky gold cuff links winked at his wrists as he shot his sleeves and sat down. The man seemed capable, and Franklin clearly trusted him. The same with Helen. Mostly WT tried to put his finger on what it was about all of this that bothered him.

With Helen in the mix, he knew he had to be careful. Thoughts of her and the past were not what he needed right now. He had a lot of lives at risk. He had to be at his sharpest and not let any personal feelings interfere.

Last night Franklin had talked them all into staying over. When WT had gone to bed in one of the many guest rooms, he'd left the rest of them in Franklin's den figuring out the best way to get the ransom money together and discussing how to handle things with the media when it was over.

WT still hadn't had a chance to talk to Helen, which was probably for the best. Seeing her had thrown him for a loop. He wasn't sure what he might have said if they'd gotten a few minutes alone. This kidnapping was enough of a mess. He had to keep his head on straight. He couldn't let his personal complications get in the way, or he'd get Thorn killed as well as the women the man was desperately trying to save.

But he didn't kid himself. He and Helen had more than a past. They had a lot of unfinished business between them. He told himself it had nothing to do with Geneva Davenport's alleged kidnapping, though, so it could wait until a better time.

He reminded himself that while he'd been shocked to see her, she hadn't been the least surprised to see him. Clearly, Franklin hadn't known about their past connection. Nor had Franklin told her who would be at the house.

Which meant that Helen had known if Franklin were in trouble, WT would be the first person he would call.

LOOKING AT JJ, Thorn knew he was treading on thin ice and not just with the judge. So much was up in the air. He had no idea what the kidnapper knew or didn't. The judge thought he was in over his head. Maybe he was.

Could he handle this? There were moments when he wasn't so sure himself. Because handling it meant handling JJ. He'd never met anyone like her, and let's face it, he hadn't given another women a thought since his wife died. So not for a very long time. Not that he had ever understood the workings of a woman's mind. Did anyone, with a woman like JJ?

She continued to surprise him, he thought now as he was taken aback by how beautiful she looked in the Montana summer morning. Nor could he believe how quickly she'd showered and dressed this morning after the past couple of days she'd had. If he'd found the real Geneva Davenport, he suspected she would have *still* been in the bathroom getting ready. She would have been a lot more high maintenance, but by now she would have been her grandfather's problem and not his anymore, he reminded himself.

JJ was going to help him find Geneva and it would be all over, he assured himself. What worried him was just the sight of her this morning had struck him at a primal level. Dressed in jeans and a red T-shirt that fit her lush body, her curves were undeniable. Her blond hair was pulled up in a ponytail. Her face, free of makeup, glowed, adding even more sparkle to her blue eyes. The woman looked young and full of life and sexy as hell.

Don't get her killed.

She'd stopped just a few feet into the main room, and was now looking at him lounging in the cabin doorway. "Something wrong?"

Just the pang of guilt he'd felt moments before, after his phone call. He had his own reasons for wanting to find Geneva, and it wasn't just to make sure she was safe. He hadn't completed his mission, and he was bound and determined to do what Judge Landusky had asked him to do. JJ hadn't signed up for any of this, and now he was dragging her along and into even more danger.

"I need to be honest with you," he said as he stepped toward her.

"*Now* you're going to be honest?" she joked.

"This will get dangerous."

JJ laughed. "Do I have to remind you that I was drugged, abducted and almost killed in a plane crash and abducted again and thrown down into a root cellar?"

"I'm serious. I need your help but—"

"I need to find Geneva Davenport as much as you do. If you're right and she set me up, then I need her to turn herself in and end all of this. If *I'm* right, then she's in danger and might not even realize it."

"You're not listening to me. I can clear you. I'll find her. You'd have to hide out for a few days, but you can walk away right now, if you want to," he said.

She chuckled. "That's big of you, but I've always been able to walk away."

He had to smile at that, thinking it was probably true. "Or take my truck when the mood hits you. It wouldn't be the first time."

JJ smiled. "I believe what you're trying to say is that I have a choice here. News flash, I always did. I could have done a lot of things differently. But now this is where I am, and I need to see this through."

Thorn studied her for a moment longer, thinking they were a lot alike and not just because they were both stubborn. She had one hand on her hip, her stance full of attitude. He loved that about her. He hadn't meant "loved."

Love was a word he'd never planned to use again when it came to any woman.

"Okay," he said, holding up his hands in surrender. "I thought we would check the airport first." He hadn't heard back from the judge. "What would Geneva have been driving?"

"Her bright red sports car."

He smiled and nodded. "Let's see if it's parked in the airport long-term parking lot. But at any point if you want—"

"Don't worry, you'll know when I've had enough of you." She walked past him and out the door to where he'd parked his bike. "Geneva's car should be easy to find. Or not find."

He followed her, relieved that she wasn't still thinking of finding Geneva on her own. Or turning herself in to the cops. He told himself that she was safer with him. At least he hoped that was true.

She was waiting next to his bike. He felt a pull stronger than gravity as he closed the cabin door and walked toward her. The morning sun lit her face. Those big blue eyes watched him approach. He hadn't wanted this job. Still didn't. But even if the judge had ordered him off, he couldn't quit now. He'd gone into the mountains to rescue Geneva Davenport. He still had to find her and get her to her grandfather.

But his main job right now was to keep Jenny Jo Foster alive. He'd never wanted to be the hero more than right now.

Just don't get her killed.

And don't fall for her.

CHAPTER FOURTEEN

THORN SWUNG THROUGH the airport parking lot on his motorcycle, JJ holding on behind him. It didn't take long to realize that Geneva's bright red sports car wasn't parked at the small Kalispell airport.

As he headed for the exit, he pulled over and cut off the motor to take a call on his cell phone. "Good morning again, Judge."

"You haven't changed your mind?"

"No, and I could really use those addresses."

WT sighed and gave him Brennan's and Spencer's addresses. "I assume you're planning to go by their houses. I thought you might want the address of Geneva's boyfriend, Zac Judson." The judge also offered him the make and model of the car Zac was driving.

"You read my mind."

"As for the other men, their families don't know yet that Wes and Kyle are dead," the judge said. "So be careful. On the news they said that there were two bodies in the plane, but their identities hadn't been released."

Thorn knew that it would take a while, since the bodies had been incinerated when the plane blew up, and neither man had identification on him.

"I'll get back to you on the other thing that you asked about," the judge said, and Thorn thanked him and disconnected.

"Zac Judson's apartment is the closest," JJ said after he told her the addresses the judge had given him.

The apartment complex where Zac rented was in the trees north of Big Fork. It didn't take any time to find his unit. The black sports car with the Texas plates that the judge had told him about wasn't parked outside. They knocked, then, scanning the area and seeing no one, Thorn picked the lock and they quickly stepped inside.

"A little talent you picked up in your youth?" JJ asked.

"One let's not mention to the judge," he said as they began to look around.

"It's like he's never been here," she said after a few moments. "Nothing personal in here."

"Because he cleaned it out either before the kidnapping scheme began," Thorn said, "or maybe when it went awry. Either way, there is nothing here."

As they started to leave, JJ bent down to pick up something that had fallen next to the nightstand in the bedroom. She held up a matchbook. "It's from a local bar."

Thorn smiled. "We might have to check the place out."

A knock at the door made them both jump. Thorn motioned for JJ to relax. She rolled her eyes as she pocketed the matchbook and he went to open the door.

The woman standing outside looked surprised to see the two of them. "I thought you were Zac," she said.

"We were looking for him ourselves," he said.

The woman looked past Thorn to JJ. "How did you get in here?"

"The door was open," Thorn said.

"I'm the apartment manager. You're friends of his?"

"Acquaintances," Thorn said.

"Well, if you see him, tell him his rent is due and if I don't get it by the end of the month, he's out." She seemed to study them both, clearly waiting for them to leave so she could lock up.

Thorn doubted Zac was worried about paying his rent. "If I see him, I'll tell him." With that he and JJ walked out of the apartment. They heard the apartment manager lock the door as she too left.

Climbing on the bike, Thorn started it and they took off toward the next address the judge had given him. With JJ guiding him, he turned away from Flathead Lake and followed the Swan River through dense trees until he spotted the address on a rusting old mailbox by the highway.

Turning down a dirt road, they meandered through the pines, coming to a dead end at a mobile home parked in the woods. An older model car sat outside. Thorn pulled the bike in slowly, watching the curtains inside the house for any movement. When he cut the motor, he didn't get off the bike for a moment, waiting to see if anyone came out.

JJ slid off to stand and look around. "This is where Kyle Spencer lived?"

"Are you all right?" he asked, climbing off the bike to join her.

"I keep thinking about the way he died." She closed her eyes for a moment, then turned her gaze on him. "Or maybe what haunts me is if he hadn't been mortally injured, I would have probably had to shoot him."

Thorn put his arm around her, drawing her into his chest for a moment. "It often doesn't feel real and then suddenly it does and..." He didn't finish. He didn't have to. "I'm sorry you had to go through that."

She nodded against his chest and then stepped back. "So we're looking for a connection to the person who hired them, right?"

"The person who hired the kidnappers will see the news

about the plane and know that two people walked away from the crash."

JJ nodded. "There should have been four bodies. But the person won't know who got away—at least for a while."

Thorn could feel the clock ticking. Maybe if they moved fast enough they could find Baker and he would lead them to Geneva.

JJ headed toward the mobile home. He could see that she was fighting memories of her harrowing brush with death aboard the plane.

He looked past the trailer to where weeds grew around several abandoned cars and a snowmobile that had been torn apart, as if Kyle had been in the middle of working on it.

JJ KNOCKED AT the door and waited. A squirrel chattered at them from one of the tall pine trees. She could hear the river nearby, and the sound of traffic on the two-lane highway. Overhead, the sky was that incredible summertime in Montana blue that she loved. The sun's rays poked through the branches, warming the morning already scented with pine.

Thorn put on a pair of gloves he'd pulled from the saddlebag on his bike and tried the door. Locked. He turned and headed for a small shed nearby, and came back a few moments later with a crowbar.

"Is this that criminal mind you told me about?" she joked.

He gave her a wan smile. "I was hoping that was all behind me. Just like I was hoping death and destruction were too."

"I'm sorry. If I hadn't been in Geneva's house that night—"

He pried at the door, the lock popping loudly as it came open, before he turned to her. "You're not responsible for this. You don't want it any more than I do, but we're in the middle of it now. All we can do is our best to, as the judge says, keep the body count down and don't get killed."

Opening the door, he took a look in and then motioned for her to enter. "Try not to leave fingerprints, but I guess I don't have to tell you that."

It took only a few moments to realize that Kyle lived alone, and had for some time from the looks of the place. She wandered to the back, finding clothes strewn over an unmade bed. She picked up one of the shirts.

"Looks like he works at an automotive shop in Kalispell," she called. "Bud's Garage." Using a hand towel she'd found in the pile of clothes, she checked the nightstand next to the bed, but found nothing of interest before she checked the bathroom and then the second bedroom. It appeared to be a storage area with guns, winter clothing and snowmobile parts that probably went to the metal skeleton in the yard.

When she came down the hall, she found Thorn going through the pile of mail on the table.

"Lots of unpaid bills," he said. "I would imagine an opportunity to make money would have been greatly appreciated. Even one highly illegal and dangerous like kidnapping."

"I doubt it was his first trip outside the jail," JJ said, remembering the look she'd seen in his eyes when she'd been fighting for her life and had broken his nose. "Anything on Baker?"

Thorn shook his head. "No one keeps an address book. Everything is usually on their phones." He sighed. "Let's try Wes Brennan's house."

Back on the motorcycle, they headed toward the town of Polson on the south end of Flathead Lake. Mile after mile, they passed cherry orchards and stands. It was too early for the stands to be open, but it wouldn't be long now. Cherry season was one of JJ's favorite reasons for living in this area. That and the lake in the summer.

Wes Brennan lived in a large Victorian house overlooking the lake on the edge of town. As Thorn parked the bike, JJ climbed off to stare at the beautiful home. It was beautifully restored to its earlier grandeur. There were flowers in the planters and the lawn was cut. It was nothing like Kyle's place in the woods.

She couldn't help but wonder how the two had known each other and how they'd become kidnappers. The night at the house, Wes had definitely been running the show. She couldn't believe that the man who lived here had drugged her and dragged her out of Geneva's house Friday night. Why would he take such a chance?

"A woman lives here," JJ said as Thorn joined her, and they walked toward the house past the flower beds. "He's married and…" Her voice broke as she saw the tricycle and small wading pool on the side of the house nearest the lake. "He has children."

Thorn opened the white wrought iron gate, and she stepped through to follow the narrow walk up to the front porch.

At the door, she hesitated. "She won't know her husband is dead," she whispered, and Thorn nodded.

He knocked. From inside the house, they heard the sound of young voices and the thunder of small feet. A few moments later, the door swung open. A pretty thirty-something woman in an apron looked expectantly at them as two identical girls of about four peered around her and giggled.

"Mrs. Brennan?" Thorn asked.

"Yes?"

"We were looking for your husband," he said.

"I'm sorry, he's not home."

"Can you tell us where we can find him?"

"He had an unexpected flight. He's a pilot for a local carrier. Can I help you with anything?"

JJ loved Montana because people were so trusting and friendly. "We were actually looking for a friend of his," she said. "Baker?"

The woman nodded and looked even more relaxed. "Johnny. It seems everyone is looking for him. His girlfriend's been calling. Did you try the bar?" At their confused look, she added, "You probably haven't heard since he only recently began managing the Pelican. They might know where he is."

"We stopped by the home of Kyle Spencer, another friend of your husband's, to ask about Johnny, but he must be at work," Thorn said.

Mrs. Brennan frowned. "Wes's mechanic? I didn't realize that Johnny even knew Kyle, but maybe he's getting his truck worked on there now, as well." She shook her head. "I can't keep track of everything my husband is involved in," she joked. "Let alone his friends."

The twins were clamoring for something to eat. JJ heard her own stomach rumble and realized she hadn't had breakfast.

"I wish I could be of more help," the woman said after promising both girls that she would get them something as soon as she finished talking to these people.

"Where is Johnny living now?" Thorn asked. "I've kind of lost track of him. That's why I was hoping your husband could help."

"He finally moved out of his folks' place over on Peach Street. He's renting a condo outside of town." The woman proceeded to give them instructions.

"But you said his girlfriend hasn't seen him, so he probably isn't there," JJ said.

"Oh, Sherry doesn't live with him. If you know Johnny,

then you know how he is with women. He's looking for the perfect one." She chuckled. "One with money."

WT WALKED ALONG Whitefish Lake at a brisk pace. He'd had to get out of the house. He'd told Franklin that he needed fresh air and to call him at once if he heard anything.

In truth, he had needed to get away from Helen. He felt like a coward, but being around her brought it all back. The past intensity of his love for her. The devastation when she betrayed him.

He hadn't thought about her in years. And yet she'd always been there, at the back of his mind, stuck in that piece of his heart that he could never give away to any other woman.

After seeing her again, the memories had come flooding back, haunting him, making him question everything. He'd been so young and impulsive, so...judgmental. That's the word that kept coming to mind. Had he wasted his life unwilling to love when it could have been so different if he had only been more forgiving?

He'd told himself that he couldn't forgive her. Things had seemed so black-and-white back then. But in truth, had he let his hurt and disappointment in her force a hasty decision that he regretted?

Sighing, he headed back toward the house. He couldn't change the past any more than he could change himself. Helen had broken his trust along with his heart. But being around her again, he saw that he'd made a decision years ago that he hadn't known would change the course of his life. It had set him on a solitary one that would leave him alone and childless.

Until he'd seen Helen again, he hadn't realized that he had missed out on anything. Now he realized that maybe it wasn't too late to change course.

THORN DOUBTED THEY would find Baker at his apartment.
But he'd memorized the address and knew they had to at
least try it. Maybe there would be something at the house
that would get them closer to finding Geneva.

He heard JJ's stomach growl loudly as they walked back
to his bike. As soon as she climbed on behind him and
wrapped her arms around his waist, he started the motor
and looked for a fast-food restaurant. He turned into the
first one, going through the drive-up.

JJ was more subdued than he'd seen her as they ordered.
He paid, then they rode over to a park where there was a
view of the lake along with a picnic table under a pine tree.
As they climbed off the bike, she said, "I feel awful for that
woman and her kids."

"I know, but Wes knew what he was getting involved
in," Thorn said as he dusted off the picnic bench. "I can't
understand why he would. Apparently, he involved his mechanic, and his friend Johnny Baker. Money can be a huge
motivator, I guess."

As they sat down, he pulled out her breakfast sandwich
and handed it to her.

"You really think if we find Baker, that he will just give
up the person's name who hired him?" JJ asked as she un-
wrapped her sandwich and took a bite with less than her
usual enthusiasm.

"It will probably take some convincing."

She chewed and swallowed as her gaze focused on him.
"Sometimes you worry me."

"I don't mean to. It sounds like he's hiding out, so let's
cross that bridge when we come to it. In the meantime, let's
talk about where Geneva might be."

"I told you, I'm just someone who arranges her travel
itinerary—not her personal friend," JJ said as she picked
up the coffee he'd bought her.

That's all she *thought* she was. But he figured she knew a lot more about Geneva's habits than she realized. If the woman was still in the area, then she would go somewhere she believed was safe. He said as much to JJ.

"What about her friends?"

She shook her head distractedly. "I doubt she'd trust any of them with the truth about anything. I could tell by the way she related to them that she had a reputation as the rich, spoiled socialite to uphold."

"She didn't have a best friend?" he asked.

"Maybe, but not one I ever heard in the background when she called. It always felt like she was putting on a show for her friends when she called to make reservations. I hate talking about her like this. I feel as if I'm betraying her confidence."

And he hated that he had to remind her. "JJ, this is the woman who could have not only just set you up, but also planned for you to die in a plane crash—if not in the explosion that followed."

WHY DID SHE trust Geneva when she had so much trouble trusting anyone? Maybe especially Thorn? It made no sense. Maybe she felt sorry for Geneva. She was so young and had everything, and yet she wasn't happy.

A boat sped past, its wake sending waves crashing onto the beach. A family was having breakfast at another picnic table. The mother was cooking bacon on a Coleman stove, the smell tantalizing. The three children were playing chase around the table, and the father was setting the table with paper plates and plastic forks.

JJ looked at the domestic scene unable not to feel an ache in her chest.

She sensed that Thorn's gaze followed hers and wondered if he had wanted children with his wife. If that could have been his life if his wife hadn't died.

She quickly looked away and finished her sandwich even though she was no longer hungry. She choked it down with the last of her coffee.

"Did you get enough to eat?" he asked. She could only nod, her throat tightening as she felt tears burn her eyes. "I've never met a woman who eats like you do."

JJ glanced over at him and bristled. "Your point?"

"I love a woman with a healthy appetite."

"Really? While you didn't even finish yours."

He shrugged. "I don't have your appetite."

"That explains a lot," she said, realizing that he was trying to lighten her mood. "Like how you live by yourself in that cabin way up in the woods."

When his gaze locked with hers, amusement played in his challenging look. "You aren't equating food with something else, are you, Ms. Foster?"

She lowered her voice. "I didn't think you'd want to talk about your…lack of sexual appetite out here, do you?"

"In broad daylight you mean?" he whispered as he leaned toward her. "I like a woman with a good appetite— in all things."

She raised a brow. "You sure about that? I suspect it's been a long time."

He grinned. "You like giving me a hard time, don't you?"

"*Me?* I haven't tied you up yet or bound you to a tree."

He chuckled. "With luck you won't get the chance. And by the way, I have a perfectly fine appetite. In all things, as well." His gaze held hers for a heat-seeking moment before he gathered up their trash.

"Maybe someday you'll have to prove it to me."

He stopped what he was doing to look at her. "Be careful what you wish for." There was a glint in his gray eyes that could have been desire. Or a warning. Whatever it had been, it sent a shiver through her.

Thorn rose to walk over to the container, where he disposed of their trash. She rose on wobbly legs. She'd been joking at first, but at what point had it turned to flirting with the cowboy? She was playing with fire and they both knew it.

But, she realized, she wasn't the same woman who'd gone to bed in Geneva Davenport's house Friday night. The events that followed had released something in her she'd kept caged while she worked to pay off her father's medical bills.

Almost dying had made her want to live. And now she felt a freedom that both excited and scared her. She felt as if she wasn't sure what she might do next. And then there was this handsome cowboy…

But when he spoke, he steered clear of their earlier flirting. "I know you're the key to finding Geneva," he said as they walked back to where he'd parked the bike, getting back to business. "Would you say she's a creature of habit?"

JJ smiled to herself, a little disappointed and yet just as relieved. For a moment she'd forgotten that she was still in danger—and maybe so was Geneva. She thought about his question for a moment. "Kind of. She knows what she likes, but she likes a lot of different things as well as places."

"She must have a favorite place in the area where she eats, buys her clothing…"

"You think she's out shopping?"

"Truthfully, I think anything is possible. She might not know about the plane crash, or Baker being on the loose or that anyone suspects her of being behind the kidnapping."

JJ climbed on behind him. "Or she could be tied up somewhere in a dark basement."

"We need to find Baker."

CHAPTER FIFTEEN

FRANKLIN PACED, TOO worked up to sit. He couldn't eat, and he couldn't sleep. He just wanted his granddaughter back.

"You are going to wear a hole in that floor," Helen said, not unkindly. "Is there anything I can do?"

He stopped pacing to shake his head. "I'm just glad you're here. Thank you for staying."

"Of course. I'm here for you, you know that."

He stopped pacing to place a hand on the back of her chair. "I just want Geneva back. I want a second chance. I'm not sure I deserve one, though."

She turned to place her hand over his. "You're going to get the chance. I'm sure the kidnappers just want the money, and then Geneva will be returned to you unharmed."

"To God's ear," he said as he forced himself to take a seat across from her. Helen had been a godsend. She seemed as anxious as he was to have this over. He suspected it had more to do with Willie than worry about Geneva on her part. He'd seen the tension between the two of them. Earlier, she'd seemed relieved when the judge had left to go for a walk.

He studied the woman for a moment. She was staring out the window with such a look of longing on her pretty face that he had to ask her. "This must be hard on you."

She seemed surprised as she turned to frown at him. "I'm not the one whose granddaughter is missing."

Geneva wasn't just missing, but it was kind of her to put it that way. "Seeing Willie again. I couldn't help but notice there was something between the two of you."

She chuckled softly and looked away again. "Like I said, we're old friends."

Helen settled her gaze on her hands in her lap for a moment. Her hands showed her age more than her face or her figure. Sometimes Franklin forgot how old he was, how old his closest friends and associates were.

Helen had come to him recently, highly recommended, when his personal lawyer had retired. She'd moved to the area and was looking for part-time employment. When he'd hired her, he'd been worried that she was looking for something more than he had to offer. She wouldn't be the first woman who'd been interested in him since his wife died. Most of them were more interested in his money than him, so he was gun-shy.

Fortunately, Helen had remained professional. Though he thought if he had been interested, she might have shared that interest. Maybe in time, he'd thought, since he did like and admire her. She was smart and a damned good lawyer.

"I'm guessing you and Willie were more than that—at least for one of you," he said, curious and surprised that Helen might be the woman who'd broken his friend's heart all those years ago.

"William and I were in love a very long time ago," she said after a moment. Tears welled in her eyes as she looked over at him. "I took off on a whim with some friends for a wild weekend in Mexico. I'd had just enough to drink, and one thing led to another. I regretted it immediately. But it was too late. William never forgave me. You know him. He said he could never trust me after that. Soon after that I married and stayed with my husband until his recent death."

"Has your life been happy?" Franklin asked, fairly sure for all of his success, he couldn't have said his had been. Successful, rewarding, fulfilling, but happy?

Helen chuckled. "*Happy?* My husband did an adequate job of supporting us. I was able to go to law school. It occupied my time."

"You never had children?"

Her eyes dimmed for a moment. "My husband was unable to have children and he didn't want to adopt. Now, of course I have second thoughts, but doesn't everyone, even those who *had* children."

Franklin let out a laugh at the truth in her words. "I loved my daughter more than life, and yet there was nothing I could do to save her from herself. And now Geneva…"

THORN FOLLOWED THE directions Wes Brennan's wife had given them. Like JJ, he hated that the woman would soon be learning not just of her husband's death, but of his involvement in a kidnapping. Which proved that you never really knew another person—even one you're married to. He'd certainly learned that lesson, hadn't he?

Johnny Baker apparently lived in what had once been a motor court with small cabins—even though the sign on the highway called them condos. He parked in front of unit number 10 and waited for a moment to see if there was any sign of life behind the curtain. There wasn't. The whole complex looked deserted.

A couple of old cars were parked nearby, but they didn't look as if they ran. Most everyone, they suspected, would have already left for work.

As he and JJ walked toward number 10, he gently moved her behind him and drew his weapon from under his jacket. Standing to the side of the door away from the window, he knocked. Then knocked harder and then tried the knob. Locked.

Motioning to JJ, Thorn led them around to the back. A large garbage can sat on a small concrete slab next to the back door. He opened the lid and saw that it was half full—everything in it, though, looking as if it had been there for a while.

He knocked, tried the knob, and when it didn't open, he stepped back and kicked in the door. The lockset was so flimsy that he figured JJ could have kicked it open. She gave him a surprised look, either impressed or shocked. He couldn't tell which as he holstered his gun.

It didn't take long to verify that the place was empty. Just as it didn't take long to know that Johnny Baker hadn't been here for some time. As they had at Kyle Spencer's, they searched.

Thorn was ready to give up when JJ said, "I'm not sure if this is helpful." She held up a scrap of paper using the hem of her T-shirt. "It looks like there's a local phone number on it."

He stepped to her, read off the number and then pulled out his phone. "Could be the girlfriend," he said as he dialed and put the phone on speaker. It rang, once, twice, three times. He was about to give up when a man answered with a hesitant hello.

"I'm sorry," Thorn said. "I'm not sure I have the right number."

"Depends on who you're calling," the man said.

"I was calling Johnny Baker?"

A long beat of silence before the man said, "Never heard of him," and hung up.

Thorn looked at JJ. "Have you heard that voice before?" She shook her head. He hadn't either. But as she dropped the scrap of paper back where she found it, he quickly called the judge.

"Can you find out who has this phone number?" he asked without preamble. He rattled it off quickly as he heard a vehicle pull up out front. "I'll call you back." He quickly disconnected as a car door opened, and he heard the crunch of gravel as someone headed for the front door of Johnny Baker's condo.

JJ BARELY GOT out the back door, with Thorn right behind her, before she heard a woman insert a key into the lock, shove open the door and yell, "Johnny? Damn it, Johnny." They heard her footfalls moving through the place as Thorn gently closed the back door with the now broken lockset.

They moved around to the front of the development to where they'd left the motorcycle. The woman came running out at the sound of the bike's motor turning over.

"Hey!" she yelled over the loud engine, and ran over to them. "Have you seen Johnny? Johnny Baker?" It appeared she thought they lived in the complex.

Thorn shut off the motor. "Who?"

"Johnny Baker." She half turned to motion to the building. "He lives in number 10."

"Sorry," Thorn said.

"You seem worried," JJ said. "When was the last time you saw him?"

"Just a few days ago," the woman said distractedly. She looked close to tears. "I am worried. He was acting…weird. Stranger than usual," she added with a humorless laugh.

"Have you called the police?" Thorn asked.

She shook her head. "He wouldn't like me doing that." She started to take a step back.

"Is there a message we can give Johnny if we see him?" JJ asked.

The woman hesitated. "Tell him Sherry is looking for him, and she's scared and mad as hell." Tears filled her brown eyes, which were ringed with mascara. "I just have a bad feeling, you know? Something bad has happened to him. We had this stupid fight." She shook her head. "Sorry, you don't want to hear this shit."

JJ reached out and touched the woman's arm. "I'm sorry. I'm sure he'll turn up."

Sherry nodded and sniffed. "I'm sure he will, one way or the other, huh." She turned and walked back to her car.

Thorn started the bike again and they pulled out. As he did, JJ saw a billboard sign across the street. She grabbed his sleeve and pulled it as she yelled into his ear, "I thought of a place Geneva might go."

Thorn slowed at the turnoff JJ had told him about. "There is this cabin Geneva had me rent for her a few times. I remember one of her friends saying she was going to write a review online about it because it was so perfect. Right on the lake, in the woods, very isolated since apparently Geneva and her crew got very noisy."

"And she returned there? That is, they *let* her return?" he'd asked after he'd pulled over down the road earlier so they could talk.

"It runs a thousand dollars a night plus a large deposit for anything that gets broken," JJ had said. "She's been there three times."

"You think you can find the place?"

"I was the one who found the place originally for her and even drew her a map how to get there, since GPS doesn't work in such a remote area, and emailed it to her. Why don't I call and see if it's rented?" She'd looked through her phone until she found the number.

It didn't take long to find out that her instincts had been right. Once she'd told the property management company her name, the woman was quite happy to help. JJ had quickly found out that on Friday, Geneva had rented the place for a week so should be there until next Thursday.

Now as Thorn followed the narrow twisting dirt road back through the thick tall pines, he felt an inkling of concern even as he told himself that Geneva was probably there with her friends partying this whole time as she waited to collect her ten million dollars.

The cabin, and Thorn used that term loosely, was four thousand square feet of glass and stone at the edge of the water in a stand of pines. The road in was private, so once they pulled off the highway, they didn't see another person.

"We're getting close now," JJ warned him.

He pulled over in a spot between two pines. "I think we should walk from here." JJ was already off the bike. "Hold up. I think *you* should wait here."

"You know I'm not going to do that," she said, and started up the road.

Well, he'd tried. "Do I have to keep reminding you that this could get even more dangerous?" he asked, catching up to her.

"You make me feel safe," she said facetiously. At least he thought she was being facetious because she was smiling.

"Keeping you safe is the problem. At least stay behind me, okay?"

They moved through the pines following the road. A few curves later he spotted the lake's gleaming green surface through the pines. The sight was spectacular. He could see why someone might want to come back here. It was isolated, and along with a huge home with all the amenities, there was this amazing lake.

Thorn slowed as they approached the structure. When he spotted Geneva's red convertible parked beside it, he looked back at JJ and gave her a thumbs-up.

A set of stone steps curved up from the ground to the first-floor deck. As Thorn started up them with JJ right behind him, he heard a woman scream from inside the house.

Drawing his gun, he rushed to the door only to find it locked. He motioned JJ back as he moved around to the front of the house, knowing that it would be a bank of windows. Whoever was inside would be able to see him—and have a clear shot.

He moved swiftly, getting to one of the French doors and trying the knob. It opened. He pushed inside, leading with his weapon. The huge living room was empty. He heard noise on a lower floor and then silence.

Thorn turned. No JJ. He quickly moved back to the deck where he'd left her. No JJ. Swearing, he stepped to the edge of the deck in time to see three people racing toward a boat parked at the dock. They jumped in and took off before he could have gotten off the deck, let alone tried to chase them down.

Glancing below, he saw JJ. She had gone around to the lower level and now stood over the body lying on the stone patio. From the color of the blood, the body had been there for a while.

CHAPTER SIXTEEN

"It's Johnny Baker," JJ said as Thorn joined her. He glanced at the body at her feet, and nodded before he stepped closer and carefully pulled the man's wallet without getting his fingerprints on it. He checked the ID and then put it back.

"How long do you think he's been dead?" she asked, feeling sick to her stomach.

"I'd say at least since some time yesterday."

She glanced up. "You think he fell from the upper balcony?" Thorn nodded. "It could have been an accident."

"Did you recognize the three people who left in the boat?"

JJ shook her head. "I didn't get a really good look at them. But they didn't look familiar. They could have just been passing by in their boat, saw the place and knew it was for rent and stopped." She looked up toward the upper deck. "You don't think she's here, do you?" If she was, then she was also dead.

"I'll go check," he said. "If you want to stay—"

"I'm going with you."

"Of course you are. Remember this is now a crime scene. Did you touch anything?"

She shook her head as she followed him back up the steps to the top floor. As he wiped the two door handles he'd touched, she looked around. "Don't worry, I won't disturb anything," she called as she moved through the massive house.

To her relief, she didn't find Geneva dead in any of the rooms. Nor did it take long to figure out that only two people had been staying here. A man and a woman, from the clothing she'd found. Only one bed had been slept in. Clothes and swimsuits and towels were thrown about as if the two had been enjoying themselves. At least for a while. There was no sign of Geneva other than all the women's clothing strewn around. No sign that she'd packed when she'd left either—without her sports car.

"What do you make of it?" Thorn said behind her, making her jump.

She turned to face him. "It looks like Geneva and her boyfriend were here since Friday evening and all was well before it apparently went wrong. I was just trying to figure out what she would do now."

"She didn't call for help," he pointed out.

"That's if she was even here," JJ said. "Baker could have come by and found only the boyfriend here."

"But it's her car parked next to the house," Thorn said.

"Her boyfriend could have been driving it."

He shook his head. "You still want to believe that she's not behind her own kidnapping or the possible murder of Johnny Baker?" He sounded past disbelieving, looking at her as if she was delusional or worse.

"She rented this place and she was here with I assume her boyfriend," JJ said, turning back to look at the bedroom and the strewn clothing. "Or at least someone wants us to believe she was here."

Thorn swore under his breath. "Face it, she's on the run from this, from the kidnappers she double-crossed, from us. Her car is parked outside the house. There is no running

from this. We can't ignore it. The cops have to be called."
As if seeing her concern, he added, "Don't worry. I'll call
the judge and let him handle it. Meanwhile, we'll make
sure we were never here. I suspect those three in the boat
are going to call this in. We don't want to be around with
the cops show up."

"WHAT IF GENEVA isn't behind the kidnapping plot?" JJ
asked as they walked back to the motorcycle in the trees.
"Her boyfriend could have planned the whole thing, and
she knew nothing about it."

"Until Johnny Baker shows up? Great theory. So where
is she? Why didn't she call the cops?" He could see that
JJ didn't have the answers any more than he did. "She's in
trouble no matter how it goes down, and we know that we
aren't the only ones looking for her."

His cell phone rang. He stopped walking to take a call
from the judge.

"I have the owner of the stolen plane. His name is Ridge
Brandemiller. He owns a construction company in the area
called Brandemiller Brothers. You asked about that property on the lake where a home is being built. The brothers
are constructing it."

"Thanks. I have another small problem." He quickly
told him what they'd found at the rental property Geneva
had booked for a week. "It appears Johnny Baker has been
dead since yesterday sometime."

"And Geneva?"

"In the wind. Her car's still here, though, but no sign of
her. Or of the man she was with. Or of a second struggle."
He knew what the judge was asking. Was it possible she
too had been killed and they had missed seeing her body
because it was in the lake or the pines?

"Thorn." The judge cleared his throat. "Franklin is anxious to talk to this woman who was staying in his granddaughter's house."

"I'm sure he is, but right now I'm not letting her out of my sight," Thorn said. "Not until I know who is behind this."

To his surprise, the judge didn't argue. Instead, the man said, "That number you had me check on? It's a burner phone."

Of course it was.

"I'll make the 911 call," the judge said. "But you need to get out of there."

"That's what we're doing," Thorn said. "We're going to check on this Brandemiller lead. I'll get back to you."

As he disconnected, he said to JJ, "Might have a lead on the man you met before you went in that old cabin's root cellar." She swung up onto his motorcycle behind him. He felt her arms encircle his waist. But before he could start the motor, her cell phone rang.

She dug the phone out of her pocket. He turned and saw her eyes widen.

"Who is it?" he asked, suddenly on alert.

"I don't know. The number is blocked. There are only a few people who have my cell phone number." Her gaze locked with his. "Geneva is one of them."

THE PHONE RANG AGAIN. JJ stared at Thorn. "I have to answer it."

He nodded in agreement. "Go ahead. Keep it where I can hear."

She cleared her voice and, fingers trembling, swiped the screen. "Hello?"

"Jenny?" The word was whispered in a breathless tone. "It's Geneva. Geneva Davenport."

"Geneva, where are you?"

"I'm so sorry." The woman sounded as if she was crying.

"Geneva, you need to go to your grandfather's and stay there until—"

"I can't. You don't understand."

"Just tell me where you are. I can help you." No answer. "Geneva? *Where are you?*" She heard the line go dead.

"Try calling her back," Thorn said.

She did, but the call went straight to voice mail, only to have the recording tell her that the number's voice mail was full. She disconnected and looked at Thorn.

"We can't stay here," he said, and started the bike. They roared up the road and onto the highway. As they headed back toward Polson, they passed a sheriff's department cruiser with its lights flashing, followed by another one and an ambulance.

JJ realized that they'd barely gotten out of there in time.

"When the kidnappers call, you need to ask for proof of life," WT told his friend.

Franklin let out a curse. "We don't even know that they have Geneva."

"Exactly."

His friend got to his feet and began to pace. "We can't keep making demands."

"We also can't seem to anxious to pay the ransom demand," WT pointed out. "The kidnappers have seen enough movies and television kidnappings. They know how this goes."

Franklin was making himself a drink when his cell rang. He dropped the glass in his hand. It shattered on the floor. He looked to the judge. WT could see that he didn't want to do it.

"Hello?"

WT moved closer to listen. The kidnapper had started talking about the ransom drop when Franklin cleared his throat and stopped him.

"I'm going to need proof of life." The kidnapper started to argue, but his friend continued. "Today's newspaper will do, with my granddaughter holding it. Otherwise, we have nothing to talk about. You can text it to me."

WT watched in surprise as Franklin disconnected and swore.

"I hate these bastards." The man's voice broke. "I want to kill them."

Helen hurried to clean up the broken glass before Franklin could step in it as he turned to make himself another drink.

He could feel his friend's frustration and anger. He just needed Franklin to hold it together a little longer.

CHAPTER SEVENTEEN

JJ DIDN'T KNOW how far they'd gone. Nor had she paid any attention to where they were going. It wasn't until Thorn slowed and pulled into Finley Point state campground that she looked up.

She kept thinking about Geneva's voice. She'd sounded scared, but not necessarily in imminent danger. She hoped the woman would take her advice and go to her grandfather's. But even if she didn't, maybe she would call back.

"What are we doing?" she asked as Thorn pulled into an empty campsite and cut the engine. She climbed off the bike, surprised how stiff she was. She'd been clinging to him for miles. The sun had topped the pines and blazed down, making the day downright hot.

"I don't know about you," he said, "but I need a swim."

She blinked as he shrugged out of his jacket, tossed it onto his bike seat and began to pull off his T-shirt.

"A swim?" she repeated.

He glanced up through the tall pines, squinting in the direction of the sun. "It's hot and if I'm not mistaken, that's a lake."

She had to admit, she could appreciate his logic. She smiled as she took off her jacket and added it to the pile on his bike seat and then stopped. "That is, if I had a swimsuit."

He grinned at her. "Come on, Foster. I've already seen it all."

"You swore you didn't look," she joked.

His grin broadened.

She cocked her head at him. "Anyway, you haven't seen it all."

"Nor will I if you go into the lake in your underwear," he said as he kicked off his shoes and socks and began to drop his jeans. "Or if you have the guts, bare-ass naked."

Laughing, she took off her shirt to reveal the lacy bra she'd put on that morning.

He let out a low whistle. "Pretty damned sexy."

She turned around to slip out of her jeans. When she turned back, he was already headed for the water. She saw that he was wearing boxer briefs and couldn't help smiling to herself. She followed in her matching underwear, telling herself that it was no more revealing than the bikini she normally swam in.

Thorn dived in with a splash. The moment her feet touched the water, she had to agree this had been a great idea, all things considered. She walked out deeper and then dived, coming up next to him. There were water droplets on his dark eyelashes. His gray eyes shone in the sunshine glinting off the lake's surface. He was smiling. She'd never seen a more appealing man.

"Race you," he said, and dived again before he began to swim along the beach.

She never could resist a challenge and took off after him.

They stopped farther up the beach, both breathless and laughing because she'd given him a race for his money. They stood in water up to their necks, breathing, laughing and just looking into each other's eyes.

JJ felt the sun on her shoulders, but the real heat was at her center under his unwavering gaze. Thorn was the first to break eye contact.

"We should probably dry out," he said, his voice sounding strained.

She nodded, and they swam back down the beach. After climbing out of the water, Thorn lay facedown on the warm green grass beside the lake. She joined him, careful to put a little distance between them.

Neither said anything for a long while. JJ relished the heat of the sun and the warm summer breeze that began to dry her body, as well as her undergarments.

"The good news is that Geneva's still alive," Thorn said, apparently going to ignore that moment between them earlier, which was fine with her.

"I wish I could have talked her into going to her grandfather's."

"I'm sure she has her reasons. If she started this whole mess…" He let those words float in the pine-and-lake-scented air for a moment.

"Maybe she thinks she can fix it. But she sounded scared to me, as if she isn't sure who she can trust."

Thorn looked at her and chuckled. "So her travel agent is the only person she trusts?"

JJ's chin shot up. "I'll have you know I'm very good at my job, and I don't just book flights and make hotel reservations. I arrange *VIP* accommodations. From the moment a client leaves her home through the entire trip. Everything is taken care of and at a very high level."

His smile broadened. "I'm sure you are great at what you do. When this is over, maybe I'll have you book me something."

She sat up a little to lean on one elbow to look at him as she raised a brow. "Domestic or overseas?"

"Surprise me. In the meantime, we need to keep digging. The stolen plane was owned by Ridge Brandemiller.

Also, not a coincidence, the house that was being built on the water near the cabin you were taken to is being built by Brandemiller Brothers Construction. I thought we would swing by their office and see if we can find out why construction workers are looking for Geneva. Maybe it's about money. But maybe they are involved in the kidnapping since it was Brandemiller's plane the kidnappers allegedly stole that night."

"It's Sunday," she pointed out. "Do you really think anyone will be there?"

"Probably not, but we can have a look around."

It seemed a long shot that Ridge Brandemiller was behind the kidnapping. Why use his own plane? Even claiming it was stolen would attract the authorities' attention. She would think that would be the last thing he would want to do if he was involved in the kidnapping.

But they had to follow up on any lead. Geneva was alive. Or had been earlier. JJ had no clue how to find her. Johnny Baker was dead, and soon the authorities would be looking for Geneva, as well. It felt as if time was running out. She certainly hoped not. All her instincts told her that Geneva Davenport was in trouble. Maybe of her own making, but nonetheless in danger.

She and Thorn stayed in the sun awhile longer, turning over and closing their eyes as the radiant heat continued to dry their undergarments. There was no hurry since the construction company would be closed. A few fluffy white clouds bobbed along in a sea of blue. It was late afternoon by the time they dressed and headed for Brandemiller Brothers Construction.

Thorn swung into the yard of a huge construction operation, most of it surrounded by a high chain-link fence.

As he stopped, JJ said, "There's a note on the door of

the office," and hopped off the bike to check it. She came back grinning. "Company barbecue." She told him the address that had been on the note. "I think we should stop by."

"After our swim, a barbecue sounds perfect," Thorn joked. "Let's go see if you recognize anyone."

JJ told him how to get to the place on the lake. The moment they turned down the private road, they began seeing vehicles parked along the sides. Thorn kept going until they could see the house.

It was massive stone and glass set against the backdrop of the lake and the Mission Mountains.

"Impressive," she said as he found a place to park the motorcycle. "The brothers must be doing all right financially. So why worry about the money Geneva apparently owes?"

"Appearances can be deceiving, I've heard," Thorn said. "They might be deep in debt and desperate. A ten-million-dollar infusion could be what they need to stay afloat."

"Maybe," she said, remembering the cocky man who'd told his men to hang on to her. He'd definitely had something going on, and yet he didn't seem desperate, just annoyed that he couldn't get his hands on Geneva. Then again, maybe he didn't want his men to know how desperate he was.

As they neared the house, they began to see several hundred people gathered on the perfect lawn that ran from the large patio to the lake and docks below.

"That's the boat I saw leaving below the cabin where you were taken," Thorn said.

"And that's the man," she said as she spotted the boss in a small crowd of people at the temporary bar that had been set up under a tree. Again today he wore shorts, a

T-shirt and boat shoes. "What do we do if he recognizes me?" she whispered.

"Nothing. We're just here for the barbecue, so let's get something to eat and let him find us."

They walked toward the smell of brisket and pork ribs cooking on the massive portable grills that had been brought in. Nearby were tables filled with side dishes and even more tables with condiments and finally desserts.

A large group had gathered down at the docks where adults were sitting in dozens of lawn chairs or on the grass. Children were swimming, and what looked to be teenagers and older kids were going out on the lake on wakeboards and tubes.

"What can I get you?" one of the grillers asked as they approached.

JJ asked for the brisket while Thorn went for the ribs. As they moved to the first table, they scooped baked beans and potato salad onto their plates.

They were carrying their meals over to one of the almost empty tables when a man approached. "Enjoying the party?"

"We are, thanks," Thorn said, and the man moved on to other guests. He resembled his brother enough that JJ suspected he was a Brandemiller. She heard someone call the name Travis, and the man turned. Travis Brandemiller smiled and called that he was coming.

"He must be the brother, but he had no idea who we were," she said after he left. "They just don't seem like kidnappers to me."

Thorn shrugged. "This little picnic has got to be setting them back a small fortune. Makes me wonder why at least one of the brothers had two of his men abduct you from Geneva's house. Seems he was a little desperate to find her."

They ate, watching the crowd. She knew Thorn was looking for the men who'd snatched her from Geneva's house and taken her to the cabin. She hadn't seen them in the crowd, but there were so many people at the party it was hard to say if they were here or not.

"Enjoying yourselves?"

She recognized the voice as the man stopped at their table. Everyone else had finished eating but them and left the table.

"We are," Thorn said as the man slid in beside JJ.

"I wondered if you would show up here," the man said.

"It's a lot nicer than the root cellar where you left her," Thorn said.

The man smiled. "I'm sorry, I don't believe I caught your name."

"Thorn, and this is JJ, but you two have already met," he said. "We didn't catch your name, though."

"Ridge. Ridge Brandemiller, but apparently you know my last name because here you are at my party."

"We saw the note on the door at your office and were hungry," Thorn said. "Also, we were wondering why a successful construction company owner would get involved in kidnapping."

"Kidnapping?" Ridge shook his head and looked around to make sure no one was nearby and listening.

"How else would you describe it?" JJ asked.

The man looked over at her with his piercing blue eyes. "I told my men to give Geneva a ride to meet me at the property because I would be there checking on a job we're doing. That's all."

"Not quite. You kept me there against my will," she snapped.

"I thought your friend Geneva might want you back,

and we could make a trade. As it was, you didn't stay long enough. You also didn't go to the cops. Why is that?"

"What do you want with Geneva Davenport?" Thorn asked, his expression fierce as he drew Ridge's attention away from JJ.

"That's my business."

"I'm making it mine."

The man laughed and shook his head. "Why don't you ask Geneva?" His gaze narrowed. "Because you don't know where she is any more than I do. But you're looking for her too. Apparently, I'm not the only one she owes money to." His gaze narrowed on Thorn. "Or is she also an old girlfriend?" He chuckled and turned to JJ again. "You must have business with her, as well." He shook his head and rose from the table, but then leaned forward, palms on the surface as he said, "I don't care how much she owes you. I intend to get my money first. If you see her, tell her I will collect one way or the other. She knows me well enough that she should have realized by now." He glanced at JJ. "You can tell her how serious I am. The next woman I have in that root cellar won't get away."

Ridge's cell phone rang. He fished it out of his pocket, excused himself and turned his back to answer it. He seemed to be listening, then said, "Thanks for letting me know." Pocketing his phone, he said, "My stolen plane's been found. Destroyed in the mountains southeast of here. Good thing it's insured." For a moment, he looked angry and then seemed to shake the news off as if unwilling to let anything spoil this day.

Smiling at the two of them, he raised his voice to say, "Please enjoy the barbecue. If you'd like a swim or…" He looked to JJ. "Do you wakeboard? If not, one of the boys down there will teach you. My treat." He waved his hand through the air. "Don't forget to have some dessert before you go. My caterer makes the most amazing fried apple pies."

THE WAIT HAD been interminable. Franklin had paced the floor, telling himself he couldn't take another minute of this. He'd threatened to call the cops, the FBI, anyone who could help.

Each time, Willie had talked him down from the edge of the cliff he'd been teetering on.

"My contact is trying to track down the kidnappers. We just have to wait. If Geneva is in on this, then getting proof of life should be simple. They probably don't want for us to think it is too easy. Just give them some time—"

"Time? With every minute I fear that I'm losing my granddaughter forever," Franklin snapped. "What if they just cut their losses, kill her and take off?"

"They want that ten million dollars too badly to do that."

"I hope you're right." He couldn't help feeling that he should have called the police and FBI right away. He trusted Willie, but all these demands… They were playing with Geneva's life.

When the text came in on his phone, he'd almost been afraid to look at it. His fingers trembled as he called it up. Tears rushed to his eyes.

Geneva, his beautiful granddaughter. There she was holding a copy of today's newspaper. He enlarged the photo. It was clear that she'd been crying. Her face was blotchy, her eyes red and her lower lip looked as if it was swollen.

But it was what he saw in her eyes that sent his heart rocketing around in his chest. She looked terrified.

THORN LOOKED AT JJ as Ridge Brandemiller walked away. "He just heard about his plane?"

"Certainly sounded that way," JJ said as they rose to throw away their trash and head back toward the motorcycle. "I told you that I didn't think those men were the kidnappers."

"If Ridge Brandemiller is telling the truth. And I tend to believe him. I wonder how Geneva came to owe him money."

"Maybe he built her house and she never paid him," she suggested.

Thorn frowned. "It sounds more like a personal loan. It also sounded like they knew each other…well."

"You think they dated? Or that he's a loan shark?" JJ was staring at the huge house.

"It might pay better than construction. Look at this place," he said, thinking the same thing. "Either he and his brother are making money hand over fist building houses or they have a sideline."

"This is the fastest growing county in Montana," JJ told him. "And his men had the passcode for her front door. I wouldn't be surprised, though, if you're right and it was more than Ridge building her house. I remember her saying once that she'd been seeing an older man with a lot of money and that he was married."

Thorn laughed as they walked back up the road, away from the party area. "See, I told you that you know more about Geneva than you think." Ahead, his motorcycle was right where he'd left it. He pulled out his phone and called the judge. He quickly told him what they'd learned at the barbecue.

"Ridge Brandemiller says Geneva owes him money. He seems very determined to get it. We're wondering if they didn't have some sort of relationship. Also, that he might have built her house." Some of the partygoers were headed their way. "Listen, we have to go. I'll call you later."

JJ groaned as he disconnected and pocketed his phone. "I know what you're thinking. If they did have a relationship at some point, Geneva could have known that Ridge had a plane."

"It did cross my mind, especially if you're right and her relationship with Ridge started off romantically. She would know where the plane was kept. All she had to do was tell Wes Brennan." He swung a leg over the bike, and JJ climbed on behind him.

As they rode away from the Brandemiller house, he looked back and saw a black pickup coming up the private road.

In his mirror, he watched the pickup turn onto the highway behind them. He told himself it could be just a tail.

But as the driver sped up, Thorn knew it could also be much worse than that.

"You need to hang on tight," he said over his shoulder to JJ, and hit the throttle.

CHAPTER EIGHTEEN

JJ HAD SEEN Thorn looking in his side mirror as they left the barbecue. When she'd turned to look back, she'd spotted the black pickup even before he'd told her to hang on.

As the motorcycle took off beneath her, the pickup seemed to hang back as if waiting for something. Was the driver following them, thinking they would lead him to Geneva? She suspected Thorn was worried, and maybe with good reason as she watched the pickup suddenly close the distance between them.

They were racing along the narrow winding road along the east side of the lake. There was no way the truck could pass for miles. But maybe that wasn't the driver's intention as it zoomed up behind them, too close now. She tried to see the driver's face, but the afternoon sun glinted off the pickup's windshield.

"Hang on!" Thorn called back, and suddenly they were leaving the road on the steep lakeside where the pavement turned to gravel as it fell rapidly toward the water.

The bike roared over the edge, leaving the pavement and flying for a few yards before it touched down. She felt the back start to slide, but Thorn hit the gas and pulled it out. Then banked around a curve. All she could do was hang on as he practically laid the bike over in the first curve and then braked for the next one. They slid, dirt and gravel flying.

She could tell they were going too fast. Worse, they were

running out of road. Ahead, it turned sharply to run parallel to the lake and the cabins along it. If he didn't slow down…

But again Thorn pulled the bike out of the slide for the next curve before he left the road to cut through the pines. She clung to him as limbs rushed past, her heart in her throat. He brought the motorcycle to a stop as abruptly as he had made the turn off the main highway. He killed the engine.

She was still hanging on for dear life and trying to catch her breath when she realized he was listening for the sound of the pickup. No way had the driver made that turn in the truck. He would have had to go up the road, pull off and come back.

JJ realized that that was exactly what he'd done. She heard the pickup's engine and looked back to catch a glint of black as it dropped down the road to the lake. But with them hidden in the pines, the driver turned in the wrong direction, away from them, and disappeared down the lake.

"You all right?" Thorn asked.

Her heart had dislodged from her throat, and she was no longer gasping for breath. "Great."

He chuckled. "That was a little hairy back there."

A little hairy? She wanted to slug him. He'd *enjoyed* that.

Thorn started the motor. "Let's get out of here."

THORN FELT SURPRISINGLY GOOD—and it had been a long time since he had. Dusk settled over the lake and the pine trees as they roared back up to the highway and then raced toward Miguel's place. Summer in the Flathead was a world apart from the life he'd been living in the mountains over Gardiner. Right now, he could barely remember that life. JJ had dragged him away from it kicking and screaming, but now that he was here, he couldn't imagine being content alone again. And that should have scared him.

He'd let this woman get too close, and he'd gotten too involved in her life. And even that didn't bother him. He could feel her cheek against his back, her arms wrapped around his waist. The heat of her body stirred a longing deep inside him. For so long, he'd told himself he didn't want to feel anything, but he couldn't pretend he didn't. This woman… What was he going to do with her? Maybe he should take her to the judge. Wasn't he risking her life keeping her with him?

And yet until he knew who was involved, he couldn't risk what a man like Franklin Davenport might do. The billionaire might turn her over to the police, who might believe that she was involved. So far Thorn hadn't found out anything that would clear her. She was twisted up in all this. Just as he was. He couldn't walk away until he was sure she was safe, because he cared about her. He'd thought he would never feel those emotions again. JJ had breached the wall he'd built around not just his heart, but also his entire life. He felt more for her than he thought possible, and while it scared the hell out of him, he felt stronger and more sure of himself than he had in years.

It was no longer a case of simply finding Geneva and turning her over to her grandfather. He had to find out who was behind this. Geneva was involved, but from her phone call it would seem that the kidnapping plot had gotten away from her. Or maybe that's what she wanted them to think.

He pulled in at the front of their cabin behind the bar and cut the motor. The faint sound of country music spilled out, making the growing darkness even more sultry. A breeze stirred the nearby pines, smelling of the lake and summer. JJ didn't move. He turned to meet her gaze. Her face was flushed—from the ride? The sun and swim earlier? Her big blue eyes were dark with something he recognized only too well. He wanted to tell her that what they were about to do was the last thing they should. It would only complicate a relationship that was complicated enough.

As warm and wonderful as the evening breeze was, he still felt a tantalizing chill as he swung a leg over the front of his bike and reached for her. Lifting her into his arms, he carried her the few steps to the cabin.

He kicked open the door, not wanting to put her down. Once inside, he kicked it closed. Her gaze locked with his. He felt an ache low in his belly, and knew they'd been headed here from the moment they met. This time there wasn't a gun aimed at his heart, but even if there had been, he knew nothing could stop this.

She leaned into him until her lips touched his. As he deepened the kiss, he let her slide slowly down his body, aware of her every curve. Her eyes widened as she felt his desire. As she broke away from him, a sly, shy smile played at her lips before she wrapped her arms around his neck and kissed him again. He cupped her wonderful behind in his hands and lifted her. She wrapped her legs around him and leaned back to look into his face, throwing them off balance.

They fell on the bed, breaking apart laughing, then quickly sobered as their gazes locked for a long moment. He stared into her adorable face as he touched her smooth sun-kissed cheek. "JJ." He said it like a caress. As his fingers reached her lips, she took his hand and pressed a kiss to his palm. Desire shot through him, racing hot and fast through his veins.

He reached for her, knowing he shouldn't, knowing he should stop this before it went any further… But also knowing it would take nothing short of a bullet to stop him now.

JJ FELT A shaft of heat race to her center as he pulled her into his hard body and deepened the kiss. She wrapped her arms around his neck, wanting this, wanting more, wanting it all. It wasn't just the kidnapping and nearly dying that had released her. Thorn had freed something inside her.

Since her father's death, she'd kept her nose to the grindstone. She'd had no time for men, not that any of them interested her. When one of her coworkers had talked her into a double date, all she'd thought about that whole evening was getting some sleep because she had to work the next day—and worrying about where she was going to sleep. Even when her date had kissed her, she'd felt nothing but relief that the evening was over.

Now though, it was as if a dam had broken. All the emotions she'd kept bottled up for the past years rushed to the surface. She felt a need like none she'd ever experienced as she felt Thorn slide his big hands under her T-shirt. His palms against her bare flesh sent a quake of desire shooting through her. She desperately wanted to feel his bare skin against her own.

Taking her hands from around his neck, she tugged at the hem of his T-shirt until he shifted on the bed to allow her to pull it off. With a low hoarse chuckle, he did the same with hers. She started to reach behind her to unhook her bra, but he got there first. He flung it away.

"JJ," he said again, his hands going to her breasts, his fingers teasing at her already achingly hard nipples, before his mouth dropped to them. She arched against him, releasing a moan of pleasure.

And then his hand slipped beneath the waistband of her jeans, into her panties, straight to her center. She heard the sound, low and deep in his throat as he realized how ready she was for him. One touch of his fingers and she shuddered, the sudden release making her cry out.

She reached for his jeans, fumbling with his buttons, and then they were both gloriously naked, wrapped up in each other's arms. She let out a laugh of joy as he pulled on protection and filled her, fulfilling her while she clung to him, the smell of the lake and the summer sun still on their skin.

IT WAS GETTING LATE. The kidnappers hadn't called back after sending the text, and WT could feel the tension in the room. As Curtis and Franklin began to discuss more about the ransom drop at his desk, Helen poured them both a glass of wine and, handing WT his, took a chair in front of the fireplace. He joined her in an accompanying chair.

She looked up in surprise and smiled as if aware that he'd been avoiding her.

He felt strangely tongue-tied around her even though they'd once been so intimate—or because of it. He still remembered what she felt like in his arms.

"So you're Franklin's lawyer," he said, wondering why he hadn't known that even though there was no reason he would have. He'd put Helen behind him years ago, and Franklin hadn't known that he and Helen even knew each other.

"And you became a judge. I understand you're retired?"

Had Franklin mentioned that when he'd been doing the introductions? WT didn't think so, which meant that she'd done some checking on him. He felt touched that she'd bothered. That, he believed, explained why she hadn't been as surprised to see him as he had her. Had she wanted to see him again?

He looked at her and wasn't sure how he should be feeling. Bewildered for one. His emotions felt all over the place, something unusual for him. "You're married," he said, noticing the plain gold band on her ring finger.

She shook her head as her gaze went to the ring. "I was. He died about six months ago. I just haven't been able to take off the ring. I know it's silly."

"How long were you married?"

"Almost thirty-four years." So she'd married not long after they'd split up. "He was a good man." Her gaze locked with his as if she knew he was doing the math. "What about you? Did you ever marry?"

He shook his head, suspecting that she already knew that. "I'm too contrary and cantankerous."

"I doubt that."

"Don't. I've only gotten worse, if that's possible, since you knew me."

"I feel like I need to say something," Helen said. Clearly, she was waiting for him to bail her out, to tell her she didn't owe him anything, let alone an explanation. "William—" Her voice broke. "I—"

"Helen, what do you think about this?" Franklin asked from the table where he and Curtis had their heads together.

As she excused herself, rose and went to join them, WT sat for a moment staring into the flames rising from the fire. Helen. After all these years. He still couldn't believe it. And *widowed*. He hated the path his thoughts had been taking since seeing her again.

Did he believe in fate? More to the point, did he believe in love anymore? He'd trusted her with his heart once. Surely he wasn't so addled with age that he would consider doing that again, was he?

And yet even as he thought it, he felt his heart beating a little faster. Had he ever really gotten over Helen?

With the answer came a rush of emotions. He still believed in second chances, didn't he?

JJ WOKE TO a low rumble. She didn't move for a moment, luxuriating in the warmth of the bed and the heat of the body next to her.

"That sounds like thunder," Thorn said. Another rumble, this one sounding closer. He sat up, taking most of the sheet with him.

She rolled over on her stomach into the hollow closest to him. "I like rain."

"Not when our only transportation is a motorbike." He made a good point. "We need to go get our vehicles from Geneva's house."

"Now?" JJ sat up, blinking. Through the curtains she could see that it was still dark outside. "What time is it?"

"Almost three in the morning." They'd made love twice before falling asleep. He turned to her. "This is a good time to go. We shouldn't run into anyone at the house."

Another good point. Still, she didn't want to leave the bed. She didn't want to put on her clothes or have him put on his. She feared if she did, it would be like waking from a wonderful dream and it would start slipping away until she realized it hadn't been real.

He turned and leaned over to kiss her. She smiled as she looked into those gray eyes. It had been real. No dream. She remembered every kiss, every touch, every lick of his tongue… She slid closer until they were touching again. She felt her nipples harden instantly.

"If you stay here like this…" he said, his voice suddenly hoarse with desire.

She laughed, knowing he was right. The storm could last for a couple of days and they would be stranded here in this cabin. Just the two of them. Right now she couldn't imagine anything better.

But as the euphoria of their lovemaking fell away, she remembered what was at stake. "We should go."

He nodded, and with obvious reluctance folded his legs over the side of the bed and rose. She followed, getting up and dressing quickly as thunder boomed as it drew closer and closer. They'd stolen a few hours to themselves, knowing it couldn't last.

Pulling on their jackets, they went outside to the motorcycle. The night was quiet except for the ominous thunder in the distance. The bar had closed an hour ago, all the cars gone. The music had been turned off, along with most of the flashing neon. The summer breeze stirred the nearby pine boughs, the air carrying the promise of rain.

JJ felt nervous about returning to Geneva's house as she swung a leg over the bike behind Thorn. That's where this had all begun. The motor sounded especially loud in the quiet. As he pulled out onto the highway, there was no traffic. He hit the throttle, opening up the motor as off to the west, over the lake, lightning splintered the clouds, illuminating the night sky before it went black again. She could practically smell the rain as they raced toward Geneva's house.

Fortunately, it wasn't far from the place where they were staying. They encountered no other vehicles along the highway. The motorcycle raced up the mountain, going so fast that JJ felt like a child again, when she believed that if she ran the rain couldn't catch her. Thorn slowed and pulled onto the road into the development as the first drops of rain began to fall.

She jumped off the bike the moment he stopped in front of Geneva's three-car garage, and, hurrying to the front, she keyed in the passcode. The moment the door opened, she stepped in and hit the button that opened the first garage stall. The door began to rise. Standing under the overhang, she watched Thorn drive the motorcycle into the garage and quickly followed him.

Once inside, she closed the garage door. Her car was where she'd left it. Just like his truck. Geneva's SUV also looked as if it hadn't been moved. She wondered what had happened to her red sports car, if the police had impounded it or returned it to her grandfather. Which left the question of how Geneva was getting around. Or if she was.

From the back of his truck, Thorn pulled out a ramp, then drove his bike into the back, pulling the ramp up after it. After tying his bike in, he jumped down and closed the tailgate. His dark hair was wet from the rain, his gray eyes shiny as they settled on her. "You want me to follow you back to Miguel's?"

She felt a cold chill that she knew could simply be the cool air of the garage coupled with the rain. She could hear it blowing against the garage doors. She'd always liked thunderstorms. She knew that wasn't what had caused the chill. It felt as if someone had walked across her grave.

Hugging herself, she looked around the garage, knowing they were alone but still sensing something ill on the wind.

Thorn stepped to JJ and wrapped his arms around her. She rested her cheek against his chest, yearning for his earlier warmth. "Everything is going to be all right." When she said nothing, he held her at arm's length to meet her gaze. "You're right, I can't promise that. But I can promise that I will do everything in my power to keep you safe and to find Geneva and get her back to her grandfather. Or die trying."

JJ smiled up at him, tears in her eyes. "It's the die trying part that scares me."

He chuckled. "Me too." She knew that wasn't true. She thought little frightened this man, and knew that he must have seen the worst in the military. Let alone losing his wife. She wondered which had been worse or if it had been a combination of the two.

"We should go. It doesn't sound like it's going to let up," she said, and extracting herself from his arms started toward her car. But as she did, she saw something pass across his face. He reached for the hand that was holding her car keys and pulled them from her fingers. "Why don't you go over and open the garage door while I get your car for you."

She started to argue that it wasn't necessary when she saw the set of his jaw. Her gaze shot to her car. Did he think someone had what…sabotaged it? Planted a bomb in it? She hadn't moved.

He stepped to the back of her car in the first stall and motioned her to the farthest corner of the three-car garage.

"No," she called to him. "Just leave it. I'll go with you in your truck." Her car wasn't worth anything. The last thing she wanted was him to—

She heard her car door groan open. She hurried to open the garage door in front of her car; fear lodged her heart firmly in her throat. Her car engine turned over, ran rough, coughed and let out a belch of carbon monoxide as the garage door slid open to the rainy night.

A few moments later, Thorn appeared at the back of the SUV, walking toward her. He'd left her car running. She tried to breathe. Just the sight of him made her want to sob with gratitude that he'd been wrong. No one had touched her car. She felt foolish even thinking that someone would blow it up—especially if Geneva was involved in this. After all, this was her house. But then again, Thorn believed that the plane had been blown up with explosives.

"I'll follow you," he said as he walked past Geneva's SUV to where his pickup was parked at the end of the three-car bay.

All she could do was nod and head for her car. As she climbed in, she clutched the steering wheel, trying to quit shaking. False alarm. And yet the fact that both of them had even considered that something had been done to her car made all this too real again.

She heard Gertrude's engine start up and let out the breath she'd been holding before backing out and heading down the mountain in the pouring rain.

The thunderstorm had dropped like a dark cloak over them. Her wipers clacked back and forth, back and forth, as she tried to see through the driving rain. The narrow road, flanked by tall pines on each side, was steep and filled with sharp curves as it fell away off the mountainside.

JJ hadn't realized how fast she was going. She'd been too busy trying to see the road ahead through the rain. It wasn't until she started to brake that she realized she was going too fast. She touched her brakes. Nothing happened.

When she'd gotten into the car and backed out, her brakes had been fine.

But this time the pedal went clear to the floor. She pumped frantically, realizing that she was going too fast, the car out of control and with no way to stop.

CHAPTER NINETEEN

THE HEADLIGHTS OF the truck shone on JJ's vehicle. Thorn was sure she was having as much trouble as he was seeing through the driving rain. She hadn't taken off in a hurry, but with growing concern, he could see her car pulling away from him.

With a shock, he realized something was wrong. He could see her fighting to keep the car on the road. His mind raced. JJ was wild and impetuous, but she wasn't suicidal. Then suddenly he knew. He'd tried the brakes. They seemed fine, but he should have done a more thorough check under the car. He hadn't seen any explosives or any sign that anyone had messed with the car.

But someone could have emptied out just enough brake fluid that it would go unnoticed—until the driver started off this mountain.

He saw his chance and, giving the old truck everything Gertrude had on a short straight stretch, he roared past her. Then he slowly applied his brakes as he saw her car coming up behind him way too fast. He gave the truck a little gas, but knew he couldn't give it much. There was a curve coming up soon. He could get them both killed if he blew this.

Her car ran into the back of his truck, jarring him. He heard metal crunch even over the thunder booming overhead. He began to brake, knowing it was going to take a lot to get both of their rigs stopped without one of them losing control and ending up in the trees.

All he could hope was that JJ knew what he was trying to do and would keep her car pointed in the same direction as the truck. He could smell his brakes, and just prayed that they wouldn't burn out before he reached the highway. If he had any hope of saving the two of them…

"Come on, Gertrude," he said as he heard the tear of metal and the truck cab filled with the smell of burning rubber and brake pads. "You can do this, old girl. You can do this." He knew he was telling himself more than the truck as he took a curve, looking back to make sure JJ was still with him.

Ahead, he glimpsed the dark strip of blacktop through the rain. They had to get stopped before that. If they didn't, they could career across the highway and into the pines. Even with traffic light, there was also the chance a vehicle on the highway might hit them before they crashed into the pines on the other side. He wasn't sure that even the pines would stop them. They could end up in the lake, if they survived crashing through the pines.

It ALL HAPPENED so fast that JJ didn't have time to think. One moment everything was fine. The next she was careening off the mountain. And then Thorn was passing her, getting his truck in front of her and trying to slow them both down. She cringed at the sound of rending metal, reminded of the plane crash, and thinking nothing could save her this time.

But she felt her car slow some, felt Thorn's determination, as the air filled with the smell of his brakes burning out. Ahead she could see the two-lane blacktop and past that pines and eventually the lake. As they raced along the last part of the road, she could feel all of Thorn's efforts finally working.

But they weren't going to get stopped before they hit the pines on the opposite side of the highway. There was no way. Thorn seemed to put everything he and Gertrude had into stopping them. She had to do something.

Earlier, she'd thought about grabbing the emergency brake, but she'd been going way too fast. Now though, she thought she had no choice. She grabbed it, grimacing as her car began to fishtail. Ahead of her, Thorn crashed into the pines next to the road and stopped, his bike slamming into the cab. The front of her car seemed to come disconnected from the back of the truck, sliding to a stop in the middle of the highway.

Through the pouring rain she saw headlights headed right for her.

She realized that her car engine had died. She tried to start it. Nothing. She tried to get out of the car to flag the person down, but her door was jammed. She unhooked her seat belt after several wasted tries with fingers that trembled too hard to operate even the simple buckle.

As she started to climb over to the passenger side, her driver's side door was jerked so hard, it broke loose on one side. Thorn dragged her out and pulled her through the rain over to the side of the road before running out into the highway to flag the approaching car.

JJ stood at the edge of the road. She was shaking so hard her teeth chattered from the rain, the fear, the relief. Tears burned her eyes. Thorn Grayson had saved her life yet again. She had to sit down, and sank into the wet grass at the edge of the road. Putting her head in her hands, she heard Thorn and the man who'd stopped.

And then the two men were pushing her car off the road and calling for a wrecker.

THORN THANKED HIS friend as Miguel dropped them off at their cabin.

"You can use my car," he told them, and dropped the

keys into the cup holder as they all got out. "I had a friend leave his pickup for me here at the bar."

Thorn shook his hand and thanked him again as Miguel left in an older model truck. He felt bowled over by his friend's thoughtfulness and help. He wondered how he could ever repay his generosity as he quickly ushered JJ into the cabin.

He was anxious to get them both into the shower even though their clothing had mostly dried and they were both warmer since the sun had come up on a beautiful summer day in the Flathead. The wrecker had taken their vehicles, but Thorn knew both were totaled. His bike might be salvageable but he had his doubts. He felt worse about JJ's car, knowing her financial situation.

As he pushed open the cabin door, he was startled to see that they weren't alone. The judge was sitting on the bed waiting for them. The older man rose as they entered the small cabin. Thorn had called him to tell him what had happened and let him know that they hadn't called the police. Right now, there would be too many questions they couldn't answer.

He hadn't expected the judge to show up here, though. In truth, he hadn't told WT where they were staying. But he realized it hadn't taken all that much for the judge to figure it out. Thorn and Miguel had met when they'd shared a cell for a short time in their youth. Miguel had gotten out and enlisted in the army to avoid prison. Thorn had gone into the judge's boot camp and later the Marines. They'd both avoided prison thanks to the judge, who pulled some strings for Miguel.

So of course the judge would know the bond the two men shared and would know Miguel would help Thorn when he was in trouble.

"I see you found us," Thorn said. "This is JJ. Jenny Jo Foster. Judge W. T. Landusky." She shook the judge's hand. "As I told you on the phone—"

"That's why I'm here," WT said, cutting him off. "I don't want either of you involved in this any further." Thorn started to argue, but the judge didn't give him a chance. "Going back into the mountains looking for the plane was one thing. It was dangerous enough. I don't like the way this has escalated."

"JJ, you should change out of your wet clothes," Thorn said. "I know you're still cold."

She looked as if she had something to say but had decided to keep it to herself for the moment. She nodded, as if seeing that he wanted to be alone with the judge. "Nice meeting you," she said to WT, and went into the bathroom.

"Nice looking young lady," the judge said, then gave him a look that said he knew there was a lot more going on between them than searching for Geneva Davenport.

"Why don't we take this outside?" Thorn said, afraid what the judge might say next. They stepped outside and closed the cabin door behind them.

"Let's have a seat in my car," WT suggested, and they walked over to where the judge had left it parked in the pines some distance from the cabin.

The moment they sat down, the judge said, "You have to stop this. For your sake. But especially for that young woman's sake. I won't have you risking her life anymore."

"Her life is already at risk. Someone planned on her dying in that plane crash. If not that, the explosion. When that didn't happen, they tampered with the brakes on her car. I don't know who is behind this, but they're using her."

"Geneva," WT said. "We both know she has to be involved."

Thorn nodded. "I agree. Or she's a pawn. Either way, whoever is pulling the strings wants that ten-million-dollar ransom money very badly. I don't think they are going to stop until they get it, no matter how many people get hurt or killed."

"My point exactly." The judge's phone rang. He took his phone from his jacket pocket, looked at the screen and said, "I have to take this." Then, "Hello." He listened for a moment. "I'll be right there." Disconnecting, he turned to Thorn again. "That was Franklin Davenport. The kidnapper called again. They've set up a ransom drop for tonight."

THE JUDGE WAS nothing like JJ had expected. For some reason she'd pictured him as short, stoop-shouldered, intelligent but withered with thick glasses. Judge W. T. Landusky, an attractive, distinguished athletic-looking man whose appearance belied his age, was a surprise.

JJ heard the two men leave. She stripped down and stepped into the shower. The warm water felt wonderful. She quickly washed her hair, still shaken from what had happened. Someone had tampered with her brake fluid? Anyone who knew that road off the mountain would know that she could have been killed. Whoever had done it…

Her heart ached. She didn't want to believe it was Geneva. But then again, the woman didn't know her. She was just some voice on the phone. Geneva knew nothing about her, while JJ had come to know the young woman. JJ was expendable.

She changed into dry clothing, growing more angry than afraid. Thorn was convinced that Geneva was behind all of this. That she had planned for the kidnappers and the woman they'd abducted from her house to die in the plane crash. So when JJ hadn't, had Geneva tampered with her car?

What would a young woman like Geneva Davenport

know about brake fluid, let alone how to empty out just enough that it would go unnoticed at first. Thorn had said there was no sign that it had been tampered with. JJ just couldn't see the young woman under her car, being careful not to spill any brake fluid on the garage floor. No, someone else was involved.

JJ pulled the last of her clean underwear from her duffel and her cleanest pair of jeans and T-shirt. The rest of her wardrobe was in the back of her car, now at some wrecking yard. Her vehicle was totaled, she had no clothes and if she didn't call work, she would be fired and have no job.

Things could be worse, she reminded herself. She could be dead right now. She pulled out her phone and called the agency, asking for a few days off because her car had been wrecked. She never took any time off, needing the money. Her boss asked if she was all right, told her to take as much time as she needed and she disconnected.

At the front window, she looked out, but didn't see the judge and Thorn. She was about to step out, when her phone rang. She saw that it was the same number that had called last time.

"Geneva?" she asked as she answered.

"You're not at work."

Did the woman really think she would be at work after everything she'd been through?

"Of course I'm not at work. Geneva, I have to see you. Where are you?"

"I only have a minute. You need to leave town. Do you hear me?" There was fear in her voice. "You aren't safe."

"Someone tampered with the brake fluid in my car. I was almost killed."

"What?" She heard what sounded like true horror in the

woman's voice before Geneva began to cry. "I never wanted any of this to happen. You have to believe me."

"I'm not the only one in danger. Tell me where you are. I'll find a way to get there. I can help you."

"No one can help me now. Save yourself. Leave town." The young woman was sobbing hysterically. And then she was gone.

JJ stood holding the phone for a moment. Geneva was scared, and not just for herself. She'd called to warn JJ, but did she know that she was also in trouble? JJ believed that the woman hadn't known about the brakes being tampered with. How much else didn't Geneva know about?

Clearly, there was someone else involved in the kidnapping. Someone who was now calling the shots. Did Geneva realize that? Or did she think whoever she'd been partnered with was now trying to make things better?

Or did Geneva want the ten million dollars so badly that she couldn't stop now? She wondered if the judge had heard from the kidnappers and what would happen once the kidnappers picked up the money.

JJ concentrated on the phone call, trying to remember what she'd heard in the background. An echo. She frowned. Some large building? Where could the woman be hiding? She thought of other places Geneva had gone with friends, places that JJ had made arrangements for them all to meet. She froze. She'd heard a noise in the background right before Geneva had broken the connection. It hadn't registered at the time. The sound of a horn, the kind that was blown at the start of a sailboat race.

The cabin door opened. As Thorn stepped in, she rushed to him. "Geneva just called. I think I know where she is."

CHAPTER TWENTY

ON THE DRIVE back to the Davenport estate, WT told himself that he couldn't do anything else but advise Franklin to go through with the ransom drop. It was that or call in the authorities. Franklin's number one priority was making sure that no harm came to Geneva—even if she was behind her own kidnapping.

What bothered him was what her long-range plan had been. This hadn't been impulsive. It had been planned. But for how long? Given the number of people involved, including the stealing of an airplane, he suspected whoever was the mastermind had been plotting this for some time. He had little doubt that Jenny Jo Foster was part of the plan. It was why Geneva had left her phone in her bedroom, knowing it had a tracking device on it.

But he supposed Geneva might not be the only one who knew all of this. The boyfriend might know, along with many others. From what Thorn had told him, Franklin's granddaughter talked freely about her personal life to not just her friends, but to a complete stranger at a travel agency while on the phone. So others could have known about JJ staying at Geneva's house when she was gone. Also known about Ridge Brandemiller's private plane at an airfield outside of town, if he and Geneva had some kind of relationship—if not personal, at least financial.

Anyone around the woman could have put the pieces

together as a way to get money out of Franklin. Maybe Geneva thought it was her brainchild, but WT suspected she'd been encouraged to play along. It wouldn't hurt her grandfather since the man was rich. Maybe he would realize how much he loved her and would give her back her credit cards and allowance, and she would give him back his ten million.

Or maybe she hadn't been duped. Maybe she was up to her pretty little spoiled neck and calling all the shots. That's what WT didn't know. He knew Thorn was suspicious that Geneva was playing JJ. But then again, he was emotionally involved with the woman. Thorn couldn't trust his instincts when it came to her.

WT thought of the young woman. She was pretty and definitely bright. She'd figured out a lot of this on her own. She was definitely capable and had proved to be a survivor. A woman like that could give Thorn a real run for his money. She could turn out to be a true heartbreaker.

He smiled to himself. JJ was definitely a woman who could bring Thorn back from where he'd been since his wife died. His smile faded from his lips. Bring him back but then possibly break his heart. WT wasn't sure the man could survive another heartbreak. Or maybe Thorn was stronger than he thought. He certainly hoped so.

He thought of Helen. All these years apart. He wondered what she'd been up to in all that time. What did he really know about the woman she'd become? Maybe it was time he found out. While he was at it, he'd see what he could dig up on Curtis Hunt.

THORN AND JJ exchanged information as they climbed into Miguel's car.

"When Geneva called, I heard a horn go off in the background—the kind they use to start a sailboat race. I checked on my phone. There is one at the north end of the lake today at Somers."

"Then that's where we're headed," Thorn said as he started the car and turned onto the highway.

"I can't believe Franklin Davenport's going to pay the ransom tonight," JJ said. "Even if he suspects his grand-daughter is behind it?"

Thorn shrugged. "Franklin is probably afraid not to in case Geneva has really been kidnapped and you were only a diversion."

"A diversion," she repeated, feeling her face heat with anger. "I could have been killed, not once, but twice."

"And you aren't out of the woods yet," Thorn said. "After what happened last night."

She shuddered as she remembered.

As they neared Somers, she looked out at the lake, awe-struck by the beauty of the colorful sails on the sleek boats against the backdrop of blue water and snowcapped mountains. She loved living here, she thought as her view was blocked by a good quarter mile of old abandoned buildings surrounded by a tall chain-link fence.

She noticed a weathered sign as they passed the gate into what appeared to be an old sawmill. She'd forgotten that Somers had been a company town back in its heyday, and the log mill had been the largest business around the area.

"What doesn't Ridge Brandemiller and his brother own?" she said as the words on the weathered sign registered. "They even own that old log mill back there."

Thorn was looking ahead to where Somers had shed its industrial past and reinvented itself. "She could be in any of those condos along the water or one of the huge lake houses," Thorn said.

JJ looked out at the sailboats with their beautiful sails against the blue green of the water.

"I doubt she's on one of the sailboats," he said, following her gaze. "But I suppose she could be." He slowed as they reached the congested area. "JJ, this is like looking for a needle in a haystack."

She looked around, trying to imagine where Geneva might be hiding out. Her grandfather had cut off most of her money. She'd rented the house on the lake for a week, but after Johnny Baker's death, she wouldn't have been able to stay there and probably wouldn't have been able to get her money back.

Being low on funds possibly, where would she have gone to hide? JJ thought of the echo she'd heard on the phone. Something large. Something open. Something…empty.

Her gaze shifted from the possibilities beside the lake, her eye catching sight of the large yellow mansion on the mountainside overlooking the water. It had been built in the early 1900s by the owner of the mill, back when Somers had been a company town.

Recently, the mansion had been in the news for some time as locals tried to save it from being torn down.

"Up there," she told Thorn.

He'd pulled over out of the traffic and now followed her gaze to the side of the mountain. "What is that?"

"An old empty mansion."

"Doesn't someone live there?"

"Not the last I heard. It was for sale but needs a lot of work. There's been a group trying to save it."

"And you think Geneva would hide up there?"

"I don't know," she said, feeling discouraged. "It's just

a thought. She knows this area. She might know that it's empty, and I suspect she's running low on funds."

He turned around, and they worked their way up the road to the mansion. As he drove onto the property, he said, "Looks like someone has been up here." He indicated the fresh tracks after last night's thunderstorm. "But I don't see another vehicle."

Pulling in behind the house, the two got out. JJ felt herself drawn to the view of the lake and the valley and the sailboat race below them.

"Is there any chance Geneva would have a key?" he asked.

"More than likely she would have had to break in," JJ said as Thorn tried the back door. "She would know the place was empty." The knob turned in his hand.

He glanced over at her, looking worried as he pointed to where someone had used what appeared to have been a screwdriver to get inside. She saw that he was wearing his gun under his jean jacket, and felt a lump form in her throat. They had no idea what they might find in this house.

While there was no vehicle parked outside, that didn't mean that Geneva wasn't alone inside. Or she might never have been here at all. Anyone could have moved in, even someone deranged or drugged up and dangerous.

Thorn went in first. The house had a musty mildew smell that came with age and abandonment. They moved through the house, JJ following Thorn's lead and trying to make as little sound as possible. They found nothing on the first floor, with its big bay window that looked out over the lake. They crossed the hardwood floor, the wood cut in a unique design. She couldn't help wondering what the house had looked like when it had originally been built almost a hundred and twenty years ago. As they headed up to the third floor, she saw more damage where the plaster had fallen off the wood lath underneath.

At a sound above them, they both froze. Thorn drew his weapon and motioned for her to stay where she was. He climbed the rest of the way to the third floor. She waited for a moment and followed.

"I thought I told you to stay," he said when she came out in a large room with even more damage to the walls and floor. In the corner birds flew in and out through the broken window, fluttering noisily around the room.

There was no one here. She wondered what had made her think Geneva would have stayed here even for a moment in these conditions. The woman would never be that desperate.

As she started to turn and go back down the stairs, she stopped, seeing something on the floor she recognized. She stepped to the flowered headband and picked it up. It still had some strands of long blond hair caught in the back of it. She held it up, filled with warring emotions. She'd been right about Geneva being here, which meant the young woman must be desperate.

"This is hers," she said to Thorn. "I've seen her wearing it in photographs at her house."

As he took the headband from her, also noticing the blond hair caught in it, JJ knew he too must be wondering how Geneva had come to drop it here and why so much of her hair had been caught in it when the band had been removed.

THORN CALLED THE judge from outside the mansion and told him what they'd found. "I thought you might want the headband since it has quite a bit of blond hair stuck in the Velcro clasp, some of it appearing to have been pulled out of her head."

"We'll work on getting the DNA right away. No idea where she might have gone?"

"None. Hopefully she will call again." He wondered if the judge was thinking what he was. The phone call. The horn announcing the sailboat race to begin. Geneva's floral headband with the blond hair stuck to it. "It feels like she is leaving us bread crumbs. Because she needs help? Or because she's trying to lead us into an ambush?"

WT said nothing for a moment. "I could argue that she made the call when she was alone for few moments. JJ heard the horn blow starting the regatta and whoever was with Geneva could have caught her making the call, grabbed for her, getting some hair and the headband when he forced her out of the mansion afraid the call would be traced."

Thorn chuckled. "It's another theory since Geneva didn't tell her where she was. JJ just figured it out."

"It's possible that Geneva was involved in the initial plan to pretend to kidnap herself using JJ, but when it went awry, I suspect she panicked and wanted to stop. But whoever she is working with is determined to see it through."

"And Geneva is involved enough that she has a phone she could use to call her grandfather or the cops and only chooses to call JJ?"

"She probably feels guilty about the woman she involved in this," WT said. "Or maybe JJ is one connection she trusts."

"Her travel agent?"

"An innocent bystander," the judge said.

Thorn wasn't sure what he believed, but he admired the judge for giving Geneva the benefit of the doubt. Otherwise, what kind of woman did that make her? "Do you want to meet to pick up the headband?" They decided on a café in Kalispell between Whitefish and Big Fork. "We haven't had breakfast and it's past lunchtime."

FRANKLIN HAD NEVER felt more anxious in his life after the judge's call. The headband Willie described was one of his granddaughter's favorites because she thought the blue in it matched her eyes perfectly. He didn't need a DNA report to confirm it. He knew, but what was she doing in that old mansion? And now they knew that she wasn't alone. Or at least suspected.

But he wouldn't rule out Geneva ripping the headband from her head and leaving it behind like some kind of bread crumb trail. Not because she wanted to be found. It could all be a game to her. He didn't want to believe that. Surely she knew that people had died because of her alleged kidnapping. Was she that reckless? That heartless?

He groaned as he paced the floor. He'd made so many mistakes with her mother that he'd told himself he was going to do things differently with her daughter. Instead, he felt he'd only made new and different mistakes. He knew he should have listened to Willie years ago when the judge had warned him he might be overcompensating.

Losing his wife had been heartbreaking, but losing his daughter had devastated him. Michelle had been such a bright, talented woman who had so much going for her, and yet she'd fallen in with the wrong crowd and gone downhill from there. He'd blamed himself for not doing everything in his power to pull her back from the disaster she had been headed for.

But she'd been a grown woman by then. There was nothing he could do but take Geneva and try to save her. He'd failed her mother, who had been killed by her boyfriend before he turned the gun on himself. Now he'd failed his granddaughter.

All he could think about were the changes he would make if he got Geneva back.

"You realize that if she is involved in this, Franklin, she's going to do some time behind bars," Willie had warned him.

His first thought was to hire the best lawyer money could buy. He couldn't bear the thought of his granddaughter in jail, let alone prison. But even as he thought it, he realized he had to stop saving her because he couldn't save her from herself any more than he could her mother. Not to mention, there wasn't enough money in the world to fix this. As Willie had pointed out, too many people had lost their lives—and it wasn't over yet.

He turned as Helen came into the room. He was struck by how attractive she was. He'd seen his friend's reaction when Helen had walked in the door. Surprise, shock and something else he hadn't seen in the man's eyes before. Desire? Was it possible Willie still had feelings for her after all these years?

"Willie called. Geneva's headband was found in an abandoned mansion near Somers," Franklin told her.

"What was she doing in an abandoned mansion?"

"Who knows? I suspect she's run out of money, so whoever is helping her must be hard up for cash, as well. Or maybe it seemed like a good place to hide out. At this point, I have no idea what she'll do next." He dropped onto the couch and put his head in his hands.

Helen came and sat beside him. "I'm so sorry, Franklin. I wish there was more I could do."

"Thank you," he said, removing his hands from his face

to look at her. He wanted to think about anything but the danger Geneva was in. "I saw the way Willie looked at you when you came in the door the other night. If it matters, I think he still cares."

Helen smiled wanly. "He definitely was surprised, but I'm not sure he still cares. Clearly, he'd never mentioned me to you."

"No, but I don't think it's too late."

She laughed at that as she rose to go stand by the window. "You should know William better than that. He swore he could never forgive me. I believe him."

"That was youth talking," Franklin assured her. "Even someone like Willie can mellow with the years."

Helen turned to look at him. "I wish that were true. I still care about him."

"I can see that. Maybe you being here is fate. Maybe this is the beginning of a second chance for the two of you. It's never too late."

"I'm sure people said the same thing to you after your wife died, and yet here you are, alone in this huge house," she said.

He chuckled. "Easier to give advice than take it, but in your case, what do you have to lose?"

She smiled at that but said no more as they waited for Willie to return with the headband.

JJ WAS SURPRISED when the judge entered the café with a young man carrying a laptop. The two slid into the booth across from her and Thorn.

"This is Zip," WT said as the young man opened the laptop and set it on the table as the waitress approached. "Just coffee for me. Black." He glanced over at Zip who only shook his head.

JJ and Thorn ordered breakfast, and as soon as the waitress left, Zip looked at her and said, "Let me see your phone."

She blinked in surprise, but dug out her phone and handed it to him.

"This the number from the burner that's been calling you?" the young man asked. She nodded and watched as he went to work on his laptop.

The waitress brought her and Thorn's meals. They ate to the sound of Zip's quick strokes on the laptop keys before he was on her phone again, his thumbs moving even quicker.

The judge sipped his coffee and said nothing.

"Want to tell us what this is about?" Thorn finally asked. He'd finished his meal, JJ had already eaten all she could of hers and the waitress had taken away their dishes.

"Zip says there is a way to trace the next call that comes in from the burner phone," WT said. "It won't be precise, but it will give you a location area that might help."

JJ glanced at the young man again. "Is he even out of high school?" she asked quietly, not wanting to interrupt Zip's train of thought.

"I'll be a junior next year," Zip said without stopping what he was doing.

The judge smiled across the table at them. "Once Zip is out of high school, he's agreed to letting me take him under my wing."

"Boot camp," Thorn said, and shook his head. "What did he do?"

"He had quite a business going manipulating grades in the school's computer system," WT said. "He was saving his money to go to an Ivy League college."

"That's admirable," Thorn said facetiously, making the judge grunt.

After a moment, Zip handed JJ back her phone and began to give the two of them instructions that went over JJ's head.

The judge must have seen her confusion. "What he's saying is that when you hit that button, with luck you should be able to pinpoint where the call is coming from. It's worth a try."

"Is there any other news?" JJ asked, not sure how much the judge had told Zip about why they needed to find the caller.

"Nothing yet. I'll let you both know." With that Zip put away his laptop, and he and the judge excused themselves and left.

"Now we just wait for Geneva to call," she said as she watched the two leave. *If* she called again.

CHAPTER TWENTY-ONE

AS THEY LEFT the café, the sun already dipping toward the west, JJ suddenly stopped walking. She'd had her hands in the pockets of her hoodie, but now pulled them out to turn to him.

"I forgot about this," she said as she opened her palm to show him.

He stared at the matchbook from the local bar that she'd found in Zac's apartment. "Where is this bar?" She told him it was in the mountains to the west of the Flathead by quite a few miles. "By the time we get there, we might be ready for a beer. What do you say?"

"Someone else could have dropped the matchbook. Or he could have stopped there on his way to town and has never been back."

"All a possibility," Thorn agreed. "I say we give it a try since right now we have no other leads."

She nodded. He could tell she was anxious. The ransom drop was scheduled for tonight. As far as he knew, the kidnappers hadn't called with directions yet. Meanwhile, all they could do was hope Geneva would call again.

They talked little on the drive to the out-of-the-way bar. The sun moved across the cloudless blue sky, the heat of the day giving way to a cool evening breeze.

The bar was located in the middle of nowhere along a two-lane highway in the mountains. From the outside, it looked like a dive. Music blared from the old speaker system as they stepped in. The place was small, just a hole in the wall with a scarred bar, a few tables off to the side and an even smaller dance floor. It smelled of stale beer and floor cleaner.

"Let's sit at the bar," Thorn suggested since there was only the bartender and an older couple at the other end. The couple gave them a smile and a nod as Thorn and JJ pulled up stools at the opposite end of the bar.

"What can I get you?" The bartender, a dark-haired man in his late fifties with a bulbous nose and watery blue eyes, set down two cocktail napkins.

"Beers?" Thorn asked JJ. She nodded, and he told the man to pour them a couple of drafts.

Another song came on, a slow country tune that Thorn hadn't heard in years.

"I love this song," JJ said.

On impulse he reached for her hand. "Dance with me."

There was a moment of surprise before she smiled, and he pulled her off her stool and into his arms as they stepped onto the tiny dance floor.

JJ COULDN'T REMEMBER the last time she'd danced. Thorn pulled her close, his hand low on the hollow of her back. She melted into his arms, resting her head against his shoulder. Like their lovemaking, they fit together perfectly as they swayed to the music. She breathed in his scent, filled with a contentment she'd never felt before.

She'd always been striving to stay alive when she was living with her mother, to be the perfect daughter when she was living with her father, and since his death, striving to pay off his medical bills and keep her head above water.

Now, she moved to the music with Thorn, the two of

them thrown together in the most unexpected way. She wanted to pocket this memory, tuck every last moment of it away. The song, the run-down bar, Thorn's male scent and the warm, secure feel of his body in rhythm with her own.

As the final notes of the song played, she raised her head to look into his eyes, not wanting this to end. Not the song, not the two of them. He drew her close again and whispered in her ear. "I'm crazy about you."

"Crazy being the key word."

"I'm serious, JJ." He drew back a little to look at her. His gray gaze met hers and held it as the last few beats of the song hung in the air. She could see that he was serious. Her heart hammered in her chest, and she felt as if she couldn't breathe.

And then he kissed her, dragging her even closer. She clung to him, wanting desperately never to leave his arms.

Then, as if hearing the old couple clapping in the silence after the song ended, Thorn released her before taking her hand and leading her back to their beers.

JJ looked down the bar at the couple and gave them a smile before climbing onto her stool and picking up her glass of beer. She felt shaken and yet warm all over. Stealing a glance at Thorn, she told herself all of this was too fast. She couldn't trust it. This wasn't real life and when it was over and they went back to their lives...

Her cell phone rang, making her nearly spill her beer. She looked at the screen and recognized the number. "It's her."

FRANKLIN STARED AT the briefcase at his feet. He'd had to buy an extra-large one to get all the money to fit. Ten million dollars in unmarked large bills. Now he thought he would lose his mind waiting for the call for instructions.

Had he been one to pray, he knew now was the time. Geneva had been alive as recently as this morning. He wasn't stupid enough to believe that he would hand over the money and he would get his granddaughter back—especially if she was truly behind all this. Worse if she wasn't.

What terrified him was that once her boyfriend or whoever she was working with had the money, the kidnapper might not need Geneva anymore. In fact, she might be a liability. Why couldn't Geneva understand that? Maybe that's why she had looked so terrified in the text photo he'd received.

He looked up as the judge came into the den. Helen and Curtis were down in the kitchen. He tried to read the judge's expression. "What's happened now?"

"I have someone looking into Zac Judson and his family," Willie said as he took a chair across from him. "I don't have the whole picture yet, but it appears Zac senior spent a small fortune trying to prop up his son only to have Zac junior lose it all in one bad scheme after another. His father finally cut him off. Zac junior doesn't have any money."

Franklin nodded, not surprised. "We already figured that, but thanks for all your help. I don't know what I would have done without you." He looked again at the briefcase. "I just wish they would call. I want this over with." He raised his gaze. "At least I think I do. If it was just Geneva behind this, I'd gladly hand over ten million to her, right or wrong. But I fear…" He couldn't say his fear out loud, and saw that he didn't have to. Willie knew because he shared the same fear.

His cell phone rang. He felt himself start as he pulled it out and checked the screen, looked up and nodded. He took a breath, let it out and tried to stay calm as he answered the kidnapper's call.

GENEVA SOUNDED BREATHLESS. "Listen, I only have a minute. Please, I need your help."

"Tell me where you are and I'll—"

"You need to tell my grandfather to pay the ransom. No police. I'm begging you, don't let him do something crazy. I know how he is. He could get us all killed if he doesn't do exactly what he's told to do. Please."

"Geneva—" But the woman's connection was broken.

She handed her phone to Thorn, who quickly tried to trace it. But she saw by his expression that the call hadn't been long enough.

He handed back her phone. "Let's get out of here."

Once outside, she took large gulps of the summer air and tried not to cry. She feared for Geneva's safety even as she feared that the woman might be behind this whole thing. Like before, Geneva had sounded scared. But she was reminded that Thorn suspected it was all an act.

If true, then the young woman had been using her from the start—and still was with these phone calls.

Thorn took out his phone. "I'll let the judge know." When the call went straight to voice mail, he said, "Call me. We heard from Geneva. She wanted JJ to make sure that Franklin pays the ransom."

WT STOOD NEXT to Franklin to listen to the altered voice giving instructions as to the ransom drop. He typed into his notes on his phone, "Demand that Geneva is there and that she's part of the trade" and held it up for Franklin. His friend read it and hesitated, his face reddening in anger before he repeated the demand and closed his eyes as if afraid that this might be the demand that got his granddaughter killed.

"You are in no position to make demands. I should hang up right now and kill your granddaughter."

"How do I know you haven't already?" Franklin said, reading what WT instructed. "You want the ten million or not? I have to see my granddaughter at the ransom drop or there will be no money."

The judge nodded even though Franklin had changed the last part a little. There was silence on the other end of the line. He could see his friend beginning to sweat, fear adding years to the media mogul's face.

"All right, but this is the last demand you make. I will bring your granddaughter, but if you don't bring the money or if you bring the cops or anyone else, I'll kill her right before your eyes. Is that understood?"

"Tell me where and what time," Franklin said. "I'll bring the money."

WT looked out the closest window. It would be getting dark soon. He figured that was exactly what the kidnappers wanted, the cloak of darkness.

"Start driving south now. I'll give you more directions as you need them." With that the kidnapper was gone.

Franklin disconnected, visibly shaking. His gaze came up to meet Willie's. "I'm scared."

The judge nodded. "I'm going with you."

"No! You heard what he said."

"I'll be in the back of your car. Don't worry, I'll stay down. I'll be able to call for help if things—"

"No, on this I am adamant," Franklin said. "It's just money."

"Even if the kidnapper brings Geneva with him, it doesn't mean he'll turn her over after he gets the money. The only way to keep that from happening—"

"I've made up my mind, and you know I can be just as stubborn as you."

The judge did know that. "It's Geneva's life if anything goes wrong."

"Exactly. That's why I'm going alone with the money."

Helen had been listening from where she was seated. "It has to be his choice, William," she said, as if seeing that the two of them had reached an impasse.

WT knew it wasn't up to him. If it had been, he would be in the back seat, calling for backup if needed. "Okay." There was nothing else he could do. "You should get going then."

As Franklin turned, the judge saw the pistol beneath his jacket. "No!" WT said, grabbing his friend's shoulder to keep him from leaving with the gun. "You're not taking a gun. I can't let you get killed and jeopardize Geneva's life, as well. Like you said, it's only money."

"You know that bastard boyfriend is behind this," Franklin said between gritted teeth. "If he gets away with the ten million—"

"The FBI will track him down. He won't be able to leave the country. He'll do time, I promise you. But right now, we have no idea who's behind this. What your granddaughter doesn't need right now is you in jail. Give me the gun."

"Franklin, he's right," Helen stated.

Franklin hesitated and then swore as he pulled the weapon and slapped it down in WT's palm. "I'll kill him with my bare hands if I have to."

"Just get Geneva to safety. That's the priority here. Going in this angry isn't going to help. I want you to call the moment it's over and you have Geneva."

His friend nodded. "I'm okay. I'll calm down on the way. No one wants this over more than me." He picked up the briefcase and headed for the door.

"I should be going with him," WT said as the man left.

"He'll be fine," Helen said as she laid a hand on his shoulder. "I don't know about you, but I could use a drink."

He shook his head. "Thanks, but I need to make a call."

Her fingers tightened on his shoulder, stopping him from

turning away. "You didn't put a tracking device on his car or the briefcase, did you, William? You didn't jeopardize his granddaughter for the sake of justice. Tell me you didn't."

WT didn't answer as he looked around the room. "Where's Curtis?"

It took Helen a moment. Like him, she glanced around, before saying, "I don't know. Now that you mention it, he left right after Franklin got the call. I vaguely remember him saying he had something he had to do."

ON THE DRIVE back to Miguel's, Thorn put his arm around JJ and pulled her over on the bench seat next to him. She felt small and vulnerable. He was reminded of her in his arms on the dance floor and what he'd said to her. He'd meant those words. He was crazy about her. But what now?

He tried not to think about it as he drove back toward the lake. "Are you okay?" He glanced over at her.

She nodded, looking close to tears. This had been an emotional roller-coaster ride for all of them. He realized that he had crossed some invisible barrier with this woman. That's when he knew he was going to tell her about Bethany.

"I want to tell you about Bethany." He felt her stiffen next to him for a moment. He took a breath and was about to say more when his cell phone rang. He swore under his breath. He'd finally wanted to tell her…

He held up a finger as he pulled over, grabbed his cell phone and took the judge's call.

"Franklin has gone to pay the ransom," the judge told him.

Thorn frowned. "You sound worried."

"I am. I'll let you know when I hear something." And the judge was gone.

Thorn repeated what the judge had told him as he pocketed his phone before he pulled back onto the road toward the Flathead Valley.

JJ had moved over a little earlier to give him space to pull out his phone. She didn't move back as he drove. "You don't have to tell me about your wife."

"I want to. The judge knows, but I haven't told anyone else." He took a deep breath and let it out. "I thought she was the love of my life. Funny how things look in hindsight. I can see what I missed, what I ignored, those red flags that seemed like nothing at the time and yet later are so glaring."

He glanced over at her. She was frowning, no doubt as confused as he'd been before the end. "I thought I was the one who went after her." He chuckled, staring at the road ahead as he drove—and reliving the first time he'd laid eyes on Bethany. "But later I realized she'd planned it all, our first meeting, everything. She feigned surprise, but she knew exactly who I was and what I did in the military. She lassoed me and roped me in, and I went like a bum calf."

"I'm sorry," JJ said.

Thorn felt her hand on his thigh, felt the warmth, the comfort, as she moved over beside him again. "My father was a ranch manager so we moved from ranch to ranch. I rebelled hard, wanting nothing to do with ranching or him. That's when I started going into town and stealing cars for the excitement of it. When I got caught, I met the judge and he turned me around even before the military did the rest of the job. But there was still some wild in me. I was like an untamed horse that had been broken to ride, but I still had a little too much spirit. Bethany seemed to like the wild cowboy in me, and I liked Bethany."

"Thorn, I can hear how hard this is for you," JJ said. "You don't need to—"

"Actually, I do," he said, glancing over at her in the dash

lights. They were coming off the mountain road, not far now from Flathead Lake. The car's headlights cut through the growing darkness. "I thought she was a free spirit, as well. I liked the wild in her, but I wasn't a complete fool. She quizzed me too much about what I was doing in the service. I caught her going through my things. I suspected she'd been on my phone. When I had a friend check it, I found out that she'd put a device on it that kept track of me and my missions."

"Are you telling me she was a spy?"

"I went to my commander with my suspicions. Looking back, I should have gone sooner, but by then she was my *wife*. It was her idea to run off and get married. I thought it was romantic." He let out a bark of a laugh that hurt. "My mission before that had gone sideways when it shouldn't have. Several of the men in my unit were wounded. Fortunately not killed."

"You loved her and thought she loved you."

He laughed. "That I did."

"I can't imagine what that did to you."

"I told my commander everything I knew about her, and what I suspected had been going on. I felt as if I was betraying her, but I had to know. I hoped I was wrong." He hesitated, this part the hardest to tell, the hardest to admit. "I got hold of her phone, doing what she'd done to me, as I continued to play along, being with her and not letting on what I suspected. It was hell."

"Oh, Thorn."

"I guess I hadn't thought it out, how it would end. Maybe I held on to the hope too long that the military would come back to me and tell me they didn't find anything suspect." He felt JJ's hand tighten on his thigh, as if she knew what was coming. "She was killed when they tried to take her and some of her associates during a raid. By then, they had a dossier on her that proved my greatest fears. She'd been working with the enemies I'd been fighting. She'd risked my life and the lives of my men, while talking about a future for the two of us when I got out of the service. She was trying to destroy me and my country."

"I'm so sorry."

He couldn't look over at JJ, seeing tears in her eyes and such compassion. It was hard enough telling her, but her reaction hit him at heart level, tearing down more of the wall he'd built around himself. "Now you know why I bought the place outside of Gardiner, built my cabin and closed off the rest of the world."

She said nothing for a long moment. "I'm glad you had Gertrude at least."

He glanced over at her, thankful that she'd lightened the mood that had settled over them. "She's a damned good mule."

"Sorry about your truck."

"It's replaceable." He slowed as he neared their cabin. "You aren't." As he pulled in and shut off the car engine, he turned to her. "For so long I worked hard every day on the place in the mountains until I was so exhausted I fell into bed at night. I lived off the land there, raising or killing what I needed, after investing what I made in the service. I told myself that I would never need anyone, let alone trust my heart ever to another woman. And it worked," he said with a bitter laugh. "Until you."

CHAPTER TWENTY-TWO

FRANKLIN GRIPPED THE steering wheel as he drove and waited for his phone to ring. He worried that his battery might have run down or that he couldn't get cell service as he drove through Kalispell headed south on the lake road as instructed.

Worry was like a vehicle resting on his chest. He tried to breathe, to calm down, to think positively. But anger boiled just below the surface. He wished he hadn't listened to Willie. He regretted leaving his handgun behind.

His cell phone rang. He jumped at the sound, took a breath and picked up.

"Where are you?" the altered voice asked.

"At Dayton." He could make out Wild Horse Island as he drove along the west side of the lake in the growing darkness.

"You're making good time. Keep going. I'll call back." And the kidnapper was gone.

Franklin put down the phone on the seat next to him and concentrated on his driving. The last forty-eight hours he'd had way too much time to think about his life, about Geneva and her mother, Michelle. He knew every parent probably wanted a do-over. Just one more chance to get it right. He certainly knew that feeling right now.

Unfortunately, he'd had his do-over with Geneva and he'd blown it, because as much as he didn't want to admit it, he knew his granddaughter was involved in all this. He just didn't know how much—yet.

His cell phone rang. This time he was ready.

"How far are you from Polson?" the voice asked.

"Almost there."

"Are you familiar with the bridge by the city park on the way into town?" He was. The park was right along the Flathead River where it flowed under the bridge and into Flathead Lake. "Leave your car at the park and climb up to the bridge. I will meet you in the middle. You're alone, right?"

Completely. "Yes. I should be there soon. And Geneva?" he asked quickly before the kidnapper disconnected.

"She'll be there."

JJ TOOK THORN'S face in her hands and looked into his gray eyes the moment he pulled in front of the cabin. Her heart ached at what he'd been through. No wonder he'd closed himself off. But even as she thought of her feelings for him, her rational mind was telling her that this was happening too fast. It couldn't be real. She didn't care. She wanted this man like she'd never wanted anything in her life.

Leaning toward him, she kissed his lips gently. She'd felt his incredible pain at finding out the ultimate betrayal of the woman he'd loved and married. That he could trust again—let alone love again—seemed impossible.

He reached for her, dragging her to him to deepen the kiss.

"Ouch!" she cried as she felt the gearshift stab into her thigh. She hadn't made out in a car since she was a teenager.

"Oh, sorry." Thorn let her go, and they both began to laugh. "We really don't have to do this in a compact car." But they stayed where they were, just looking at each other, for a few more moments, as if they'd both felt it. Something had changed between them. A wall had come down that even their lovemaking hadn't been able to topple. She hadn't moved to a mountaintop, but she'd been hiding from intimacy, as well. She'd used her father's medical bills as an excuse to lock herself away. But no more.

As they opened their doors and started for the cabin, Thorn swept her up in his arms and carried her inside. Just looking into his eyes made her heart beat even faster. She could see that he didn't know where they might go from here—any more than she did. Nor was he ready to say those three little words—any more than she was. But what they had between them… It was nothing short of amazing. They'd brought each other back. She'd never felt such a strong emotion as he gently lowered her to the bed.

The small old cabin was their harbor away from the rest of the world—at least until the phone rang, dragging them back. But right now. It was just the two of them.

"I want to make love to you," he whispered, his gaze never leaving hers.

And he did.

Thorn listened to the sound of the shower running. He stretched, smiling to himself as he thought about JJ and their earlier lovemaking. He felt like a new man, and that made him laugh. This woman had rescued him from a dark place—a place he'd thought he could never escape.

His stomach growled, and he knew JJ must be starving. He climbed out of bed and dressed. Moving to the bathroom door, he called, "I'm going to get us something to eat over at the bar. I'll be right back."

He remembered that she'd left her phone in case Geneva called. He pocketed it along with his own. Neither phone had rung since she'd gone to take a shower after their lovemaking.

As he started toward the bar, Miguel pulled up in a pickup, jumped out and opened the back. Thorn couldn't believe what he was seeing. Miguel had retrieved his motorcycle from the salvage lot where his truck and JJ's car had been taken.

"I thought it was totaled like the truck," Thorn said.

Miguel smiled. "It took a little work. I wouldn't say it was as good as new, but it's running like a top and most of the dents have been beaten out of the body."

Thorn didn't know what to say. Before he could say anything, Miguel said, "Help me get it out of the back of the truck."

He did and then hugged his friend. "I don't know what I would have done without you. I owe you."

Miguel shook his head. "We're friends." He shrugged as if that said it all, then climbed into his pickup and pulled up to park behind the bar. "The special tonight is chicken enchiladas," he called as he entered the back.

Thorn laughed, thinking how much JJ would like the special as he walked over to the bar.

Back at the cabin, he put the food on the table and wondered if the judge had heard anything from the kidnappers about the ransom drop. Probably not, because WT had promised to call.

As he pulled the phones out of his pocket and set them on the table, he wondered at the fact that no one but Geneva had called on JJ's phone since she'd retrieved it from her bag more than twenty-four hours ago. At least she hadn't gotten any calls that he knew of.

Thorn felt bad for her. JJ had cut herself off from the rest of the world to keep her head down as she worked to pay off her father's medical expenses. He saw so much of himself in her. He'd told himself that he didn't need anyone. It had been a lie he'd lived with. Until JJ.

That repressed passion had certainly come out in the past few days with her. He smiled. They were like two people who had washed up on a deserted island after thinking their lives were over. That alone should have scared him. He knew how intense something could feel when mixed with a healthy dose of fear and danger.

But every cell of his body argued that this was real.

He thought she'd appreciate him bringing the food back to the cabin. She had to be as anxious as he was. Nothing could go wrong with the ransom drop, and even as he thought it, he feared something might already have.

Shouldn't they have heard something by now? The judge had promised to call. He thought about calling him, but knew better than to tie up WT's cell phone.

Suddenly he froze. The shower was still running? His chest tightened. JJ had always been so quick in the shower. He tapped on the door, telling himself not to panic. "JJ?" No answer. He tapped louder. "JJ?" Still no answer. He tried the knob.

As the door fell open, he saw that the shower was on, but JJ wasn't in it. His gaze shot from the torn shower curtain to the window that now hung open, the summer night blowing in.

JJ was gone.

CHAPTER TWENTY-THREE

IT WAS DARK by the time Franklin pulled into the lot at the small park on the Flathead River. There were no other cars, but there were signs that people had been here earlier. The trash containers were full and coals still burned in the raised grills, the scent of charred hot dogs hanging in the air as he climbed out of his vehicle and looked up at the bridge.

He couldn't see anyone. Only a few cars passed as he reached into the sedan for the briefcase. He had to go up the hill to reach the bridge, climbing slowly, looking around, half expecting to be ambushed.

When he reached the bridge, he stopped as if to catch his breath. In truth, he was breathing hard but not from exertion. He was scared, fearing what might go wrong. Geneva's life was at stake. It was a thought that hadn't left his mind since the kidnapper had called Friday night.

He could hear the lap of water beneath him and smell the summer scents that floated on the breeze. The briefcase felt heavy in his left hand. He shifted it to his right as he heard a boat in the distance. Several cars went past, their headlights temporarily blinding him.

Why meet here? he wondered. Would they try to snatch the briefcase from him as they drove by? He knew that he didn't expect them to live up to their end of the bargain.

They were criminals, he thought angrily, and reminded himself that his granddaughter might be the leader.

As headlights washed over him from behind, he caught movement at the other end of the bridge. The car passed him, illuminating two figures. Heart in his throat, he began walking.

The bridge didn't span a great distance, but the darkness made it seem farther to the middle. The wind coming down the Flathead River buffeted him as he walked. The briefcase seemed to grow heavier with each step. He changed hands every so many feet as he tried to remain calm and not to think too much.

He could make out the larger figure moving toward him in the front. A smaller figure was behind him. Geneva? He got only glimpses of the person behind the man. Both wore hoodie sweatshirts, the hoods up. He could only hope the other one was Geneva. But if it was, her blond hair was covered. Otherwise, he would have seen it when a car passed.

Traffic was light tonight as the hour got later and the sky darker. Development around the lake and town cast multicolored lights over the water, but none near the bridge. Still, when he did look down, the river's surface had a gunmetal sheen as it flowed past.

He was getting close to the middle of the bridge and began to slow, determined to make the kidnappers come to him. Gauging the distance in front and behind him, he stopped to wait and set the briefcase at his feet. The summer air was cool off the water. He crossed his arms, knowing that it wasn't the temperature that had him shaking.

The two figures kept coming. He could definitely make out the man in the lead. Broad-shouldered, wearing a dark hoodie that matched his hair. Zac Judson. Franklin still hadn't gotten a good look at the smaller figure behind him.

It could be a smaller man, in which case this could go south quickly, and he could end up dead.

He wished again for his gun. But he knew that if it was two men headed for him and they had tried to trick him, he would have pulled the weapon and shot them both. That alone should have made him glad that Willie had insisted on him leaving the weapon behind. He didn't want to spend the rest of his life in prison.

But damned if he wanted these bastards to screw with him any further. Once he got Geneva back safe, he would go after everyone involved with all the power and money he had, and it was a hell of a lot.

And if Geneva is involved?

That thought made him sway a little in the breeze that seemed to have picked up with the growing darkness of night.

The two figures were almost to him. The man's face was in shadow, but he was positive it was Zac Judson.

Zac stopped a dozen yards away. "You bring the money?"

Franklin reached down and picked up the briefcase. "Where's Geneva? *Geneva!*"

Zac reached behind and shoved back the hoodie just enough to reveal her hair. Blond strands caught in the breeze, whirling around her face. The man was still blocking Franklin's view, but he saw that her mouth had duct tape over it and her wrists were bound in front of her.

"Let her go!" Franklin demanded. "Let her go now!"

Zac started to speak, but Franklin was no longer interested in anything the man had to say. He threw the briefcase as hard as he could. Zac saw it coming and tried to dodge out of the way, but had nowhere to go as a car sped past with the bridge's concrete railing on one side and a vehicle rushing past on the highway. The briefcase caught him at gut level, bending him over.

Franklin was moving the moment he threw the briefcase. He charged like a wild animal, a guttural sound coming from his mouth that filled the night air. He saw his granddaughter's eyes widen in alarm just an instant before Zac dropped the briefcase to the bridge walkway and turned.

From only yards away, Franklin watched in horror as the man grabbed Geneva and threw her off the bridge before scooping up the briefcase and jumping after her.

He heard the first splash and then the second. He'd been moving so fast that it took him a few steps to stop. He grabbed the concrete railing and looked down in the water and saw nothing. Realizing that the current had already carried them both to the other side of the bridge, he turned to run across when a car swept past, nearly hitting him.

All he could think of was Geneva, her hands bound, duct tape over her mouth. She would drown. Another car swept past before he could rush to the other side. He was planning to jump into the river, save his granddaughter, but before he could reach the opposite side of the bridge, he heard a boat motor come to life.

By the time he reached the downriver side of the bridge, he watched in the boat's lights as first the bound woman and then the man and briefcase were pulled aboard. Zac turned, glanced up and saluted him.

But Franklin's gaze was on the woman, the blond hair wet against her face. He finally got a good look at her before the boat sped off across the wide expanse of Flathead Lake.

It wasn't Geneva.

CHAPTER TWENTY-FOUR

THORN HURRIEDLY TURNED off the shower and ran to the bathroom window to look out into the darkness. There was no movement, no sound. It verified what he'd suspected. JJ had gone out the window while he was over at the bar getting the food. But she hadn't gone willingly, he saw as he took in the torn shower curtain, and to his horror, drops of blood on the bathroom floor.

He hurried out of the bathroom, telling himself not to panic. But his thoughts were out of control right now. He'd been in abduction situations before, but never involving someone he loved. He rushed around to the back of the cabin. Through the light coming from the open bathroom window, he could see two sets of man-size footprints in the still muddy earth.

Taking out his phone, he started to call the judge, but it rang before he could. He'd forgotten for a few minutes about the ransom drop. The judge could be calling to tell him that they had the kidnapper—and Geneva.

"JJ. They have JJ," he said into the phone without preamble.

"I know," the judge said to his surprise. "Franklin just called. He'd demanded that the kidnappers bring Geneva to the drop. Instead, it was a blonde woman who looked like her."

"JJ." His voice broke. "But they already had Geneva. Why take someone who looked like her?" Thorn had been thinking out loud but now stopped, realizing what he was saying.

"We don't know why they didn't use Geneva. Maybe… I don't want to speculate."

He knew exactly what the judge didn't want to say. Geneva was dead. They had to have someone show up for the exchange. Why not the woman who'd already been mistaken for her? But how had they known that he and JJ were staying at Miguel's?

He couldn't worry about that now. He listened as the judge told him what he knew, cringing at the part about Zac throwing JJ off the bridge with her bound, her mouth taped. He must have let out a furious sound because the judge quickly added, "The last he saw of her, she was fine. One of the men in the boat pulled her on board. She left with Zac and the money."

"She's not involved, if that's what you're thinking."

"I wasn't thinking that," the judge said quickly. "But maybe that was their plan, to sow that seed of doubt in Franklin's mind."

Thorn swore. His brain screamed, *Find her before it's too late.* They'd needed her and now they didn't, and that's what terrified him.

Trying to pull himself together, he drew on his strength. He couldn't lose JJ. He had to think clearly. He had to behave the way he'd been trained. He couldn't let his personal feelings paralyze him or worse, force him into a mistake that could cost her her life. If she was still alive…

He shoved that thought away. "We couldn't trace Geneva's last call. But it did ping on the closest cell tower. I'm going there now. If I find something…"

"Be careful, Thorn. I have a bad feeling about all of this. Also, Franklin's chief financial officer disappeared right before the ransom drop. Helen's had no luck trying to reach him."

Thorn grabbed up JJ's phone and, pocketing both his

and hers, strapped on his gun and headed for the door. The night was clear and cool. He took his motorcycle and sped northwest toward the town of Somers. That's where they'd found Geneva's headband in the old mansion overlooking town. That's where her last call had pinged a cell tower—somewhere around the small town that had once been known for its lumber mill.

THE JUDGE SAT for a moment in the guest bedroom at Franklin's estate, too upset to move. He didn't believe JJ was involved in the kidnapping and hadn't for some time. Instead, what had him upset was wondering how the kidnappers had known that JJ and Thorn were staying in one of Miguel's cabins.

The place was so out of the way. He knew he hadn't mentioned anything about it to anyone. But with a start, he realized that he had been forced to put the address into his vehicle's navigation system. Otherwise, he would never have been able to find it.

Now all he could think about was who'd been in his vehicle. He recalled Curtis's interest in the car. He'd handed the man his keys so he could check it out. He'd stopped short of telling him he could drive the sports car. But he had told Curtis that he could start it up because the roar of the huge engine was part of the fun. He'd watched from the window. Helen had gone out and climbed in it as well, kidding him about the car being his midlife crisis.

Had Curtis pretended an interest in the car? Or had Helen climbed in only to check out his navigation system? Or had both of them wanted to know where Thorn and JJ had been staying so they could tell the kidnappers where to grab JJ?

He shook his head and looked down at his phone. It was

synced with the car system. He laughed. All anyone had to do was look at his phone. WT tried to remember if he'd left it lying around where it could have been picked up, and realized that he'd put it on the charging station a few times in the kitchen. He'd forgotten about it until he went into Franklin's den and had to go retrieve it.

But would that have been enough time to check his phone? He'd turned the passcode off, finding it a pain in the neck.

Did he really suspect Helen? Or even Curtis? Maybe there was an even simpler explanation. He'd been followed from the Davenport estate. He swore, realizing that he hadn't checked for a tail. Probably wouldn't have recognized one if he had. Had he led the kidnappers right to JJ?

He felt sick, fearing that he was responsible for getting her abducted. He could see how Thorn felt about her—and knew what it would do to him if something worse happened to her. WT would be responsible for whatever happened to the two of them. But he also felt relieved that he had come up with an explanation that didn't include Helen.

At a tap at his door, he forced himself to rise from the end of the bed to answer it.

"Are you all right?" Helen asked, looking concerned from the doorway.

"Is Franklin back?" he asked, not about to share the bad news he'd received even though seeing her in the flesh, he had trouble believing the suspicions he'd had about her only moments ago. This was Helen, a woman he'd loved so desperately that he'd never loved another.

She shook her head. "Curtis hasn't returned either. Should we be worried?"

"No, I'm sure he's on his way back," he told her, suggesting they wait in the living room. The bedroom felt too intimate. She smiled almost ruefully, as if she too felt that old chemistry stirring between them. Apparently, it was something a person never outgrew.

Last night lying in bed alone in this huge house, he'd wondered if what they'd felt for each other so long ago had been the real thing. It had certainly felt that way for him—back then—and even now with everything that was going on.

In the living room, Helen poured herself a drink. She seemed as nervous as he was as he waited for Franklin to return and Thorn to call after he'd followed up the only lead he had on JJ. Maybe it was time to call in the authorities. Maybe it was past time.

"Sure I can't tempt you with a drink, Judge?" Helen asked from the bar.

He shook his head and looked down at his phone, willing it to ring with some good news. The fire crackled in the fireplace as Helen walked over to it, her lovely body silhouetted in the light.

"Do you ever think about us?" she asked quietly, her back to him.

His heartbeat kicked up at the soft seductive tone of her voice, let alone her words. She turned slowly to look at him. He felt young and foolish again. He almost felt tempted. "Helen—"

She cut off whatever else he might have said as she stepped to him, standing on tiptoe to kiss him. Just the touch of her lips ignited a need he'd thought long forgotten. Her free hand cupped the back of his neck, drawing him down as she deepened the kiss.

He took her in his arms, pulling her into him. It had been so long and yet he remembered her mouth on his, her body melded to his. She smiled against his lips as she felt his evident desire and drew back to look into his eyes.

"You haven't forgotten," she said, still smiling that

Cheshire-cat smile of hers, something else that he belatedly remembered. Helen had always loved having the upper hand.

He let go of her. "This isn't the time or place," he said, his voice sounding unusually gruff. In truth, he was half afraid of what would happen if they took this any further right now. Only moments ago, he'd been suspicious of her and hadn't trusted her. She'd broken his heart. How did he know she wouldn't do it again? Maybe he was too old for this.

"What's wrong, Judge?" she teased. "You can't tell me that you don't want me as much as I want you." He shook his head. She was right about that and she knew it. "William, we could have this time together. You aren't really going to let a misunderstanding from so long ago keep us from a second chance?"

His cell phone rang, and she turned away, her back a steel rod of disappointment—or was it anger—as she moved to the bar to freshen her drink.

JJ WIPED HER bleeding nose and sat up, the blanket that had been wrapped around her falling to the floor. She didn't know how long she'd been out. She touched her neck where the man had choked her into unconsciousness. Her throat hurt. Who was she kidding? Her whole body hurt. She felt as if she'd been beaten. But why wouldn't she, after everything that had happened to her, including being thrown off a bridge into the river? She'd almost drowned.

She'd been surprised when she'd been hauled into the boat to race across the lake through the darkness. At first she'd thought she'd been rescued even though she was with the same men who'd dragged her naked from the cabin shower. They'd tossed her in the back of the van along with some clothing to wear and told her if she did as she was told, she would live.

She was alive, but for how long? she'd wondered after

she'd seen where they'd taken her after pulling her out of the water. She'd looked up to see huge hulking buildings, piles of logs and old machinery etched against the night sky. Brandemiller Mill near Somers. She'd recognized it the same instant she'd been filled with terror.

The place had an eerie feel to it that had told her it had been abandoned for a very long time. It was the kind of place a body could decompose and never be found. She hadn't been able to hear the traffic on the highway on the other side of the mill, and realized just how alone she was—with three dangerous men. If they'd brought her here to kill her, they'd picked the perfect place.

She'd tried to run only to be grabbed and thrown to the ground. She'd felt the viselike arm around her throat, seen stars flash before her eyes and then nothing. She hadn't even gotten a chance to scream. What little fight she'd managed to put up had gotten her a bloody nose.

Blinking now, she tried to see where she was in the total blackness. The floor under her felt freezing cold. She touched it with her fingertips. Concrete? The rough surface almost felt like rough metal. At least she wasn't back in the root cellar. That alone buoyed her spirits. And the clothing someone had put on her was at least dry and warm. They'd even given her a blanket. That had to be a good sign, right?

Pushing to her feet, she swayed as she managed to stand, the floor feeling as if it wasn't quite level. Lifting her arms over her head, she could feel nothing. As she took a step, her bare foot made a scuffing sound. It echoed, giving her the feeling that she was in a fairly large room.

She swallowed back the panic that rose in her sore throat. She had no idea where she was, let alone what they planned to do with her now. They'd forced her to go with them to the ransom drop after dressing her in some of Geneva's clothing. Her wrists had been bound and duct tape slapped over her mouth.

"You do anything to let Franklin Davenport know that you aren't his precious granddaughter, and the man I have stationed near the bridge will shoot you," Zac had told her. She hadn't seen the man and yet she hadn't doubted that he would kill her if he didn't get the money. What worried her was why they hadn't brought Geneva to the exchange. Also, she'd worried about what they planned to do with her once they had the money.

Now she had a pretty good idea. All they had to do was leave her here. One day, if this sawmill were ever leveled for new development, they'd find her skeletal remains, but by then Zac and his cohorts would be long gone with the briefcase full of money.

Tears filled her eyes. Was this nightmare never going to end? She thought of Thorn and felt a surge of anger. She wanted to live. She would live. She had to. She wiped furiously at her tears as she turned back to retrace her footsteps so she could find the blanket on the floor. She wrapped it around her, determined not to lose her shit. Life had thrown her a few obstacles. The thought made her laugh at how mildly that was putting it. So what if she'd had to improvise a lot to stay alive for at least half of her life? She'd gotten this far, hadn't she? She couldn't give up.

She felt her anger warm her almost down to her bare feet on the cold floor. These people wouldn't get away with this. Somehow she would—

JJ spun around at a sound behind her, trying to see in the total blackness. She'd been so sure she was alone. Now she heard something moving toward her, a steady scrape on the floor headed in her direction.

CHAPTER TWENTY-FIVE

THORN OPENED UP his motorcycle, letting it run through the dark night as fast as he could go. He'd gone through Big Fork headed north, then turned west, taking a road along the north end of Flathead Lake. He had no idea what he was looking for, believing he would know when he saw it.

Where would they take her? To a place where her screams couldn't be heard. Not to kill her, he assured himself. They could have let her drown in the river. Instead, they'd pulled her into the boat. And taken her somewhere boat accessible.

He'd almost reached the town of Somers when he spotted the lit cell phone tower and slowed. Off to his left was Flathead Lake. He thought of the boat the kidnappers had escaped in. Ahead, he could see the lights of Somers and all the new development.

But closer he saw the skeletal remains of the abandoned old sawmill. There were numerous large buildings and rusted equipment next to the lake, along with a huge pile of old logs.

He slowed his bike. The mill was surrounded by a high chain-link that had seen better days. A thick stand of bushes had grown up along the outside of the fence. He hadn't gone far when he saw the wide gate into what had once been a bustling sawmill. He pulled in, his headlight revealing a chain and lock on the gate, but the chain was hanging down, the lock open.

He read the name on the weathered sign: Brandemiller. It appeared to be another connection between Brandemiller and Geneva, and maybe ultimately Zac Judson and the kidnapping—if he was right and JJ was inside here somewhere.

He could see tracks where someone had driven in after the recent thunderstorm. His heart began to pound as he looked at the hulking buildings—so close to the cell tower that had pinged on Geneva's last call. All his instincts told him this was where the call had come from, and that JJ was in there.

But what if they were wrong? If he was wrong, he would be wasting valuable time. He knew he couldn't second-guess himself. He had to go with his gut. He cut his motor and pushed the bike into the bushes to hide it. Taking the small flashlight from his saddlebag, he turned it on and spotted a hole in the chain-link.

Praying his instincts were right this time, he slipped through the hole and into the abandoned sawmill property.

JJ MOVED SLOWLY BACKWARD, her fear growing as she tried to understand who or what was in the room with her. She had no weapon, no real way of seeing what was coming toward her. Nowhere to run.

That became even more clear as she backed up against a cold wall in this windowless room. If that's what it was, a room. The edge of the floor sloped downward. What was she in? Something bowl-shaped.

She didn't have time to think about that. It had been bad enough thinking she was in a room alone. Was there a sick animal in here with her? Something that had crawled in and couldn't find a way out?

JJ tried to still her pounding pulse so she could hear above the sound whatever it was now made as it approached slowly—cautiously? Whatever had been moving across the rough floor toward her stopped. She heard a sound like something alive taking a breath. Her eyes stared into the complete darkness for movement, feeling as if she'd gone blind and deaf, as well.

JJ wiped her nose as it began to bleed again and took a breath of her own, and then froze. Whatever it was in the room with her was moving again. Growing closer. A slow, tenuous sound.

She took a couple of quick steps to the side, hoping to circle around whatever it was—until she stepped in something wet, making a splashing sound. She froze in place, realizing that she'd been heard. Whatever was in the room with her had heard her and now knew exactly where she was.

The smell of the liquid rose around her—stagnant water? She hoped that was all it was as she held her breath and listened. If she moved, she would be heard.

"I know you're there." The low whisper echoed ghost-like through the space.

Goose bumps rippled over JJ's flesh.

FRANKLIN FELT NUMB. He didn't remember calling Willie after the bungled ransom drop. Nor did he remember driving home. Now as he walked in his front door, he headed directly to the bar and poured himself a drink. He took a swig of it, swallowed and turned to see Helen and Willie staring at him.

"I suppose you've heard," he said, his voice rough with emotion.

"I was waiting for you," Willie said. "I haven't told Helen anything."

She moved to Franklin to put her hand on his arm. "Is Geneva...?"

"I don't know," Franklin said with a defeated sigh. "They didn't bring her. They brought her dead ringer. I didn't get a good look at her until they were getting away."

"Getting away with the money?" Helen asked.

Franklin nodded, finished his drink and poured himself another.

At the sound of the front door opening and closing, they all turned. Curtis stopped at the edge of the living room. "I'm sorry. I knocked but when no one answered I came on in." His usually impeccable attire was filthy.

Franklin frowned. He hadn't even realized that his chief financial officer hadn't been in the room. "What happened to you?"

"I went to run an errand and had car trouble in the middle of nowhere," Curtis said.

"An errand?" the judge asked.

Curtis looked around as if confused. "Helen asked me to pick up some Advil for her. What's happened?"

"I might have mentioned..." Helen began and stopped. Franklin saw Helen turn to the judge and shake her head as if she hadn't asked Curtis to pick anything up for her.

"What's going on?" Franklin demanded at the undercurrent in the room.

"What kind of car trouble?" WT asked.

"I didn't get very far and I had a flat. I changed that, and not far up the road the engine just quit running. I had to call a garage. The mechanic said one of the wires had come undone?" Curtis shook his head. "I just bought the car. The mechanic said I shouldn't be having these kinds of problems." He turned to Helen. "I'm sorry, I completely forgot about your pills I was so anxious to get back here."

"I'm sorry I mentioned them," she said.

"The ransom drop didn't go well," the judge said. "The kidnappers got away with the money."

"What about your granddaughter?" Curtis asked.

Franklin shook his head and excused himself. He heard Willie follow him into his den. "What was all that about out there?" he demanded the moment his friend closed the door.

"Curtis left right after you and just returned."

He frowned. "He said he went to get Advil for Helen and had car trouble. What of it?"

"Helen said she didn't know where he'd gone, that he'd made an excuse and left in a hurry."

"What are you saying?" Franklin demanded.

"That it's suspicious. Are you sure you trust him?"

He raked a hand through his hair. "I'm not sure I trust anyone." He met Willie's gaze. "Tell me Geneva isn't dead."

As THORN HEADED into the mill, keeping to the shadows of the dilapidated buildings, he heard seagulls squawking overhead, then an eerie silence. He passed a building with a huge rusted saw blade sticking up from a rotting wooden table. Large rusted equipment sat silent and unused.

As he passed other cavernous buildings, he found them empty and dark and cold. The mill felt unearthly quiet, forgotten and desolate enough that anything could happen here without the rest of the world knowing.

He came around the corner of one building to see a black sports car ahead. His instincts had been right. Zac was here. But was JJ with him? The men could have dumped her in the middle of the lake.

Thorn shoved the thought away. His gut couldn't be

wrong. Not this time. But where was everyone? This place was huge. He walked over to the sports car, not surprised to find it empty. He considered all the buildings he would have to go in to find JJ and whoever had taken her. His instincts told him there wasn't time and there was a faster, more efficient way of getting whoever was here to come to him.

He saw the glint of a lighter lying on the console and tried the door. Unlocked. Taking the lighter, he moved to the gas tank. As he did, he tore a strip of his shirt off. Lighting one end, he dipped the other into the tank, then he ran to dive behind the closest building. He barely got behind it before the car blew.

The loud explosion lit the sky, sending a cloud of smoke and debris into the air.

JJ LET OUT the breath she'd been holding as she recognized the whisper. "Geneva?"

The woman began to cry in huge quaking sobs that echoed in the chamber. JJ stepped out of the pooled water on the floor and moved toward the sound, feeling her way in the blackness. She found the woman crouched on the floor and knelt to put an arm around her. She felt as if she knew this woman, maybe because she'd once been this young. Or because she'd been living vicariously through this woman for some time. Not to mention sleeping in her bed when necessary.

"What's going on?" JJ asked. When Geneva kept bawling, she gently shook her. "Tell me. What are you doing in here?"

It took the young woman a few minutes to pull herself together. JJ couldn't see her face, but she could hear her sniff, wipe her nose on her sleeve and sniff again before she spoke. "I was tricked. He tricked me. I thought he loved me."

"Zac." JJ had seen how cold-blooded the man was when he'd forced her to follow him over the bridge to collect the ransom and later tossed her over the side into the river. "Do you know where he is now?" With her arm still around Geneva, she could feel her shaking her head. "Do you know why he put us in here?"

That made the young woman begin to cry harder.

"Do you know what kind of room we're in?"

In between her sobs, Geneva managed to get the words out. "It's not a room. It's a water tank."

She felt her eyes widened in alarm as she recalled the stagnate water she'd stepped in. Why would the man put them in a water tank? The question made her heart race. "Did he tell you anything when he put you in here?"

"He said he would come back for me, but I knew he wouldn't. Then he drugged me."

JJ wasn't about to tell her that Zac already had the money.

As THE FLAMES of the burning sports car began to diminish, Thorn stayed where he was and waited. The first man who appeared in the glow of the burned-out car wasn't Zac Judson.

But he would do, Thorn thought as he crept quickly through the dark shadows and circled to come up behind the man just as he started to turn. There was that instant when the man's eyes widened in alarm, but by then Thorn had his arm around the man's throat.

"Where is JJ?" he demanded. The man seemed to be trying to speak. He loosened his hold a little. "Where is the woman?"

"Zac has them in the tank room."

Them? "Where's the tank room?"

The man motioned toward the west. With a twist of

the man's head, Thorn knocked him out and then dragged him back into the darkness. Whoever else was here would have heard the explosion, but only one man came to check it out. That meant whoever was left was busy. Busy tying up loose ends.

As he headed deeper into the mill, he heard what sounded like machinery start up. He thought of the saw blade he'd seen, then reminded himself that the man had said the women were in the tank room.

It wasn't a saw blade that had started up. It was a pump engine.

Heart in his throat, he ran toward the sound.

JJ LISTENED. That boom earlier. It had sounded like an explosion. Was Zac planning to burn this whole place down with them inside? Not likely, since they were in a water tank.

So had someone else caused the explosion? She knew better than to hope. But she couldn't help herself. Thorn Grayson had come to her rescue so many times already. Why not one more time?

"What was that sound?" Geneva whispered. "Do you think they're trying to open the door to get us out?"

"It sounded like an explosion."

"An explosion?" Geneva started to cry again. "This is all my fault. I just wanted it to stop. I told Zac I was done. He was so angry. He said I had to go with him to pick up the money, that my grandfather was insisting and that I wasn't going to ruin this for him. When I refused, he hit me and then…" She began to cry again.

"He took me instead," JJ said. Geneva quit crying. She could feel the woman's gaze on her even in the pitch-blackness.

"He took *you*?"

"You're lucky you didn't go. He threw me off the bridge

into the river with my hands bound and my mouth covered with duct tape. I almost drowned."

Geneva began to cry again, heart-wrenching sobs.

"Stop crying, so I can listen," JJ snapped.

She'd heard a loud clank just outside. Maybe Geneva was right, and Zac was coming for them. He'd put them in here because even if they had screamed their hearts out, no one would have heard.

JJ knew she was clutching at straws. She waited for the door to open. There had to be a door. How else had Zac gotten them in here?

Geneva seemed to be listening, as well. At least she'd quit crying. There was another clank, then another. Then a sound that turned JJ's spine to jelly. A roaring sound as if a huge valve had opened.

She pulled Geneva to her feet only an instant before water gushed in, nearly knocking them both off their feet.

CHAPTER TWENTY-SIX

THORN RACED TOWARD the sound of the running pump. As he came closer, he heard yet another sound. The roar of water. His chest tightened, making it hard to breathe as he ran. The man had said JJ was in the tank room. As in *water* tank?

A huge building loomed in front of him. He turned on his flashlight as he shoved open the door. The sound of his footfalls on the old wooden floor echoed through the large empty building. He kept running, burst through another door that led along a walkway to yet another old structure.

The sound of the pump and the roaring water was growing louder. It couldn't be that far now. Fear had him breathing hard. He rushed through the musty smelling building, his flashlight beam skittering over the dusty floor as he followed the footprints. He had no idea how many kidnappers were still on the property.

But he knew there had to be at least one more—the person who'd started the pump and had now turned on the water. Thorn couldn't be sure how many people Zac and Geneva had involved or how many of them were now dead. The man had said they were in the tank room. They. Did that mean that Geneva was still alive?

He suspected that the kidnapping hadn't gone as Zac and Geneva had planned. It went awry that first night when Baker and JJ hadn't died in the plane crash. Otherwise, they could have collected their ten million and been long gone by now.

But now Zac had the money. So why was he here tonight in this desolate abandoned sawmill? And how many cohorts were with him? Franklin had said there were two in the boat that picked up Zac and JJ.

One of them was now out cold near the burned-up sports car. One of them had been driving the boat. Had he left? Or was he still here, the boat pulled up on the shore? He assumed if the man was still on the property he would have come running when he'd heard the explosion. So hopefully, that only left Zac.

So where was the man?

As Thorn burst out of the building, he came around a corner and got his answer.

THE WATER ROSE QUICKLY, lapping up their legs. JJ pulled Geneva over to the side where she found what felt like an imperfection in the inside of the tank. A piece of the metal stuck out like a very narrow step only wide enough to put a foot on. She searched frantically for more but found only one—just large enough for one person to balance on.

"Stand on this," she ordered, reaching down into the water to guide the younger woman's foot to the step. "Don't move, okay?"

JJ knew there had to be a door that they'd been brought in. She moved through the water as quickly as she could, feeling her way along the sides of the tank as the water continued to rush in and rise around them.

She searched for something, anything to use to get them out of here. She wouldn't let herself accept that it was futile. Or that no one knew they were here.

What would Thorn have done, though, when he found

her missing? The thought broke her heart. They'd gotten so close in such a short time. She thought of his heartbreak. Now he was about to lose another woman he'd cared about unless she could find a way out of this.

She found the seam in the wall where the door opened and pounded on it with her fist. Then felt around under the water for something to use, anything she could pry with. She found a small jagged piece of what felt like rock, but quickly realized it was useless at opening the door. She pocketed the rock and continued around the tank, not sure what she hoped to find. Some way to stop the water or to escape.

Was Zac out there listening to the water rise? Was he waiting until the tank filled completely before he walked away?

The water was already up to her waist. Soon they would be swimming, but how long could they do that? Maybe it wouldn't matter because if the water kept rising, it would completely fill the tank and they would drown.

Heart dropping, JJ realized that she might have finally found herself in a situation where there was absolutely nothing she could do about it.

ZAC JUDSON CAME at him with a large wrench. Thorn had just enough time to leap to the side, the blow catching him in the shoulder as he swung his flashlight. It smashed into the side of the man's face.

He heard Zac let out a cry of pain and started to pull his weapon. But the man moved faster than he'd expected, coming at him again with the raised heavy wrench gripped in both of his hands and blood running down the side of his face.

Thorn ducked under the man's outstretched arms and

the heavy wrench, plowing into him and driving him back. Zac lost his balance, flailing for a moment before he went down. Thorn went with him, smashing his fist into the man's face as they hit the ground.

Zac brought the wrench down on his back. The blow stole his breath, but he still managed to pull his weapon from its holster. He shoved the barrel into Zac's neck, but was knocked off balance as the man rolled to the side and brought down the wrench once again, this time aiming for Thorn's head.

Zac was strong, and he was a fighter. He had ten million reasons why he needed to win this one. Thorn had only one: JJ. That made him even more determined. He feared he was fighting for her life.

He pulled the trigger. The wrench clattered to the ground next to his head an instant before he rolled to his side away from Zac. As he got to his feet, he looked over at the dead man. His shoulder and back hurt as he holstered his weapon. He picked up the wrench and limped toward the sound of the grinding pump.

As he came around the side of the building in front of him, he saw the water tank and what Zac had done to the door into it and felt his heart drop.

"HE'S GOING TO kill us!" Geneva cried as she swayed on the tiny step, her head still way above water.

"Stop!" JJ ordered. "You're safe for the moment. Just stay where you are and keep quiet. I think I heard something."

JJ thought she'd heard a gunshot over the sound of the water filling the tank. Maybe she had imagined it. Her eyes filled with tears. *Don't let anything happen to Thorn*, she prayed silently even as she couldn't help but hope that he'd found her and that he was coming to save them.

But as the water rose to her chest, she knew time was running out. Soon they would be swimming, and she could feel Geneva getting more panicked by the moment. She tried to hang on to the side of the tank next to Geneva. Her body wanted to float away from the side as the water lapped higher and higher.

THORN TOOK ONLY an instant to assess the situation. He rushed to the pump next to the large water tank. The moment he did, he saw that he wouldn't be needing the wrench. Zac had seen to that. He'd sabotaged it so there was no stopping the water now.

With a curse, he could hear the water filling the tank. It didn't sound as if it had completely filled yet. He knew JJ had to be inside, and yet he tapped on the side of the tank with the wrench and pressed his ear to the cold metal. He tapped again, praying for a sound from within.

And then it came. A distant *tap, tap, tap.* His heart soared, but how was he going to get her out? He tapped again and heard the answering tap before he rushed to the door and tried to open it, only to find Zac had broken off the latch, a piece of pipe still jammed into it.

But there had to be a drain. He had to move some debris away, but managed to find the drain and open it. Water gushed out in a steady stream, but more was being pumped in than was coming out.

His mind raced. There had to be another way.

He backed away to look toward the top of the tank. He spotted a large cap with a hatch on it that could be opened— if he could get to it.

Hurrying around to the side of the tank, he saw that the

old metal stairway to the top of the tank lay in pieces on the ground.

But at the back, he spotted a stone structure adjacent to the tank. It was a few yards from it. If he could climb up the rough rockwork... He reached up, grabbed the edge of the stone, his fingers digging into the decaying mortar, and began to climb.

JJ HAD FELT her heart soar when she'd heard the taps on the tank. She'd pulled the rock from her pocket and answered. Someone was outside. Someone knew they were trapped in here. It had to be Thorn, she told herself as tears burned her eyes. He'd come to save her again.

But the water was up to their necks, splashing into their faces. Geneva could no longer stay on the tiny step. They were forced to swim to keep their heads above water, and she wasn't sure how much longer they could last.

The water had risen to the point where she could tell from the sound that there wasn't that much room above their heads.

"He's going to save us," she told Geneva, who was beginning to get hysterical again. "You have to believe me. You have to hang on."

"I don't know that I can. I'm so tired," she cried and sputtered as her head went under. JJ grabbed hold of her and pulled her to the surface.

"Fight!" she yelled at the young woman. "You have to fight."

But she could feel that Geneva didn't have much fight left in her.

THORN PULLED HIMSELF up the last few stones. He could see where there used to be a catwalk across to the top of the tank. But the boards had rotted away over the years, leaving only a little of the original framework.

He considered trying it, feeling time running out, but decided not to trust it. His only other option was to leap across the expanse and grab hold of the edge of the cap on top of the tank. If he missed it...

Missing it wasn't an option, he told himself as he considered the drop to the ground. There was no way to get a run at it as he teetered on the edge of the stone building, which like the rest of the place was eroding. He was able to take one step back, and no longer hesitating, he jumped.

For a moment, he thought he'd misjudged the distance. One foot landed on the rounded top of the tank and began to slide, the other dangling in midair. He scrambled, like he'd never scrambled before. His right hand found purchase, locking down on the rusted edge of the tank's cap.

He held on for a moment to catch this breath before he pushed with his one foot on the tank and managed to grip the edge of the cap with his other hand and pull himself to the apex. The top of the tank was slightly flattened and large enough that he could stand. He worked to open the cover, feeling time running out.

CHAPTER TWENTY-SEVEN

WHEN THE LID on the top of the tank opened, JJ heard the sound and looked up. For a moment she was shocked at how close the water had already risen. She saw stars in the night sky and heard Thorn's voice and began to cry. She'd known that if anyone could rescue them, it would be him. And yet, like Geneva, she had been losing hope.

"How do we get out?" Geneva cried, swimming over to look up.

"I think I can reach you," Thorn yelled as JJ heard him sprawled on the top and extend his arm into the tank.

"You go first," JJ said to Geneva, who reached up. Thorn clasp her arm and pulled as Geneva kicked her feet frantically.

"Easy," Thorn told her as he pulled her up.

JJ trod water, feeling the water and exhaustion taking its toll. And then Thorn was reaching for her. The moment he grabbed her arm, she knew she was going to be all right. He pulled her up and into the starry night, as in the distance she heard the sound of sirens over Geneva's crying.

She sat on the edge of the tank's opening along with Geneva and Thorn, the three holding on to each other, as the rising water in the tank spilled over. JJ breathed in the summer night and leaned into Thorn's strong body. She'd never been so glad to be alive.

AS THE JUDGE pocketed his phone, he turned to the others waiting anxiously for the news. "Thorn found JJ and Geneva. They're both alive and safe."

Franklin looked as if he was about to collapse with relief. He leaned on the back of a chair as if to catch his breath.

"What about the kidnappers?" Helen asked.

"One dead, another taken into custody," WT said. "There is a third, but I'm sure they'll find him. Thorn had to call the police because the three of them had to be rescued from the top of a water tank."

"Is Zac the deceased?" Franklin asked.

WT nodded.

Helen sighed, looking relieved. "Thank God it's over, then," she said, before adding, "I could use a drink. How about the rest of you?"

"What about the money?" Curtis asked.

The judge shook his head. "I don't know. It could be gone."

"I don't give a damn about the money," Franklin said as he followed Helen to the bar. "I just didn't want that bastard Zac getting it."

"I think you should be ready for the fallout," WT said as he waved off a drink. "The police will have all kinds of questions. I'm sure the FBI will be involved. They won't be happy that we didn't call them right away."

"I just want to see my granddaughter," Franklin said, his voice breaking. "Until I see her…" He took a gulp of the drink Helen had made him and then cleared his throat. "Then I'll deal with whatever I have to."

WT knew his friend was strong and could handle what he had to know was coming with the conclusion of this affair. He just wasn't sure Franklin realized how bad it would get before it was truly over.

"Will you be needing me?" Curtis asked as he picked up his briefcase.

Franklin nodded. "Please stay a little longer. There are a few things I need you to take care of. Let's talk in my office."

"You're going to just let him leave?" Helen asked WT as Curtis left the room and Franklin followed him down to the hall.

"I've verified that he was where he said he was during the ransom drop," WT said. "He wasn't one of the kidnappers, Helen."

She raised a brow. "Well, you know best." She let out a laugh, before adding, "Judge." She took a sip of her drink, studying him over the rim of her glass, her blue eyes dark with emotion.

"I trust Curtis," Franklin said, weighing in as he came back into the room and heard the conversation. He also must have felt the tension between them. "I never trusted Zac." He walked to the window and looked out. "Shouldn't they be here by now?"

"I think that's them now," WT said as he saw the police vehicles pull up along with Thorn on his motorcycle. JJ and Geneva climbed out of the back of a police car. "Let me talk to law enforcement. I'll hold them off as long as I can." He went to the door as Geneva and JJ came up the walk. They were both soaked to the skin. "Helen, can you find some clothing for these women?" he asked over his shoulder as he went out to speak with the police officers and then Thorn.

DAYLIGHT CREPT THROUGH the large window that looked out over the lake. JJ realized she'd lost track of time. She felt exhausted, empty and cold inside, as if everything that had happened to her had finally hit home. She was still shivering after the hot shower and the change of clothing even though she was standing in front of the fireplace. It felt as if someone had been trying to kill her for days—and almost had. Just the thought of being in that tank... She shuddered and Thorn stepped to her to put his arm around her.

Like her, he'd been given dry clothing to wear. She suspected it was Franklin's given the look of it—golf shorts and matching T-shirt. JJ again found herself wearing some of Geneva's clothing that apparently she'd left at her grandfather's house for when she visited. After all, he had a large swimming pool, hot tub and sauna out back. JJ had never seen such a huge place. It was like a castle. She wondered if he got lonely here, all by himself except for the staff.

Franklin had been pacing the floor since hearing from Thorn and JJ about what had happened. After wrapping his granddaughter in his arms, rocking back and forth with her for a few minutes, Helen had taken a sobbing Geneva to one of the guest bathrooms so she could also get a shower and change into dry clothing.

Now as Geneva came into the living room with Helen following her, she was no longer crying. She'd fixed her hair and even applied makeup, JJ saw. The young woman was nothing if not resilient, she thought.

"We need to talk," Franklin said. "Please sit down. We don't have much time." Geneva looked as if she might argue, but something in his tone must have warned her not to. She sat on the edge of a chair as if not planning to stay long.

While Geneva had been showering and changing, the judge had taken Franklin aside to talk to him. When the two had returned to the living room, JJ had seen that Franklin had been upset.

"I need to hear your side of the story, Geneva," her grandfather said now. "But—" He stopped her before she began to speak. "*Do not lie*. I need the truth if I am going to be able to help you."

Geneva looked around the room for a moment as if not wanting to say anything in front of the others gathered there.

"All these people helped save you," Franklin said, cutting her off as if seeing where her thoughts had been headed. "We all need to hear it."

The young woman took a breath and let it out slowly. "None of this is my fault."

"I said don't lie. Are you telling me you had *nothing* to do with the kidnapping?" her grandfather demanded. "Geneva, you're in enough trouble. Lying right now would be a very bad mistake."

"I was almost killed!" she cried.

Franklin's voice remained calm. "I need to know what part you played in the kidnapping, Geneva. I can't keep the police at bay much longer."

Geneva glanced toward the window as if in surprise that they hadn't left. JJ realized that the young woman had no idea how much trouble she was in.

"It started as a joke. I wasn't *serious*." Geneva began to cry. Her grandfather handed her a tissue and waited. Slowly she raised her head, wiped her eyes and lifted her chin indignantly. "I was angry. I didn't feel you were being fair with me. I *jokingly* suggested kidnapping myself."

"How did it go from a joke to so many people dying?" Franklin asked, sounding tired and old and brokenhearted.

Geneva looked away for a moment, licked her lips and sighed. "Zac asked me how I would do it. I had no idea but the more we talked about it, a plan kind of emerged." She looked at her grandfather. "I knew you wouldn't want me to ever be in danger, so I had this idea." Giving JJ a sheepish look, she said, "I never dreamed anything would actually happen to her."

"Other than being abducted by force from your house?" her grandfather said in obvious disgust. "How was it you thought no one would get hurt?" Geneva shook her head and began to cry again.

"Whose idea was it to steal the plane?" the judge asked.

"Zac said the thing to do would be to get the kidnappers and the pretend me far away from here until we picked up the money. Then they could come back, but by then we would be long gone with the money. It was Zac's idea to ask for ten million. I would have been happy with five."

"How frugal of you," her grandfather said.

"No one was supposed to get hurt," she said plaintively.

"Whose idea was it to leave your phone in your bedroom?" JJ asked.

"Mine," Geneva said, brightening. "I knew my grandfather had put a tracking device on it. So I always left it behind when I didn't want him to know where I'd gone." She smiled and shrugged.

"So it was your idea to have the kidnappers pick it up when they took JJ?" Thorn asked.

Geneva frowned. "Did they?" She looked confused. "I guess I never thought about it. Why would they do that? I mean, then my grandfather would know where they went."

"So you didn't know the plane was supposed to crash with your phone on board?"

Her eyes widened. "No, I swear. Zac promised that no one would get hurt. It was an accident. He said it was an accident. He was really upset about it."

"No, Geneva," Franklin said. "It wasn't an accident. He was really upset because one of the kidnappers survived— and so did your double."

"I don't understand what you're saying," she cried.

"We believe the plane was disabled and the pilot given the wrong coordinates to the airstrip, and it crashed in the mountains. Everyone—including what was thought to be you—was to die," the judge said. "There were explosives on board."

She was shaking her head. "That's crazy. It doesn't make any sense. Eventually, someone would realize it wasn't me in that plane."

"But by then, you and Zac would have the ten million dollars and have disappeared. Wasn't that the plan?" Thorn asked.

"Zac said they would come back safely," Geneva said. "We never wanted anyone to be hurt otherwise I would never have gone along with it."

"You weren't aware of the phone calls Zac made to me demanding the ransom money even after the plane crash?" her grandfather challenged.

"Well, yes, but…" She looked around the room as if hoping to find someone who would help her and, finding none, looked at the floor.

"What about the man who fell off the balcony at the house you rented on the lake?" Thorn asked.

"The man was threatening Zac!" she cried. "They got in an argument and the man fell. I didn't see it, but Zac told me about it."

"The man was the one of the kidnappers who survived the plane crash," the judge said. "They argued because John Baker had figured out that Zac had set him up, planning for him to die when the plane went down—if not in the explosion."

Geneva's expression crumpled. "But I didn't know any of this. I was a victim too."

"Why does Ridge Brandemiller think you owe him money?" Thorn asked.

The young woman avoided her grandfather's gaze. "I haven't paid him yet for building my house. It wasn't my fault. When my allowance got cut... Ridge has been a real jerk, threatening me."

"Is that why you told Zac about the Brandemiller plane?" Thorn asked. "You did know about the plane."

Geneva squirmed on the edge of her seat. "I'd been up in Ridge's plane when we were dating—"

"*Dating?* The man is married," Franklin said. "Not to mention old enough to be your father."

She waved that off. "Zac was trying to figure out a way to get his friends and the woman they kidnapped—"

"JJ," Thorn said. "The woman who helped save your life."

Geneva's eyes filled with tears again. "Why are you all so angry with me? I almost *died.* Zac never planned to take me with him. All he wanted was the money." She bit her lower lip for a moment. "He *used* me."

"Well, you got that part right," her grandfather said.

"But now it's over," she said brightly as she wiped at her tears.

"Geneva, it's far from over," Franklin said. "You are facing criminal charges. People have died because of you. Others have risked their lives to find you. You'd be dead now if it wasn't for these people."

She swallowed. "*Criminal charges?* But I didn't really *do* anything."

Her grandfather sighed. "You were part of a kidnapping scheme. At any point until almost the end, you could have stopped it."

"But by then—"

"There are no excuses for what you've done," Franklin said, getting to his feet.

"We have lawyers," Geneva cried. She looked to Helen.

"You can get me out of this. Isn't that why you're paid so much?"

"Not nearly enough," Helen said as she put down her drink glass. "I wasn't going to tell your grandfather until later, but now is as good a time as any. I quit. I'm going to let you handle this from here on out without my help."

Geneva mugged a face as Helen walked out. "You have other lawyers," she said to her grandfather. "Probably better lawyers than her. You can't let your only granddaughter go to jail."

"I'm afraid it is worse than jail," he said. "You're looking at prison."

"Prison?" she cried. "No." She laughed, shaking her head. "I know you're angry and I don't blame you, really. You must have been worried about me. But you wouldn't let me go to prison."

"It won't be up to me, Geneva."

"But I was…*manipulated.*" When she saw she was getting nowhere, she said, "Fine. I'll throw myself on the mercy of the court. No judge or jury can look at me and think I belong in jail, let alone prison."

Silence filled the room.

She looked around at everyone for a moment, before her expression turned sour, marring her pretty young face as she turned on JJ. "What about *her*? She got herself kidnapped. She was in *my* house. She had no right to—"

"Shut up, Geneva," her grandfather snapped. "I've never struck you. I'd like to leave it that way. But if you say one more word against this woman…"

The judge stood. "I think we're done here." He turned to Franklin. "The police are outside, and the FBI has been called. They will be here soon. With Helen gone—"

"I'll take care of everything," he said, suddenly looking

his age. Geneva looked shell-shocked, as if this couldn't be happening to her. JJ knew the feeling.

As she walked out with the judge and Thorn, she heard Geneva begging her grandfather to save her. To blame it on someone else. To bribe the police or a judge who owed him a favor.

"I'm so sorry I got you involved in this," WT said to Thorn. He looked to JJ. "Are you going to be all right?" She nodded and hugged herself. "The police and FBI will want to talk to you, but I know Franklin will see that you get the best lawyer money can buy if it comes to anything. I don't think it will. He won't let you be charged. You helped save his granddaughter's life." He turned to Thorn. "They'll want to talk to you too. But I would imagine you're anxious to get back home. You have livestock, right?"

"I've had a friend looking after my horses and mule." He didn't sound anxious to get home, but he didn't deny it either, JJ noticed.

"I'll explain that to the police and FBI. You can go home and take care of your place. I'm sure we'll talk soon," the judge said, and walked toward the officers waiting at the curb.

As she and Thorn started to head toward his motorcycle, it finally hit her that she had no clothes, no car. Hopefully, she still had a job, but that could change if it came out how she was involved in Geneva Davenport's kidnapping.

The door opened behind them, and Curtis Hunt came out calling JJ's name. "Mr. Davenport wanted you to have this." He handed her an envelope. "This is for you," the man said to Thorn as he tried to hand him an envelope, as well.

"I don't want his money," Thorn said.

"It's merely reimbursement for your pickup," Curtis assured him.

Thorn laughed. "I will miss Gertrude, but she wasn't worth much. Tell him thanks anyway. I'm fine."

"Thorn's right," she said, looking down at the envelope in her hand. None of this was anyone's fault but her own. She didn't deserve any money, and said as much around the lump in her throat.

"The two of you saved Geneva's life. I can assure you Mr. Davenport would give everything he has to have his grand-daughter safe. He owes you both a lot more than what is in these envelopes. He will be very upset if you don't take them."

"He's right. You lost your car and all your clothing," Thorn said as he took the envelope Curtis was still offering him and handed it to her. "Stop feeling guilty," he said as he put his arm around her and led her toward his motorcycle.

"How does a person do that?" she asked, her voice breaking as she heard Curtis go back inside the house.

"One day the sun comes out and you realize you're only human," Thorn said. "And you cut yourself some slack."

At least that was his philosophy, Thorn thought. Or had been. Right now, he wasn't sure of anything except one truth. He didn't want to leave this woman, and yet he also didn't know what he had to offer her.

"We should get your duffel bag from Miguel's," he said.

On the drive back to the cabin, he realized that he'd been so involved in finishing this job for the judge and making sure JJ and Geneva were safe, that he hadn't thought past the next minute. He had no plan.

When he stopped the bike behind the bar, JJ hopped off. He shut off the motor and saw that she hadn't started toward the cabin. She stood with her hands in the front pockets of her jeans, balancing on her toes nervously.

"You don't have to stay," she said. "You need to get home to your animals."

That much was true. "Where will you go now?" he asked.

"I have a friend I'm going to stay with until I get a car and some clothing."

He looked at her, not believing a word of it. But it was clear that she was trying to get rid of him. "Let's get your duffel bag and I'll take you there."

She shook her head. "I already sent a text to my friend. She's picking me up here."

"Then I'll wait until she comes," he said.

"No." Her voice softened. "You need to get to your animals." *Back to your life.* She didn't say it, but he heard it in her words. She'd been trying to get rid of him since he first laid eyes on her. But he'd thought all of that had changed. He thought...what did he think? It wasn't as if she'd said she loved him. He hadn't said the words either. Three little words he'd sworn he would never say again.

"Jenny Jo—"

"Please, Thorn." She sounded close to tears. "We both need time. It's best if we say goodbye now."

"I don't want to leave you." His voice broke.

She looked away. "We need time to process all of this."

He couldn't argue that, logically, but his heart ached at the thought of not waking up next to her. They'd been through so much together. They'd shared so much in such a short time.

JJ finally looked at him. "You need to get back to Gertrude and not worry about me. I'm going to be fine."

He smiled then. "I know you are."

JJ WAITED UNTIL Thorn left before she walked over to the bar. Miguel was serving food to one of the tables. When he spotted her, he hurried over.

"Thorn?" he asked.

"He's gone home."

Miguel nodded sadly. "The special?"

She chuckled. "Please, then I have a favor to ask."

"The cabin is yours as long as you need it."

"You didn't tell me you could read minds as well as cook."

"I'm a man of many talents. Have a seat. I'll get you a beer. You look like you could use one."

She took a chair at the bar. The place was empty this time of day—too early for lunch for most people—except for the two men Miguel had just served. She put her elbows on the bar and propped her head on her hands, feeling the weight of the world on her shoulders. Thorn had gone home. It was where he needed to be.

Tomorrow she would find a cheap car to buy, pick up what clothing she needed. She hadn't even looked in the two envelopes stuffed in her jeans pocket. Hopefully, it was enough to last her for a while until she got her next check. Then it would be life as usual—except that she would find a cheap place to live. Maybe she would stay here, depending on what Miguel charged. It wasn't that far from the travel agency.

He slid a beer in front of her. "You're going to be all right."

Tears burned her eyes. She nodded and took a drink. "I'm a survivor."

"Yes, you are." He headed back into the kitchen.

By the time he came back out with two cheese enchiladas, beans and rice, she was sound asleep, her head on her arms. The smell of the food stirred her, and she sat up. Miguel looked at her with such compassion as he put down the plate.

"I wasn't sure I should wake you," he said.

"I'm glad you did. I'm starved." She picked up her fork and took a bite, savoring the flavors. Her stomach growled. "Any chance I could rent the cabin?" She saw him start to offer it to her at no charge. "I pay my own way so don't insult me."

He laughed, shaking his head. "Fine." He gave her a ridiculously low price. "And that's my only offer, so if you are as smart as I think you are, you'll take it without argument."

"Thank you. Thank you for this too," she said as she took another bite.

He left her to check on his only other table. She ate, feeling her strength and resolve come back. She would do what she had set out to do. With the low rent of the cabin, she would be able to pay off her debt much sooner.

By the time she finished most everything on her plate, she almost felt like her old self again. She left money on the bar for her meal and a tip. Franklin had given her way too much money. Then add the same amount that he'd given Thorn that Thorn had insisted she take, she knew she could find a used car and some clothing and still have enough left to pay for the cabin and food here at the bar.

Outside, the sun had come up on another summer day. She breathed in the scent of the pines as she walked to the cabin. She could do this. She really was a survivor.

But as she pushed open the cabin door, she felt a sharp tug at her heart. Thorn was everywhere in this room. For a moment, she hesitated, fighting the memories of being in his arms.

Then she stepped in, knowing that it wasn't just this cabin he lurked in. He'd imprinted himself on her. She would carry those memories always.

She closed the door, stumbling to the bed. As she lay down, she could smell his scent on the sheets. She pulled them over her and drifted off to sleep.

CHAPTER TWENTY-EIGHT

JJ woke to the sound of a horn outside the cabin. She sat up, seeing that she had fallen into bed fully clothed—in Geneva's clothing. She moved to the window and looked out. Curtis Hunt stood next to an SUV, the driver's side window down, his hand on the horn.

Before he could lay on the horn again, she stepped out and blinked at the brightness, still not fully awake. "Mr. Hunt?"

"Oh, good, you're awake," he said. "Franklin wanted this delivered early so you'd have some way to get to your job. He said you would need new clothing, as well." She stared at him, uncomprehending.

"The SUV," he said, motioning to the one he stood by. "He thought you'd like this color, but if you don't, he insisted you take it back. The name of the dealer is inside. Also, there is a voucher for a year's insurance and license plates."

"Wait, what?" she demanded as he started to walk toward what she realized was a waiting vehicle. "I can't accept that."

Curtis stopped and turned back with a sigh. "Here are your options. You can accept his kind generosity, send him a thank-you note or even call. But, if you refuse it, he will come here himself and believe me, he isn't going to take no for an answer. So please, help me out here. Take the car."

She stared at the pretty pearl-colored SUV. She'd never

owned a new car. Her father had bought her the used sedan when she graduated from high school. But now it was in a wrecking yard somewhere here in this valley with what little clothing she owned no doubt ruined in the back.

When she looked toward Curtis, he was making a fast getaway. "The keys are in the ignition," he called back as he was whisked away by an unseen driver.

She sighed, touched by Franklin Davenport's generosity. At the same time embarrassed by it. She knew she should accept it graciously, but it was hard to accept help.

Glancing at her watch, she saw that she had just enough time to shop for clothing before her first day back at work.

EVERYTHING LOOKED JUST as Thorn had left it when he returned to his place in the mountains. He'd parked his motorcycle in the barn, covered it with the tarp, and after checking his animals, headed for the cabin.

The air smelled just as it always did. The sun had swung across the sky as he'd traveled home, racing along as if running from something rather than racing toward it. Exhaustion pulled at him, making his footsteps slow now. He'd pushed open the door to his cabin. Just like he'd left it.

Had it only been a few days since he'd been woken up in the dark of early morning by the judge's phone call? It seemed a lifetime ago. He'd shuffled in, closing the door behind him, and had stood in the center of his cabin not knowing what to do next.

He'd been content here. Now, he felt lost. He knew he would get back into his routine before long. But right now, it seemed impossible. Everything had changed. He'd changed.

However, for the life of him, he didn't know where to go from here.

Common sense told him not to try to figure it out as

wrung out as he was. He stumbled toward the bed, kicking off his boots before falling on top of the old quilt. He lay there, staring up at the ceiling, JJ haunting his every thought. He saw snapshots of her in his head. Laughing. Cutting those big blue eyes at him. Smiling. He thought of her appetite—in all things. He thought of that moment when he'd seen her in that tank, water up to her neck, and he'd reached for her and she'd grabbed hold and he'd pulled her into his arms. He thought he was too tired to sleep.

It was his last thought before he dropped off into something close to unconsciousness.

It FELT SO strange to be back at work, JJ thought. She'd gone straight to her office and had barely sat down when she got a call from a client wanting to book a trip to New York.

It was as if she'd never been gone. Nothing had changed at her job, in her office, out the window. And yet everything had changed for her. She'd changed.

"It's so good to have you back," her boss said, sticking her head in when JJ had a moment free. "You could have taken more time off if you needed it."

What would have been the point? Thorn had left to get back to his animals on his side of the mountaintop. The judge had come by to get a statement from her to give to the FBI, telling her not to worry.

She'd bought some work clothing and called Franklin Davenport to thank him for the car. He'd sounded tired but glad that she liked the SUV, including the color.

All of what had happened now seemed a blur. The time she'd spent with Thorn had been insane. She told herself that it would have been ridiculous to make any kind of life-changing decisions until she was able to sort it all out in her mind.

She needed to give it some time. At the time, it had seemed like the smart thing to do. After all, she and Thorn had only known each other a matter of days. A person didn't chuck his or her life after a brief love affair, especially one as intense as that one had been, with people trying to kill them.

That's all it had been. A brief love affair. Love. The word made her ache inside because it might have been brief but it had been love she'd felt for Thorn. Still felt for Thorn. She hadn't said the words. And neither had he. But she'd seen it in his gray eyes, felt it when he touched her, heard it in her heartbeat at just the sound of his name. She'd fallen in love with the cowboy.

Love didn't care that their lives were as different as night and day or that they lived miles apart or that they hadn't known each other long. They'd shared so much in such a short time. To not be together after all of it felt as if her heart had been ripped out of her chest.

But she moved through her day, telling herself this was what she had to do.

THORN WOKE TO DAYLIGHT. For a moment, he was confused. Had he only slept a few hours or had he slept almost twenty-four hours? He rose, determined to get back into his routine. That meant feeding his animals. On the way home when he'd stopped for gas, he'd called his friend in the area who'd been feeding his stock and thanked him, assuring him he was headed home and would be taking care of things from here on out.

He pulled on his boots now and headed for the barn. He was glad to see his critters, but found himself going through the motions. He needed to get his garden in if he was going to have one this year. There was that old shed that needed to be torn down and lime to be bought for the outhouse.

At the sound of vehicles coming up the road, he looked out the barn door to see Curtis Hunt pull up in the brand-new gray pickup. Another vehicle pulled up beside it. Thorn didn't recognize the driver.

As Curtis got out, he looked around before taping an envelope to the pickup before heading toward the other rig.

"Hold up there, Curtis!" Thorn called as he stepped out of the barn.

But Curtis didn't hold up. He hopped into the other vehicle, and the driver quickly did a highway patrol turn and took off down the mountain.

Thorn cursed as he walked to the new truck and pulled off the envelope stuck to the window. A set of keys jangled inside. He dug out the note and read:

There isn't enough money in the world to thank you. Nor any way to thank you. Please, at least let me replace your truck. I consider this a favor.
Franklin

Thorn swore again before considering the shiny new rig. It wasn't Gertrude, but he supposed it would do. Taking the keys, he opened the door and slid behind the wheel. The inside smelled like soft new leather instead of dust, oily rags and that hint of mud mixed with manure he'd grown accustomed to. He turned the engine over, revved it and turned it off.

His cell phone rang. Seeing it was the judge, he picked up.

"You all right?" the judge asked.

He'd been better. But he'd been worse too. "I'm fine. Franklin bought me a truck."

"I heard he bought JJ an SUV. Accept the gift," WT said without hesitation. "Don't be pigheaded and cut off your nose to spite your face."

"I can afford to buy my own truck."

"See what I mean? Be gracious. The man feels he owes you. You could make it a little easy on him. It's just a truck."

It wasn't just a truck. It was a damned expensive one, much more than he needed, but he held his tongue.

"How about you? Are you all right?" Thorn asked.

"I'm fine."

He chuckled. "We both had a hell of a few days there, didn't we?"

"What now?" the judge asked.

"I'm back at my place in the mountains. What about you?"

"Home. Have you heard from JJ?"

Thorn looked out at the mountain. The breeze stirred the pine boughs, the sun warmed the pickup cab and in all that big blue sky, he saw a hawk catch a thermal and rise out of his sight.

"She suggested we take some time to let it all sink in."

"Not bad advice, I guess," the judge said. "I would imagine she's back at work."

"Hopefully, she won't be couch surfing."

"She's staying in the cabin at Miguel's."

That surprised him. He thought there would be too many bad memories there. For him, it would have been too many good ones. "So she's all right?"

"Probably as all right as you are," WT said. "I'm not one to give advice, but you'd be a damned fool if you let her get away."

Thorn laughed. "Never one to give advice, right? Why

don't you take some of that advice for yourself when it comes to Helen."

"Don't worry," WT said. "I won't let her get away."

That surprised Thorn. "I'm glad to hear that." He started to tell the judge that as for him and JJ it wasn't that simple, but realized the man had already disconnected.

Idly, he ran his fingers over the leather steering wheel before he pulled out his phone once more, made a few calls and then pocketed his phone before starting the engine again. "Come on, Gertie," he said. "Let's go for a ride."

JJ WAS IN her office the next day when her phone rang. She picked up. "Jenny Foster, Big Fork, Montana Travel Guides. How may I help you?"

"I'd like to book a trip," said a familiar male voice. Her pulse leaped, and for a moment she couldn't speak. Her heart thumped wildly against her ribs. She hadn't realized how much she'd missed the sound of Thorn's voice.

"Where would you like to go?" she asked, her voice breaking.

"Surprise me," Thorn said. "But only if you're coming with me."

Tears rushed to her eyes. "How long are you planning to be gone?"

"As long as it takes."

"Takes to what?"

"Figure out how the two of us can take the next step."

"The next step?" She felt like a parrot repeating everything he said, but she could barely get a breath out, her chest was so tight.

"I'm not good at long distance relationships."

She swallowed the lump in her throat. "How would you know?"

"You got me there," he said with a chuckle.

"I'm sorry, don't you have some animals that need to be tended to?"

"That's something else we have to work out—where we're going to live."

"I guess that's where it gets complicated." Her line buzzed, signaling there was a client waiting in the outer office.

"I'm going to have to put you on hold. Unless you want to call back and discuss this."

"Put me on hold. I'll wait as long as it takes."

She buzzed the receptionist to tell her she was free and to send the client back. As she started to rise, she was surprised when Franklin Davenport filled her doorway.

"Mr. Davenport," she said as the intimidating figure closed the door before approaching her desk. "What can I do for you?" To her surprise, the man looked nervous. "Would you like to sit down? It's not Geneva, is it?"

He shook his head. "She's fine. Well, as fine as she can be under the circumstances."

"If it's about me talking to the police, I already gave them and the FBI my statement."

Again he shook his gray head. "It's about the reason you were in my granddaughter's house that night."

Her heart dropped. She'd feared that this wasn't over, hadn't she? "Mr. Davenport, I'm so sorry. I know I shouldn't have been there."

"Please, call me Franklin. And that's not what I meant. You were there because of your financial situation. I hope you don't mind, but Willie told me. I can't tell you how much I admire your tenacity in paying off your father's medical debt, but I can't stand by after everything that has happened and do nothing. I know you resisted taking even a little money let alone the vehicle."

"I really appreciated both, but they were too much."

He waved a hand through the air to cut her off. "I didn't come here looking for another thank-you, JJ. I've done something a bit reckless since I didn't ask you first. I paid off your father's medical bills."

She stared at him. "Mr.—"

"Franklin."

"Franklin." She had to sit down, her legs were suddenly too weak. "I… I don't know what to say."

"Say you'll allow me this, since I've already done it. What you did to save my granddaughter…"

She opened her mouth, but nothing came out. "I didn't do it for money or—"

"I know. That's why you have to let me do this."

"It's too much," she finally managed to say, tears filling her eyes.

"It's not near enough. You risked your life because of my granddaughter. You and Thorn both. I will always be in debt to the two of you." Another line rang, signaling that she had another client waiting in the lobby. "You're busy. I'll see my way out. And I insist on paying for the honeymoon."

Honeymoon?

Franklin winked at her. "Anywhere in the world you and Thorn would like to go for as long as you want." With that he left.

The man was delusional. There was no honeymoon without a wedding. And she hadn't heard from Thorn since he'd left. That was, until a few minutes ago. And he still hadn't said those three words. Nor had she even though she knew she loved him.

Her line buzzed again, but before she could answer it, her

doorway filled again. She recognized the cowboy standing there, holding his Stetson and smiling like a fool.

"Want to go for a ride in my new Gertrude?" Thorn asked. "I just checked with your boss. She said you could. When I told her what I had in mind, she said you should."

"What you have in mind?"

"Asking you to marry me." He reached into the pocket of his jean jacket and pulled out a velvet box. "I know you said we should take some time to think about things. If you need more time—"

JJ shook her head as she stepped around her desk and threw herself into his arms.

"I love you, Jenny Jo," he whispered into her ear. "I *love* you."

She drew back to look into the cowboy's gray eyes. She didn't need even another minute. How many times did a man have to rescue a girl before she knew he was the one? Only once, unless she was a fool. And JJ was no fool.

"I love you, Thorn Grayson. But how are we—"

"We'll figure it out. Together," he said, and kissed her, lifting her off her feet. As he set her down again, that grin she loved so much was all over Thorn's face. "You wanna see the ring?"

CHAPTER TWENTY-NINE

THE JUDGE SPOTTED Helen the moment he entered the Kalispell airport. He'd cheated and called ahead so he knew what flight she would be taking and what time she would be boarding. She sat alone near the window at the gate, waiting for her flight. There was a book in her lap, but it was clear she hadn't been reading it. Instead, she was looking out the window as if lost in thought.

He wondered if she might be wishing she'd done things differently in the past. He knew it had certainly been on his mind. He approached her slowly, enjoying just looking at her. She was a beautiful woman, dressed immaculately and with a poise and self-assurance he'd always admired.

She seemed to sense him and turned from the window. He tried to read her expression as she saw him. Definitely surprise registered, but what other emotions she'd felt at seeing him there, she hid well. It was a talent of hers, he realized. The woman was good at hiding her true feelings.

"William," she said, smiling as she moved her large purse for him to sit next to her. "I didn't know you were also traveling today."

He shook his head. "I'm not flying anywhere, Helen. I just came to see you."

"That was very nice of you, but I don't think I mentioned that I was planning to take a trip."

"The way you mentioned your pills to Curtis? No, you didn't."

Her smile faltered. "I'm sorry? Are you keeping tabs on me, Judge?"

"I never really understood what happened between the two of us," he said.

Helen chuckled and seemed to relax. "So that's what this is about? Closure? What do you want me to say, William?" She turned more toward him, her expression one of sympathy. Or maybe it was pity. "I cared about you. I might even have loved you. But it was so long ago, and you made it perfectly clear earlier that you no longer feel anything for me."

"It would have helped back then if I had known you were pregnant with another man's child."

Her expression froze for a moment. "I don't know where you got your information, but—"

"Helen, by now you must realize that I wouldn't be here unless I knew everything." He watched her swallow and look toward the gate longingly. She must have been so sure that she would be getting on a flight today that would eventually land her in South America, where she couldn't be extradited. In another twenty minutes, she would have been gone.

"I don't know what you're talking about."

He chuckled, thinking of all the innocent—and guilty— people who had come before him when he was a judge. He'd been seldom fooled, and yet he'd let Helen and the past blind him in a way that made him feel old and unwise. He resented that the most, he thought. It didn't matter that she'd pulled the wool over Franklin's eyes, as well.

"The man you had the affair with in Mexico was Zachariah Judson," he said. "Your name is on Zac's adoption papers as the lawyer who handled it for the birth mother. All I had to do was the math."

She pursed her lips, her skin paler than it had been only moments ago. "Didn't you question, then, that the baby could have been yours?"

WT shook his head. "No. I knew that if it had been mine, you would have had an abortion. You had no faith that I was going to ever amount to anything. But what I don't know was how Judson and his wife ended up raising your son."

Helen looked away for a moment, her slim throat working. He watched a vein in her neck throb before she finally spoke. "He paid me," she said simply, and turned to glare at him, daring him to say something. "I needed the money."

For a moment, neither of them spoke. Flights were announced overhead along with warnings not to leave bags unattended. Some of the people at her gate had started to stand, anxious to board. He knew none of them were as anxious as Helen, though.

"Why Franklin's granddaughter?" he asked. "Or were your aspirations much larger? His wife had died, and he hadn't remarried. Why settle for ten million when you could have had the whole ball of wax? Franklin, at his age, could fall down the stairs at any time and die. But he wasn't interested in another wife, was he?"

Her eyes narrowed to angry slits. "You think you're so smart. You think you have it all figured out. You know *nothing* about me and never have. Yes, I wanted more than I got. But you're right, Franklin and I did get close. Unfortunately, he wasn't interested in me as anything more than his personal lawyer."

"You got to know Geneva, though."

She let out a bark of a laugh. "What a spoiled, obnoxious brat." Helen practically spat out the words. "If I had married Franklin, I would have gotten rid of her first thing."

WT felt a chill rattle through him. He'd never imagined

that under this beautiful exterior lurked such cold-blooded hatred. "So you'd been in contact with Zac over the years?"

She shook her head. "I'd heard that he was more like me than his father. I'd also heard that he could use some money. He never knew we were related. He merely thought I was his father's lawyer who took care of his adoption. I told him I had a proposition for him. All I had to do was throw him and Geneva together. With his boating background, he had no trouble getting a job teaching sailing up here on the lake. It was just a simple matter of purchasing Geneva sailing lessons for her birthday. Zac did the rest."

"Why wouldn't he opt to simply marry into the family and cut you out of the deal?"

"Because Franklin hated Zac from the moment he laid eyes on him. He was also threatening to cut off all of Geneva's money if she continued to see Zac."

"So the kidnapping."

Helen chuckled. "It was the kind of thing she would have done—if she'd been smart enough. I watched the way Franklin was with her. It was difficult being around someone so wealthy. Didn't you ever want to live like they do?"

WT shook his head. "It always looks better from the outside."

She scoffed at that. "I wanted an easier life. Zac was enough like me that I knew he'd do whatever had to be done. The acorn doesn't fall far from the tree, as they say. You should appreciate that, William. You with your perfect, righteous and law-abiding mother and father. Is that why you had to help all those misguided young people who came before you on the bench? Did you feel guilty that you'd had such an easy life?"

"Again, Helen, it only looked perfect and easy from the outside. Haven't you learned that as you've aged? Things are seldom as they appear. But no matter, it doesn't allow you the excuse to be the way you are just because your life was a little rough. You became a lawyer. How bad could it have been?"

Anger transformed her features into an ugly mask. "I wanted your life and Franklin's all rolled into one," she snapped. "I wanted prestige or at least to have people respect me for the wonderful things I'd done, like you, William. Since I couldn't have that, I went for the money." She lifted her chin. "Don't you dare judge me."

He heard the woman at the gate call her flight. "I'm retired, Helen. I'm not going to be the one to judge you." He stood and saw her grab her purse, as if afraid he would take it from her. But he already knew that she'd had Zac wire the ten million to a Swiss bank account as per her plan. And now she was going to lose a lot more than ten million dollars. "I used to tell those young people who came before me in court that we all reap what we sow. That seems to be a lesson you didn't learn. Until now. I'm sorry, Helen, but I don't think you're going to like prison."

She looked past him as two men in uniform and two FBI agents in plain clothes headed toward her. With that poise she'd perfected, she rose to her full height. "You could have let me go. For old times' sake," she said quietly.

"You know me better than that."

Helen turned to smile at him. "Yes," she said, her voice breaking. "Unfortunately, Judge, I do know you. Otherwise, I might have tried to pass off the baby as yours. I knew you would have married me for better or worse. I spared you, William. You should be thanking me."

EPILOGUE

"CAN I OPEN my eyes now?" JJ asked as Thorn took her hand and helped her from the pickup. Spring had come to the Flathead Valley. She breathed in the sweet, familiar scents, filled with a love for this place and this man.

"Not yet," Thorn said. "Just a few more steps." She could hear the excitement in his voice, feel it in his touch. The man had swept her off her feet—literally. Whisking her away in a whirlwind of wedding and honeymoon. Franklin had insisted they do something amazing, and they had. Over three months cruising around the world.

They'd gone to places she'd never dreamed she would ever see, eaten amazing food, explored old ruins, climbed mountains and swum in turquoise seas. They'd laughed and danced and watched sunsets on deck chairs.

"What about my job?" JJ had demanded when Thorn had told her what Franklin wanted to give them.

"Your boss told me that you never even took your vacations. You have the time coming. She's happy for you."

"But how can you be gone that long? What about your critters?"

Thorn had kissed her and said, "Let me worry about that, okay?"

For all the amazing places they'd gone, she was thrilled to be back in Montana, back to the Flathead Valley that she loved. She could feel the breeze stir her hair, the sun kissing her face as she waited, her hand in his. He'd said he had a surprise for her. Last night they'd flown into Kalispell and stayed at a hotel near the lake. He'd promised that the honeymoon was never going to end. It certainly felt that way.

"Okay," he said with what she knew was a grin on his handsome face. "Open your eyes."

JJ breathed in the sweet scent of pine and spring in the Flathead Valley before she slowly lifted her lashes. Her breath caught in her throat. Tears welled in her eyes. "It's a house?"

"It's our house."

She couldn't speak for a moment. "How?"

"I know how much you love this area and the lake. I sold my place and bought us this."

"All those questions on our honeymoon about what I would want in a home…"

His grin broadened. "Whatever you had in mind, I then would call the contractor and tell him to add what you wanted."

"Oh, Thorn." She threw herself into his arms. "I never dreamed…"

"I know how hard it was on you when you had to sell your father's house and how much you missed a roof over your head."

"You mean how much trouble it got me into," she said with a laugh.

"But if it hadn't, we might never have met."

It was a sobering thought.

"Ready to see inside?" he asked.

She nodded, feeling like a kid on Christmas morning. Well, at least the kids she used to see on television on Christmas mornings until her father saved her.

The moment she stepped in, she fell in love with all of it. Thorn had listened to her dream of what she would want in her own home. The Craftsman-built house was light and airy with lots of windows.

He led her through the house, pointing out small things he'd had added for her. It was too much to take in. "But this is what I really wanted to show you," he said as he drew her over to the front window.

"The lake," she cried. She could see Flathead Lake.

"It isn't as good a view as from Geneva's."

"It's wonderful." He put his arm around her and she leaned into him as they admired the sliver of glistening surface seen from their home. Their home. JJ couldn't believe it. She looked up at her husband, wanting to pinch herself.

WT TAPPED AT the bright red front door, finding himself smiling. The house looked like JJ, he thought, and knew that Thorn had built it especially for her. It was bright and cute and perfect.

JJ opened the door, smiling as if happy to see him standing there. "Judge," she said. "I'm so glad you could make it."

"A housewarming present," he said as he handed her a wrapped package.

"Thank you." She beamed, the happy bride. He couldn't have been more delighted for her and Thorn.

"Nice place you have here," he said, looking around the Craftsman-style house that Thorn had told him sat on twenty acres at the foot of the Mission Mountains. The cowboy had been so excited, wanting to surprise his new bride once they returned from their honeymoon.

"There's even a view of Flathead Lake from the living room," she said with obvious pride. "Thorn thought of everything."

"I'm happy for the two of you," the judge said. "I knew you'd work things out."

"Thorn's out back grilling steaks. I was so glad you were free for dinner."

"Me too. I knew about the house. Thorn let me in on his

surprise for you. I can see why you love it. It's you. And he has a place for his animals. He said Gertrude loves it here."

She smiled and then sobered. "I'm sorry about Helen."

He started to say that it hadn't been serious, his feelings for the woman, but the denial wouldn't come out. He'd been head over heels in love with Helen all those years ago. He would have married her—just as she said. Even if she had been pregnant with someone else's baby. And he had no doubt he would have regretted it. So Helen was right. She'd saved him from more heartbreak.

Nor could he deny that seeing her again had rekindled a lot of those old feelings.

"I know you cared about her," JJ said, touching his hand.

He nodded. "For a few minutes, she made me feel like a teenager again. I wanted to forget the past and trust her." He shook his head. "Love and lady justice are definitely blind."

How had he not seen who Helen truly was? Just as Thorn had not seen the real Bethany. It was as if there was an important missing component that had gotten lost at conception with those two women. A piece of the heart missing that held compassion, love and truthfulness. He and Thorn had both been stung badly by women, but at least Thorn hadn't given up. He'd found JJ, and she was definitely worth keeping.

She squeezed his hand. "It's scary, but I hope it doesn't make you not want to try again."

WT laughed. "At my age—"

"Love is no different," JJ said. They had been making their way through the house, and had reached the glass doors leading out to the patio. Her gaze went to Thorn. The cowboy was at the grill, his back to them. "It's terrifying," she said of love. "But sometimes, it works."

He smiled as she opened the door to the patio and Thorn.

"Yes, sometimes it does," he agreed. And he had to admit, even at his age, these two gave him hope.

THORN PUSHED BACK his Stetson as he watched his wife make her way up the shore. His wife. He'd never dreamed he could be this happy. Hell, he never planned to get married again. But JJ wasn't like anyone he'd ever met. She'd opened his heart again and now it swelled with such love for this woman that he often thought it would burst.

JJ walked along Flathead Lake's shore picking up rocks. He loved watching her. She was so intent, picking up pretty ones that caught her eye. Some were tossed into the waves. Others, she pocketed as keepsakes.

Now as he watched her, he felt a tug at his heart at how close he'd come to losing this woman even before he'd met her. How different his life would have been if the judge hadn't called him and asked him to find a plane that had gone down in the mountains behind his cabin. He'd thought nothing could dislodge him from that mountaintop. Certainly no woman.

But then he met Jenny Jo Foster, now Grayson. She was one of a kind, and all he wanted to do now was spend the rest of his life making her happy. They'd spent months after the kidnapping traveling and talking about their futures. He'd known how much she loved this valley and how hard it would be for her to leave it.

He'd surprised her with the house here in the Flathead Valley because he'd known how much it would mean to her. He loved that he could give her something she'd yearned for since her father died—a roof over her head. It seemed a small thing. Their home wasn't large or fancy and yet seeing how much she loved it—and him… It still choked him up.

In the aftermath of everything that had happened, they'd come to know Franklin Davenport better. They had him and the judge over for dinner often. WT stopped by when he was at his place in Montana.

They seldom talked about the kidnapping. Geneva had thrown herself on the mercy of the court. She'd gotten five years, but she would be up for parole in three and with good behavior, possibly serve even less.

She'd been forced to sell her house to pay Brandemiller Brothers what she owed them. She'd had just enough left over to hire her own lawyer. There wasn't enough money to pay for the plane that had been destroyed, but Travis Brandemiller had said that his brother had insured the plane. Travis also said that he wasn't interested in suing for damages.

Ridge Brandemiller and his two construction workers who'd abducted JJ were now behind bars.

The other two men Zac had used the night of the ransom drop had also been arrested and were now serving time in Deer Lodge at the state prison.

Zac Judson Sr. had flown up to take his son's body back to Texas. Thorn had heard he also stopped by the prison to see Helen. According to the scuttlebutt, it was fortunate that there was heavy Plexiglas between them, since he blamed her for his son's death and rightly so.

Helen had confessed to her part in the kidnapping plot. She got twenty years for both the kidnapping and the resulting deaths.

Franklin recovered the ransom money and donated it to a variety of charities in the valley. He said he didn't want it. He was trying to put the memory of the kidnapping and his worry over Geneva in the past. Most of the media coverage had died down after the funerals of John Baker, Wesley Brennan and Kyle Spencer.

There were many nights now that Thorn didn't have bad dreams. His dreams had changed because of JJ and the future they had planned. She'd changed his life, he thought now as he watched her pick up a small stone, turning it in the sunlight before pocketing it in the beach cover she wore.

She was beginning to show, and he'd noticed that she often would stop whatever she was doing to place her hand over her stomach and smile. Their son or daughter would be born around Christmas. Just when he thought he couldn't possibly be happier, they'd found out that they were pregnant.

He was already planning the swing set and tree houses and forts he would build for the kids. JJ said she wanted three children. Maybe more. She'd gone to part-time at the travel agency, and would soon be a full-time mother. Thorn had found he loved working with animals, and was considering becoming a farrier. He wanted a job where he could spend as much time as he wanted with his family. He had his military retirement, and since they lived simply, they could both concentrate on each other and their kids. *Kids*, he thought, excited about the future. He couldn't wait to see their first baby.

JJ looked up, as if feeling his gaze on her. Her face broke into a wide smile as she began walking toward him. He felt the sun on his face, the breeze whispering in the pines near the shore and felt the soft lap of the warm lake water at his feet as he headed toward her.

Thorn chuckled to himself. JJ thought he'd rescued her, but in truth, this woman had saved him.

* * * * *

Look for the conclusion in B.J. Daniels's Montana Justice series—Heart of Gold. Available wherever HQN books are sold.

"I'm curious," Jinx said, her voice sounding strange even to her. "How
did you get that scar?"

She watched Angus swallow, then seem to relax, his blue eyes bright
with humor. "Well, it's kind of an amusing story." He smiled. "I got
pushed out of a barn loft when I was eleven."

"That's awful."

He sat up straighter until they were eye to eye. "It was my fault. I asked
for it."

"You asked to be pushed out of a barn loft?"

"I was teasing her. She warned me that if I didn't stop she would knock
me into tomorrow."

"She?" Jinx felt goose bumps break out over her skin and for a moment
she could smell the fresh hay in the barn, feel the breeze on her face,
remember that cute cowboy who'd taunted her. Her heart began to pound.

His smile broadened. "She was a spitfire, as fiery as her hair back then."

Jinx felt heat rush to her cheeks. "Tell me her name wasn't
JoRay McCallahan."

"Sorry, I'm afraid so," he said and laughed. "I wondered if you would
remember."

"When I saw you, I thought I'd met you before, but I couldn't think of when that might have been. Then Max told me that my mother took me up to the Cardwell Ranch for a short visit when I was about nine." She groaned. "Your mother must have been horrified by what I did to you." Jinx didn't think she could be more embarrassed.

He shook his head. "My mother said, 'What did you do, Angus?' I confessed that I'd been giving you a hard time and that you'd warned me what would happen if I didn't knock it off."

"Oh, I can imagine what my mother said."

"Actually, both mothers had trouble hiding smiles, once they realized that no one was hurt badly. Your mother told you that you couldn't go around pushing boys just because of something they said or you'd spend the rest of your life fighting them."

"You'd think I'd have learned that lesson."

He grinned. "When your mother said that, you replied, 'Well, if the boys are smart, they won't give me a hard time—especially standing in front of an open window two floors up.'"

She laughed with him. "Oh, that sounds so much like me. I'm so sorry."

"Don't be," he said as he seemed to fondly touch the scar. "It was a good learning experience for me." His blue eyes hardened. "And I never forgot that girl."

"I suppose not." She shook her head in disbelief. "Still, you came down to help me get my herd up to the summer range."

"Like I said, it's what neighbors do," he said and grinned again. "Also, I was curious to see the woman that girl had grown into."

She couldn't help the heat that rushed to her cheeks, wanting to blame it on the sun beating down on them. "Now you know."

Don't miss
Ambush before Sunrise *by B.J. Daniels,*
available June 2020 wherever
Harlequin Intrigue books and ebooks are sold.

Harlequin.com